STAR TREK

THE NEXT GENERATION

D1584159

STAR TREK:
THE NEXT GENERATION NOVELS

STAR TREK:
THE NEXT GENERATION GIANT NOVELS

STAR TREK
THE NEXT GENERATION

NIGHTSHADE

LAURELL K. HAMILTON

TITAN BOOKS
LONDON

STAR TREK **THE NEXT GENERATION 24:**
NIGHTSHADE
ISBN 1 85286 426 5

Published by
Titan Books Ltd
19 Valentine Place
London SE1 8QH

First Titan Edition December 1992
10 9 8 7 6 5 4 3 2 1

British Library Cataloguing-in-Publication Data. A catalogue record for this book is available from the British Library.

Printed and bound in Great Britain by Cox and Wyman Ltd, Reading, Berkshire.

Chapter One

DEANNA TROI stood at a viewport gazing at the stars. They were utterly still—cold, harsh light without a planet's atmosphere to make them twinkle. Troi had sought out this empty corridor and its fine view of the stars. She wanted a few minutes to compose herself before going to the bridge.

The ship was orbiting the planet, Oriana. Generations of civil war had nearly destroyed the planet and its people. Troi wanted to take the unperturbed peace of the stars with her onto the bridge. The ship's counselor had to be calm, relaxed, ready to serve.

"What are you looking at, Counselor?"

She jumped and whirled. "Worf, you frightened me."

The Klingon officer frowned, which was a fearsome sight all on its own. "I did not intend to."

Troi smiled. "I know."

The frown deepened, causing the ridges on his forehead to wrinkle. He nodded.

His emotions, as always, were close to the surface of his thoughts. The Klingon made very little pretense in his own mind. Unlike humans who often lied even to themselves, the Klingon thought what he thought, and did not care that she knew it. It didn't make Worf uncomfortable to be around an empath the way it did some of the crew. Worf had no secrets to keep because secrets implied shame.

Troi appreciated his openness. She smiled. "You asked what I was looking at." She motioned him to the window.

Worf stood beside her, hands clasped behind his back, broad shoulders filling the window. Troi knew she was not tall, but beside the Klingon she felt tiny. "Aren't the stars beautiful?" she asked.

He shifted, slightly. Troi could feel his puzzlement. "I do not understand."

A human might have lied, but at least this Klingon said what he felt. "I was gazing at the stars and thinking how lovely they are."

Worf stared out into the cold blackness, the stars like chips of ice caught in velvet. "I see stars," he said at last.

"But don't you think they're beautiful?" She glanced up at him in time to see the same fearsome scowl.

"They are stars. I suppose some might think they are . . . pretty."

Troi smiled. "I think they are."

He nodded.

Troi could feel laughter at the back of her throat.

But she swallowed it. You did not laugh at friends, especially when they were trying to be polite.

Captain Picard's voice came out of empty air, "Counselor Troi, please report to the bridge."

Troi hit her communicator. "I'm on my way, Captain."

"Worf here, Captain. Is my presence required?"

"It would be most appreciated, Lieutenant."

Troi felt the smile in the captain's voice.

"We are on our way, Captain," Worf said.

Worf strode toward the nearest turbolift. Troi had to quick step to keep up with him. "We weren't scheduled to speak with the Orianians for another hour," she said, "What could it be?"

"I do not know." Inside the smooth whiteness of the turbolift Worf said, "Bridge." The lift vibrated, then began to move.

Troi could feel Captain Picard's agitation. He was worried. She did not share her findings with Worf. She could read the emotions of everyone on board. It was simple courtesy not to reveal what she felt to others. It would have been like telling secrets you had learned eavesdropping.

The turbolift door whooshed open. The bridge of the *Enterprise* spread out before them, all graceful curves, neutral carpeting. It looked like an executive boardroom more than the bridge of a starship. A place for conferences not confrontations.

On the main viewscreen was the picture of a man. The skin was pale gold. The facial bones were high and delicate, almost birdlike. The face was dominated by huge liquid brown eyes. The large eyes and the delicate face made the man seem childlike. The

3

effect was spoiled by his deep voice and the injuries to that lovely face.

The right side of his face was battered and bleeding. He held stiff one arm at his side. His pain hit Troi like a physical shove. She staggered. Worf caught her arm.

"Are you all right, Counselor?" he asked.

She nodded. Troi realized that it wasn't just the general's physical pain but his anger. He was full of a great roaring outrage at what had been done to him.

Worf's hand was a steady, solid presence. She took a deep breath and stepped away from him. "I'm fine." Now that she was prepared, Troi could ride the pain and the rage. Everyone's attention was fixed on the viewscreen, no one but Worf had seen her momentary weakness. Troi was grateful for that. It was inexcusable to allow other people's emotions to throw her so badly. Composing herself, she moved to take her seat on Captain Picard's left.

The battered man on the screen said, "I have honored you beyond our customs by allowing you to see my face. I hoped it would convince you. Our enemies, the Venturies are determined to stop these peace talks. Captain Picard, please reconsider. It is far, far too dangerous to risk a Federation ambassador. You see what they have done to me." He raised his good hand to emphasize the cuts on his face. "If it had not been for my bodyguards, I would not be speaking to you now."

"I assure you, General Basha, that I will take all precautions for my safety. But I do not intend to allow terrorists to derail these negotiations before they even begin," Captain Picard said in his careful accent.

"Captain, please, I want these talks to go on as scheduled. Our scientists say we have only a decade at most before our planet can no longer sustain life. This civil war has devastated our lands and our people. But I cannot ask you to give your life in our war."

"That is commendable, General, but . . ."

"At least promise you will bring bodyguards," the general said.

Captain Picard sighed. "If you believe it to be necessary."

General Basha stared at Picard, his brown eyes looking suddenly tired. "My second in command was assassinated yesterday evening, Captain Picard. If you insist on coming down here, then yes, by all means, bring bodyguards."

Captain Picard nodded. "I am sorry for your loss."

Basha made a small push-away gesture with his good hand. "It happens, Captain. Our war has lasted two hundred years, it happens. I will meet you as soon as I have been attended to."

"Do you need any medical assistance?" Picard asked.

"Thank you, but no, our medical facilities are quite good. I pray that you do not find out how good." With that the screen went blank.

"Well," Picard said, "what do you make of that, Number One?"

Commander William Riker's round, bearded face frowned. "I request permission to act as ambassador to Oriana."

"Why, Number One, trying to steal some of my thunder?" Picard smiled slightly as he said it.

"Captain, two assassination attempts in twenty-four hours, one death. It's too dangerous to risk your life."

"I disagree. This planet is dying, Will. If this war is not stopped, the Orianians are facing genocide. I have been requested as ambassador, and that is what I am going to be."

"With all respect, Captain," Riker said, "it is too dangerous."

"I agree with Commander Riker," Worf said, leaning over his console to loom above the captain's chair.

"I appreciate the concern, but I will not be frightened off."

Riker frowned. "Then at least take a full security complement."

"I have every intention of taking security with me, Will. I am not eager to fall prey to an assassin's attack."

"It is still very dangerous, Captain," Worf said.

Picard scooted his chair so he could see his security officer. "Are you saying, Lieu . nant Worf, that your security personnel could not see to my safety?"

Worf stiffened. "I did not say that."

Picard smiled. "Good. Pick three people and meet me in the transporter room in an hour."

"Very good, Captain," Worf said. He didn't salute, of course, but Troi could hear it in his voice, a growl of respect. He left the bridge to gather his security team.

"Only two guards, Captain?" Riker asked.

"I am not going to take another army down on the planet. There are quite enough armed camps down there already." He turned to Troi. "What did you think of General Basha, Counselor?"

"He was in a great deal of pain, but hid it well. He is very strong, both physically and emotionally. He feels sorrow over the death of his second-in-command. He is full of great rage, and he was lying about wanting the talks to go on as scheduled."

"In what way?"

Troi tried to put into words something that would have been so much easier to just share. If the captain had been a Betazoid, Troi could have simply let him feel it. She always struggled to explain what was to her very simple. "Much of his anger was about the attacks, but there was also anger about the treaty negotiations."

Picard steepled his fingers, tips touching his chin. "He is a military general, Counselor. Without a war, he is out of work."

"True, but I felt . . ." she spread her hands in a helpless gesture. "He was hiding something. Some deception. Something to do with the negotiations."

"Perhaps the general's faction plans to retaliate for the death of his second-in-command," Riker suggested.

Picard glanced at him. "More assassination?"

Riker nodded.

"Could that be it, Counselor?" Picard asked.

Troi tried to recall the feelings. It was like trying to remember dreams: Some things were clear; others faded the harder you tried to catch them. "It's possible."

Picard nodded. "The sooner we get these talks underway the sooner we can put an end to this nonsense. Counselor Troi, please accompany me to the surface. I think your insight may be invaluable on this mission."

7

Troi smiled at that. She followed Picard's lean figure into the turbolift. The last thing she felt as the doors closed was Riker's worry over her safety. Duty and friendship made him worry over the captain, but there was more to his worry over Troi. They were no longer a couple, but the thought of her in danger troubled him a great deal, she knew.

Troi sighed. The past was past. The future was Oriana and its two waiting armies. If Captain Picard failed, it meant not just the death of an entire race of people, but of a planet as well. Everything would die. Every animal, every plant. It was only a matter of years. Deanna Troi wondered what the minds of a dying race would feel like. If she were an Orianian, she would be afraid, very afraid. Afraid and full of hate. Yes, if General Basha was typical, there would be hate.

Chapter Two

THE PLANET ORIANA filled the viewscreen. It was a great shining, silverish ball. Occasional bands of sickly green swirled through the cloud cover, like gangrenous fingers. Picard and Troi stared at the small viewscreen in the transporter room. The captain touched his communicator. "Data, what is the atmosphere of Oriana like?"

"It is outside the acceptable range of breathable atmosphere without some sort of filter or breathing apparatus. The atmosphere does not protect the surface from the sun's radiation. Blindness is possible within hours of surface exposure. Skin cancer would be almost a given in such a radiation field, after an exceptionally short exposure."

Picard sighed. "What about animal life?"

"Surface life is restricted to a few species of anthropoids, two species of reptilianlike predators, and one larger mammalian predator. And two hundred thousand Orianians."

"Only two hundred thousand, Mr. Data, are you sure?"

"Yes, Captain."

"Thank you, Data," Picard said. He turned to Troi. "Well, Counselor, now I know why General Basha's coordinates are indoors. It seems this planet is on the verge of death."

She nodded. "Now that we are orbiting the planet I can feel many minds. They are very afraid, Captain."

He gazed down at the poisonous gray-silver ball that had once been a class-M planet. "They have a right to be afraid."

The doors whooshed open, and Lieutenant Worf stepped through. Three security guards were at his back. "Captain, we are ready."

The three security guards fanned out and stood at attention on either side of Worf. Ensign Kelly was a woman nearly as tall as the Klingon himself. Beside her stood Ensign Conner, a slightly shorter man with skin the color of ebony, almost purple in its darkness. His broad shoulders led into a thick neck, signs of weight-lifting. The last guard, Lieutenant Vincient, was tall and thin, with short-cropped hair.

Picard pulled a breathing mask from the small plastic box in front of the transporter pad. It would cover the face completely. Goggles were sewn into the breathing mask to form one protective unit. It didn't look particularly comfortable. He had wondered why they needed breathing masks if they would be beaming indoors. The answer had been, in case of accidents. They could survive for a time without protective clothing, but no time at all without the masks.

Picard slipped the mask on. It fit tightly, and there was a faint medicinal smell to it, but Dr. Crusher had assured them all that it was not only safe but necessary. Picard agreed with the doctor especially after hearing Data's previous description of the planet's atmosphere.

The others pulled their own masks into place. Troi stood to Picard's left, much as she always did on the bridge. Worf had moved just behind the captain, again unconsciously taking his position on the bridge. Finally, the three security people took up stations to either side.

Glancing at the white-masked face, Picard noted that the masks made his people look . . . impersonal. He suddenly realized how very much humans relied on facial expressions.

He nodded to the technician at the control panel. "Engage." There was the same high-pitched sound as always, then a sensation as if a hand were tickling the inside of his body, where no hand could ever reach. Then Picard's eyes refocused to see a stone courtyard covered by a multicolored dome. Bits of colored glass and ceramic tile formed a pattern under their feet like a rainbow gone mad. Just looking down at it was dizzying.

A dozen armed figures stood around the courtyard. They wore swirling black-and-gold robes, their faces hidden behind breathing masks and goggles. Riflelike weapons were held at attention but not pointed at them.

Worf and his security people had moved to stand

around Picard and Troi like a cage. Phasers were out, but not pointed—yet.

"Who is in charge here? We did not intend to beam down into an armed camp," Picard said.

A robed figure stepped from the circle.

Worf stepped in front of the captain.

The robed figure slung the rifle over one shoulder. A black-gloved hand sketched a salute. "Welcome, Captain Picard of the Starship *Enterprise,* Ambassador of the United Federation of Planets. I am Colonel Talanne, wife of General Basha. As for the weapons, they are for your protection as much as my own. My husband feared you would not take enough precautions. But I see he was wrong."

Picard stared at the woman. Her face was completely hidden. If the voice had not been so distinctly female, he would not even have known that. "At ease, Lieutenant."

Worf stepped back grudgingly. His people followed his lead but did not holster their phasers. The robed guards did not holster their rifles, either.

"I am honored, Colonel Talanne. We share your sorrow for recent events."

"Thank you, Captain, you are most kind." She waved her hand, and the armed figures fell into two lines, one on either side of the group.

The four security guards formed a phalanx around the captain and Troi, facing slightly outward. "Put up your weapons, Lieutenant Worf."

"Captain, I do not think that is wise. If assassinations are so simple then how can anyone be trusted?"

Picard stepped close to Worf, coming barely to the Klingon's chest. "You will not insult our hostess by insinuating she is a traitor."

"It is not her I am worried about, Captain," Worf whispered, his deep voice made more so by the effort not to be overheard.

"We cannot begin a peace mission with weapons drawn, Lieutenant."

Troi said, "I sense no treachery in these people, Worf."

Worf frowned at her.

"Put up your weapons, Lieutenant Worf. That is a direct order."

"Aye, Captain." He holstered his phaser, as did his people.

"His caution is commendable, Captain Picard," Talanne said. "I would trust the people here in this circle with my own life. But finding a dozen people who cannot be bribed is getting to be a chore."

She turned and walked toward a low doorway. The door was painted to resemble a dark red flower complete with yellow stamen and a tiny insect on one petal. The image clashed with the bright courtyard. Individual tastes did vary.

Picard started to follow her, but Worf moved in front of him. Picard sighed as he followed his security officer's broad back. The three remaining guards took up their posts to either side of Picard and Counselor Troi. This mission was going to be hard enough without Worf taking his safety so terribly seriously. It was not that Picard did not appreciate his own possible danger, but how was he to negotiate peace when his own people were so obviously ready to fight? He wondered if Commander Riker had had a parting word with Worf. Riker took his duty to protect his captain very seriously.

Of course, if Picard insisted on lesser safety mea-

13

sures and was killed for it . . . Well, he would never hear the end of it, so to speak.

Troi followed the captain. The security guards to either side obstructed most of her view. The filter mask was uncomfortable, cutting into her face.

The robed guards were a mixed bag of emotions: resentment, anger, fear, anticipation, worry, hope. General Basha's wife, Talanne was worried, frightened. Her husband had almost been killed—it was a normal reaction—but Troi felt the fear was more than that. Colonel Talanne feared them. They were the newcomers, an unknown. It was normal to fear the unknown, and yet . . . Troi shook her head. She had no words for it, or even a specific feeling. Talanne meant them no harm, in fact was worried for Picard's safety, yet . . . Something was wrong, but what?

They were led into a low-ceilinged hallway. The walls were a brilliant buttercup yellow. It was at least one solid color, which was a relief after the courtyard. Worf and the three security guards had to stoop to enter the door. It was only then that Troi realized that all the Orianians were small. None of them were as tall as the captain. While Worf, Kelly, Conner, and Vincient towered over them.

They towered over Troi as well, but she was used to it. Once in the small enclosed space of the hallway, the size difference made the robed guards nervous. Troi could feel the guards judging them, anticipating treachery.

Worf's eager attention was like a pressure on Troi's mind. She often felt the emotions of people she knew stronger than strangers. Worf was, to an extent, in his

14

element. A warrior among warriors, with violence threatening to erupt. But Troi trusted Worf not to act irresponsibly.

Captain Picard's irritation at Worf's solicitousness made Troi smile. It would be a battle of wills between them.

There was only one door at the end of the hall. The pale walls stretched back toward the outside door smooth and perfect. Talanne stood to one side of the door. Two robed guards moved in front of her. The door opened. The guards went in weapons at the ready. They didn't hesitate, or doubt. They just went in ready to kill or be killed. They did not fear death. No, Troi thought, that wasn't it.

She could feel their minds as they searched the room. They were not afraid, that was true, but they thought of nothing but their task. Their concentration was purely on the situation at hand. If they concentrated hard enough on just their duty, Troi guessed, there was no time for fear.

All the guards waited, their emotions going into hold, their senses alert for . . . duty. Troi suppressed a shudder. She had been among warrior races before but nothing like these people. They didn't know any other life. The war had consumed them as surely as it had consumed the other resources of the planet.

The guards came back to the door. "All clear."

"Good," Talanne said. "Captain, welcome to my home." She entered the room.

Picard tried to follow her, but Worf was still in front of him. "Lieutenant. I trust our hostess and her people. I do not think these extra precautions are necessary."

A variety of emotions played over Worf's mind. Troi felt them like waves over her body; anger, loyalty, respect. "As you like, Captain."

Picard took a deep breath and straightened his uniform, just a bare pull on his jacket. "Thank you, Lieutenant."

Troi followed him inside the room. Worf and his people followed behind. Three of the robed guards entered the room as well.

It was a small room. Ten people filled it nearly to capacity. Tapestries covered every wall. Woven images of tall graceful trees, red flowers like the outer door. Grass as bright yellow as the hallway flowed through the wall hangings. A vine exploded around the edges of the scene, heavy with thick purplish-green leaves and oblong orange fruit. Every color looked fresh, as if when touched it would still be wet. It wasn't just lifelike, it was brighter, bigger, richer; more than the real thing. Or so Troi thought.

She couldn't imagine nature giving such colors in one place at one time. One thing about naturally occurring plants, they always seemed to match. The colors melting together, completing each other. Mother Nature did not clash.

Picard pulled off his mask, and the rest of the Federation party followed suit. Troi was relieved to feel the air on her face again. The straps cut into the sides of her face.

"You honor us with bare faces. I can only return the honor." Talanne pushed back the hood of her robe. Close-cropped brown hair curled around her face protection. She lifted the mask off in one smooth, practiced motion. Her skin was a slightly darker shade of gold than Basha's had been, a deep amber, but her face was nearly identical in bone structure. There was none of the smaller jaw, or narrower face that differentiated human males and females. "It has been a long time since I have been in a room full of this many bare faces."

"Is it your custom to cover the face even indoors, where the air is breathable?" Picard asked.

"Yes, Captain. In times of war you must expect the unexpected, like a bomb blowing out the wall and exposing you to poison."

Worf stared round the room. "Is this common?"

"It hasn't happened in over fifty years, but too many children were injured. It is one of our few rules."

"Then we can safely go without the masks indoors," Picard said, with only the hint of a question to his words.

"Yes, Captain. Our people will stare, and think it strange, but with their faces covered you will not be able to see them stare, and they are all too well trained to question your customs."

Picard wasn't sure how to take that. "If we are breaking a sacred custom, we can wear the masks."

"No, Captain, please, let it remind my people of what we have given up. Enough of this," Talanne said, "I noticed you admiring our wall hangings."

"Yes," Picard said. "They are extraordinary."

"It is an art form at which we excel. One of the few nondestructive things we do well on this planet." The bitterness in her voice was thick enough to cut. To Troi, the emotion was like a twisted thing, almost painful.

"The wall hangings are what we have instead of windows. None of us wish to be reminded of what we

17

have done to our world. Looking out upon this desolation, this death . . ." Talanne shook her head. "Allow me to offer you some refreshment."

She moved to a small table that held a crystal decanter and five glasses. The liquid inside was a deep purple. "I will send for more glasses. My husband was unsure how many of you there would be."

They had to practically huddle around the table to have room to lift their glasses. "I mean no disrespect, Colonel Talanne, wife of Basha, but is it really necessary to have so many people in the room?" Picard said.

The three robed guards were instantly alert. Hands tightening on weapons. Worf noticed it, and was reaching for his phaser.

Talanne raised a hand. "At ease. I am sorry, Captain. You have my bodyguards worried. It is customary that if one leader has bodyguards, the other has an equal number. It is only wise."

Picard nodded. "Ah, because I have three guards you must have three guards."

"Exactly."

"I too am a guard," Worf said.

"But you are a commander, an officer, are you not?"

"I am."

"We cannot have equal numbers of officers. The crowd would grow too large." She smiled and raised a glass. "Besides, if you have too many officers in one place, it is too great a temptation."

"For assassinations you mean?" Picard asked.

"Yes, Captain. We lost five officers in one bomb attack some three months back."

"And do the Venturies also have to watch how many officers they have in any one place?"

With a brilliant smile, she answered. "Yes, Captain, they do."

"Assassination is not an honorable way to take your enemy," Worf said.

"Lieutenant Worf," Picard said, voice sharp.

"No, that is all right, Captain. Even we have heard of Klingon honor." She turned to speak directly to Worf. "We would do anything to bring this war to a close. Anything, even treachery, if the fighting would just end."

"Do you not wish victory over your enemies?" Worf asked.

"Some still do, but most just want an end. Our planet is dying. Our children are dying. Neither side seems able to win even by treachery, so we must talk peace before we all die."

"Seeing the necessity for peace is the first step to achieving it," Picard said.

Talanne smiled. "I hope so, Captain Picard, I very much hope so."

The door opened, and every weapon in the room whirled toward it. A small, blond boy, perhaps three years old, raced into the room. The features that were lovely on his parents were nearly unreal on the child. He looked carved from aged-goldened alabaster with eyes a startling shade of jewellike blue. He came to a skittering halt, eyes wide, staring at the guns.

"Put up your weapons," Talanne said. She moved toward the small boy. Two guards moved with her. "Jeric, where is your sentinel?"

"Don't know, Merme," he said. His eyes were still wide, his pulse hammering in his thin neck.

His fear had been pure and total when he had seen the weapons. Troi had felt his desperate sure knowledge that he was about to die. Only a little older than three, but he knew what dying meant. He knew what weapons could do. The memory of such things stained his mind, colored his emotions. Troi had never met anyone so young with such an old mind.

The boy stared openly at Worf.

Talanne knelt in front of the boy. "Jeric, listen to me." She touched the boy's cheek gently forcing him to look at her face. "When did your sentinel go missing?"

He frowned. "Missing?"

Troi felt the woman's impatience. Talanne swallowed it back and kept her voice normal, calm. "Where were you just before you ran in here?"

"Is something wrong, Colonel Talanne?" Picard asked.

"I don't know yet, Captain. Jeric's sentinel should be with him at all times."

"What exactly is a sentinel?" Picard asked.

"A personal bodyguard." She stared at her son's frightened eyes. "Where were you just before you came to here?"

"In the playroom."

"Good. Was the sentinel with you then?"

The boy frowned again.

Talanne gripped his arms gently. "Jeric, were you alone in the playroom?"

He nodded solemnly. His mother's seriousness finally sinking into him, or perhaps it had been the guns.

"Where were you before you went inside the playroom?"

20

"Outside."

"Outside," she whispered it, as if it were some obscenity. Her hands must have tightened because the boy wriggled in her grip. "You are not allowed outside ever. Who took you?"

"Bori took me. You're squeezing my arms, Merme."

She hugged him to her chest. "I'm sorry, Jeric. Merme didn't mean to hurt you. Where did the sentinel take you?"

"Outside."

"Where outside?"

"Outside." He struggled away from her arms. "Just outside, Merme."

"Did you see anyone else outside?"

The boy nodded. "A man, Merme."

"Did you know the man, Jeric?"

He shook his head.

"Did your sentinel or the man come back inside with you?"

"No, Merme."

Talanne hugged her son to her. "Check the corridors. Spread the word that we may have a security breach."

Two guards moved to the door. One hesitated. "What of the newcomers?" It was a man's voice. Without some clue every figure was neuter, a soldier neither male nor female.

"I trust them. Go, find out what has happened. See to my husband's safety."

The guard still hesitated.

"Go, now!" She swung the rifle into play in one practiced motion, the boy shoved behind her back with the other hand. "Do not refuse a direct order."

He bowed from the neck. "I hear and I obey." He was gone with the other guard. The door closed behind them.

"I appreciate the trust you have placed in us, Colonel Talanne," Picard said.

She stood, rifle still loosely grasped in her hand. Jeric clutched her other hand. "Do not be, Captain. I know what your starship is capable of. If you wished to do us harm, you could, and nothing on this planet could stop you. That is one of the reasons we called upon the Federation. One thing we Orianians respect is strength."

"Your honesty is refreshing, Colonel Talanne, but I'm afraid I am a little lost. Why is your son's missing security guard so very important?"

"It is not just the guard. Jeric is never allowed onto the surface of the planet. His safety is too important for that. No one would take him outside, no one, least of all his own security guard."

"You think it was a kidnapping attempt?" Worf asked.

"No, Lieutenant, I fear worse things."

Worf frowned. "You do not mean that . . ." He stopped in mid-sentence, glancing at the boy.

"You make war on children," Worf said in a low voice.

"Worf," Picard said, his voice soft with warning.

"It's all right, Captain Picard. No, Lieutenant, we don't normally make war on children. But there are factions that are desperate to win this war rather than have peace. They would do anything to stop the peace talks."

"The Venturi would use your son as a negotiation tool?" Picard asked.

"Not the Venturi," she said. "They are as eager as most of us to end this conflict, but there are factions on both sides that consider peace without victory worthless."

The child looked from one adult to the other, trying to follow the conversation. He knew it involved him, Troi sensed, but not how.

Talanne led her son toward the center of the room. "You see how desperately we need your intervention, Captain." She gentled her son against her leg. "Do you know that no one can even actually agree on what began this war? Two hundred years of fighting, and we don't even know why we're doing it."

Tears glimmered in her eyes. Her sorrow was full of anger, outrage at what had almost happened to her son. Without any solid facts Talanne was doing what any mother would do, thinking of the direst possibilities.

"We are here to see the fighting stop, Colonel Talanne. To allow your children to grow up to be more than soldiers," Picard said.

"The children," she said softly, "the children." She hugged Jeric tight against her. "You will find Jeric is the exception, Captain."

Before Picard could ask what that meant, the door opened. The two remaining guards took their posts, weapons on the door. Worf went forward with Conner. He left the others in a triangle around the captain.

Talanne shoved Jeric into Troi's arms and took her place with the guards.

A black and gold robed guard stepped through. "It is I, Colonel."

"Take off your mask, slowly."

23

The man did, pushing hood back to reveal short brown hair. With the same hand he scooped off his mask to reveal a plain, pale face with brown eyes. He had the same delicate features as General Basha and his son, but not quite. He seemed a little less perfect, almost ordinary, though still delicately pretty.

"What have you to report?" Talanne asked.

"We found Jeric's sentinel dead in the garden. There was a second man in our colors, also dead. We believe Bori planned treachery, then could not go through with it."

"Why do you think that?"

"Why else take the boy outside? We all know your orders on that. Under no circumstance is the boy to go outside."

Talanne nodded. "Very well. Is the building secure?"

"Yes."

"Triple the guards."

"They have already been doubled, Colonel."

"Did I ask your opinion? No, I gave you an order."

"Aye, Colonel Talanne." He turned on his heel and left the room. Guards could be glimpsed on either side of the door. They were three deep on either side.

The boy pressed in against Troi's legs. She placed her hands on his shoulders. He was trembling, and Troi's skin felt cold with his fear.

From Talanne there was no fear for herself. Worry over the boy and her husband; for herself, nothing. Troi tried to feel something from the guards around her. Some hint of fear, but there was nothing. It was as if they had hit a switch inside themselves: on, fear; off, soldier. Colonel Talanne was full of emotions, all crowding near the surface, but the guards seemed emotionless.

Troi knew she could have concentrated, searched below the surface thoughts, but that was an intrusion. Without good reason she did not peel away the layers of someone's carefully built protection.

There was also the possibility that there was nothing inside the guards, nothing to find. No, surely not. Surely the emotionally dead guards were the exception. Could a race of people destroy their inner-selves along with their environment? Did the barren, polluted world reflect the barrenness of the people themselves? If that were true, then the peace talks were going to be very difficult. Troi needed to know if there were deeper emotions in the guards. If Colonel Talanne was the exception, Picard would need to know. It was those deeper emotions that Picard would appeal to for peace. If most of the Orianians were closer to Vulcans in their emotional makeup, it would change how Picard approached them. Troi needed to know.

She chose a guard near her and began to concentrate gently. She didn't want to startle him. There were races that could sense an empathic intrusion.

Picard's communicator burst into life. The sound made Troi jump. Her concentration shattered.

"Riker to Picard."

"Yes, Number One, what is it?"

"We've received a distress signal from an alien vessel. They call themselves the Milgians. The Federation has no record of a first contact. Their engines are in danger of exploding. Lives have already been lost. Even at maximum warp we are two days from them, but we are the nearest ship." Riker's voice hesitated, "There are over four hundred lives at stake."

"I understand," Picard said. He glanced at his hostess and her guards. "You have to answer the distress call, Number One."

"Will you and the away team be all right?"

Troi felt Picard's doubt. "We will be fine, Number One. In fact beam up the three security personnel."

"Would you repeat that, Sir?" Riker said.

"Captain, you can't," Worf said.

Picard stared at his security chief. "Colonel Talanne has done us the great honor of trusting us. We will return that honor."

"Permission to speak freely, Captain," Worf asked.

"Denied, Lieutenant. Beam up the security personnel, Number One."

"Captain, I . . ."

"That was an order, Commander Riker," Picard said.

"Aye, sir."

The three security personnel shimmered, then vanished. The room suddenly seemed much less crowded.

Talanne shook her head. "I do not know if you are very brave or very foolish, Captain."

"We must negotiate peace, and that only comes through trust."

"You are hoping to lead by example," Talanne said. "You give up some of your bodyguards, and others will follow."

Picard smiled. "It might be a start."

"It may well work. If the Federation ambassador

26

trusts his safety without a phalanx of guards, then it seems cowardly for the rest of us to hide behind our own."

"Riker, here, Captain. We have the security team on board. If we are going to answer the distress call, we have to go now."

"We'll be here when you return, Number One."

"I don't like this, Captain."

"Nor I," Worf said.

"I appreciate your concern, both of you, but trust must begin somewhere. I think it has to begin with us."

"I was going to suggest we increase security after what has just happened, Captain."

"I cannot negotiate a peace treaty behind a wall of armed guards." Picard shook his head. "No, we will be fine as we are."

"What's happened down there, Captain?" Riker asked.

Picard hesitated, then said, "There have been two more deaths, and some talk of bribery."

"Captain, I request that you beam back to the ship immediately. When we have aided the alien vessel you can return and continue the talks."

"No, Commander, if these talks only work because I have the *Enterprise* to back me, then what happens to the peace when we leave?" Picard smoothed his hands down his jacket. "Perhaps this is all for the best. Return as soon as you can, Picard out."

"Captain . . ." Riker said.

"That was an order, Commander."

"Aye, Captain. Riker out." Will's voice was well controlled, but his anger was like a small slap to Troi. How was Will ever to guard the captain if the captain

27

would not listen to reason? A question without an answer.

"I see that I am not the only one to have their orders questioned," Talanne said.

Picard smiled. "No."

"I do not think that your chief of security approves of your refusing reinforcements," she said, nodding at Worf.

Worf shifted his stance, jaw clenched tight. His dark eyes glanced at Talanne, then back to empty air. He was careful not to look at the captain.

"I am sure that Lieutenant Worf does not approve," Picard said.

Worf made an abrupt sound, almost a snort.

Picard ignored it. "But if every official we meet has to have an equal number of bodyguards . . . it could get rather crowded."

"Very true, Captain," Talanne said.

Picard smiled. "You trusted me first, Talanne, by giving up two of your own guards."

"Perhaps, or perhaps I think you are outsiders and would have no reason to harm me. It would be very different if you were a member of the Venturi faction."

"Peace must be based on trust. Armed camps cannot trust one another," Picard said.

"I will give you one of my guards, Captain. No matter how good your Lieutenant Worf may be, I do not wish to explain to the Federation how their ambassador met his end."

"I am sure that Lieutenant Worf will be glad of the help."

Worf gave a curt nod. "As of now, yes, I would." His voice held an angry thread of growling.

Talanne smiled, then laughed, a sharp, abrupt sound. "I like you, Picard. And that is good. You are right about the mistrust. It is thick in the air like the poison we have to breath outside."

She held out one hand, and Jeric ran to her. His warmth lingered against Troi's legs, the feel of the boy's thin shoulders on her hands.

"I will go see to my husband now, Captain. I hope you and your people find this room comfortable. We will move your quarters every few days, as a matter of caution."

"Where will the rest of my people be staying?"

Talanne frowned. "I assumed you would want everyone in the same room. I am sorry. It is our custom to share rooms with our most trusted guards. If you wish other rooms, I can provide them given some time."

"Please . . ." Picard began.

"Captain," Worf said, "perhaps it would be best to share rooms."

Picard took a deep breath, to protest, then thought better of it. "Very well. We accept your hospitality and your customs. Thank you."

"Sleeping mats are rolled against the wall underneath the wall hangings," she said. "I will leave you to settle in. I will bring your evening meal personally."

"That is most gracious."

She gave a small smile. "Not at all, Captain. I just don't want to come back tomorrow morning and find you've all been poisoned."

"Poison," Worf said, "is a coward's weapon."

"Lieutenant Worf," Picard said evenly.

"No, that is all right, Captain. As it turns out, I

29

agree, but not all my enemies have such fine distinctions. I will send Breck to you as a guard. He is the one whose face you saw." With that she turned and left. Jeric glanced back once before the door cut off his view.

"Well," Picard said. "What do you make of that? Counselor?"

"Colonel Talanne wants the peace talks to work. But the guards . . . I don't know what the guards want."

"Explain."

"On the surface their minds are almost clean of emotion like machines." Troi hesitated.

"Go on, Counselor."

"They seem to be able to hide their emotions almost completely, as if they can function independently of their . . . feelings."

"Theories on that?"

"I don't know, Captain. I've never felt anything like it. It is as if they are as desolate as their planet."

"A race of people is not tied to their planet, Counselor. The fate of one is not necessarily the fate of the other."

"I know that, but . . ."

"But?"

"I have no other explanation for what I sensed in them, Captain."

"Lieutenant Worf?"

"These are warriors without honor, Captain. I have never seen a race where treachery is so commonplace."

"We will be on our guard, Lieutenant. Believe me, I do not wish to end my days here."

30

"With all due respect, Captain, it is not a matter of being on guard."

"Explain."

"These are assassins without a code of honor. They seem to have no rules. If this is true and they are determined to kill you, they will succeed."

"You cannot stop them?" Picard asked.

"I will give my life to stop them, Captain, but if they are truly determined and do not care how many of them die in the attempt, we will be overrun. There are simply more of them than there are of us."

The captain nodded. "I see. Well, we will just have to make the best of it. As far as we know, there have been no attacks on us personally."

"We have been here less than an hour, Captain. Even assassins need time to plan," Worf said.

Picard smiled. "Of course, Worf."

Troi felt the captain's humor—humor in the face of danger. It was a very human trait. But she also felt Worf's utter seriousness. He believed that it was only a matter of time and planning before a direct attack was made on the captain.

Chapter Three

DEANNA TROI WOKE TO DARKNESS. She sat upright, clutching covers to her chest, her breathing loud and ragged in her ears. Troi waited for the nightmare's fear to recede, but it didn't. She whispered, "Light," but nothing happened. Had the computer not heard her? She reached out and her hand brushed heavy cloth and under that a hard flat surface. A wall and a wall hanging. She was on Oriana, on a peace mission.

The fear was like a hand squeezing her heart. Her pulse thudded in her throat until she could barely breathe. It wasn't the lingering taste of nightmare. Rather, it was someone else's ongoing terror. It screamed along Troi's nerves, roared through her brain, until she had to press her hands to her mouth to keep the screams inside.

She had to make it stop. Crawling out of the bedroll, she saw a dim light coming from somewhere.

Without windows it would have been too dark to even move around, but the glow showed the sleeping form of the captain.

Worf was sitting quietly in a corner, and Troi could just make out the shape of the Klingon's face. She felt rather than saw his eyes upon her. Soundlessly, Worf moved toward the counselor.

They met just beside the door. Worf leaned next to her. His breath was warm on her cheek as he whispered. "Counselor, what is it?"

The terror beat through her like a second heartbeat. Troi wasn't sure she could talk without the fear spilling out into screams. She shook her head slightly, trying to think of how she could communicate the terror.

"Are you ill?" he whispered.

Yes, Troi thought, yes, I'm ill. All she could manage was a nod.

"I will wake the captain."

Troi started to say no, but then nodded. She did not wish to involve the captain in her own problems. There was a price to be paid for being an empath, and yet it might be something important. Until she knew where the terror originated, Troi had no way of knowing if the others needed to know or not.

Worf knelt by the captain. Picard woke instantly, one hand gripping Worf's arm. "What is it?"

"Something is wrong with Counselor Troi."

The captain rolled over. "What is it, Worf?"

"She is ill."

Troi was beginning to shake as if cold. The terror was mind-bending, horrible. Captain Picard was suddenly beside her. "Counselor, what's wrong?"

"I . . . I don't know. Fear . . . horrible fear." She shook her head. "I can't . . . Must stop it. Must stop it!"

"Could this be some kind of attack?" Worf asked.

Troi shook her head. "No. Must find . . . Captain!" Troi pressed her hands over her face. If something wasn't done soon, she would begin screaming. Once she started, she wasn't sure she could stop.

Picard gripped her upper arms, his strong hands digging into her flesh. "Counselor Troi." He shook her gently. "Counselor, what can we do to help?"

She did her best to swallow the fear, to breathe past the screams in her head. "Must find . . . and stop it. Fear, must stop it. Find it. Please!"

Picard nodded. "Worf, tell the Orianian guards that something is wrong. Explain as little as possible to them. Tell them the Counselor needs medical attention, and we will accompany her."

Worf nodded. "Yes, Captain." He moved to the door and opened it. Two guards were outside the door. One was Breck, the guard Talanne had sent to them.

Troi could not hear what was said. There was a far-off murmuring sound in her head. Not the screams, but a babble of voices, echoes. The fear was fading, changing. Sorrow, such unending sadness. Her throat tightened with unshed tears. Was it the same person or was it someone else?

Her mind felt raw from the terror, abused. Her empathic abilities were dulled by the emotional assault, but the sorrow . . . the sorrow remained.

Picard took her elbow gently and led her through the door. One of the Orianian guards led the way.

Worf led their own party, Troi and Picard in the center with Worf and Breck, bringing up the rear.

"Are you better?" Picard asked softly.

She nodded. "The fear has receded, but it isn't over. Whatever caused the fear is still very real. I . . . I can't explain it, but something is very wrong."

"Can you lead us to the disturbance?"

"Yes."

The guard that led them hesitated outside a narrow corridor. This close, Troi should have been able to feel what caused him to pause, but the emotional battering she had received, was still receiving, had dulled her senses. It was as if all her powers were concentrated on this one person's sorrow.

"We must be very quiet. There was a birth scheduled tonight," the guard said. His voice was bland, ordinary, but something in the way he stood at the head of the corridor, as if afraid to go down, made Troi wonder.

They hurried down the corridor, past several doors all painted to resemble exotic flowers in livid, Day-glo colors. Troi stopped, almost stumbling. Only the captain's hand kept her from falling. She placed her hand against a door on the right-hand side of the hallway. "In here, Captain." The tears finally crept down her face. "In here."

Breck said, "That is the nursery. We are not allowed in there."

"Something is wrong, Captain, very wrong," Troi said.

"My ship's counselor is skilled at healing emotional wounds. She wishes to help whoever is behind this door."

He shook his head. "That is not allowed."

"You can't just ignore it," Troi said. "She's hurting. They've given her something to make her sleep, but it isn't enough." She pulled away from Picard's hand and went to the guard. "Please, I must help her. I must try."

The guard stared at Troi. His masked face gave no hint of what he felt. "Can you truly help?"

"I want to try, please."

He glanced across at the other guard. "What were our orders on restricted areas?"

"No restricted areas. Colonel Talanne said the ambassador was to have full access."

Breck took a deep breath. "Very well, if you truly believe you can help." He hit a code into the door keypad, and the door whooshed open.

There were voices in her mind, whispers, echoes. She shook her head trying to clear it, to follow the sorrow, the tears. But it was like the voices of ghosts.

Picard touched her arm. "What is happening to you, Counselor?"

"Voices in my head, but not voices. I don't know." She looked at the captain. "It's like I'm hearing ghosts."

The guard made an odd sign with his left hand—two fingers pointing out towards Troi. "You can hear the voices of the lifeless, can't you?" His voice was hushed, choked.

Troi could only nod. It made sense of a sort.

"What do you mean, the voices of the lifeless?" Picard asked.

Breck shook his head. "We have gifted ones in our people, too, Captain. I do not envy them. This place is haunted enough without mind-voices."

36

The room was huge, cavernous like a warehouse. But it was empty. The floor stretched smooth and unbroken toward the distant back wall. Their footsteps echoed in the emptiness. The walls were divided into small rectangles. Wires and clear plastic tubing ran in and out of each individual rectangle. Liquid slurped through the tubes. The wires hummed with electricity. "What is this place?" Picard asked.

"It is the room of lifeless children," the guard said. This time there was no mistaking the catch in his voice. Troi did not need to feel it to hear the sadness.

Troi moved toward the right hand wall. Picard let her go, staying close by in case he was needed. Worf and the Orianian security team were being alert, searching for enemies.

The Orianian said, "No one will attack us here. It is a place of neutrality."

Worf nodded, but his hand stayed near his phaser just the same.

Troi touched the cool metal of the walls. Liquid ran through two tubes, a rainbow of wires fed into the small rectangle. The whispering in her head was louder. It was like the sound of water running, or wind in leaves, continuous, monotonous, but . . . There was meaning here, intelligence. It wasn't just wind or water. There were thoughts captured behind these walls. Thoughts, like ragged bits of dream.

She laid her hands flat on one rectangle. The thoughts were stronger when she concentrated, but still made no sense. "I don't understand. What are they saying?"

"Who, lady?" one of the guards asked.

"I don't know. I . . ." Then suddenly, Troi knew what was behind all those rectangles. There were

37

hundreds of them like boxes in a warehouse. Liquid slurped in and out of the tubes. The wires hummed, and there was the faintest smell of electricity, a sharp ozone smell.

Troi backed away from the wall, clutching her hands to her stomach. "Oh, my god," she whispered.

"Counselor, what is it?" Picard asked.

"Babies . . ." she whirled to look at all the holding tanks, "babies."

"These are the lifeless children," Breck said. "I told you that."

"But they're not dead," Troi said. She walked up to him, staring up into his face. "They're alive inside there."

He shook his head. "They are lifeless."

"No, I can feel them thinking, dreaming. I know they're alive."

"You are mistaken, lady," the guard said.

Troi shook her head, backing away from the guard. "Captain."

"I'm here, Troi," Picard said, coming to stand beside her.

"They are alive."

"I believe you, Counselor, but why would the guards lie?"

"I don't know." She stared at the warehouse of dead children. It was impossible. They were keeping them alive. The tubes and wires were feeding them— why did they say the children were dead? It made no sense.

"Is this what woke you, Counselor?"

"No." She started walking through the huge room toward a small door at the end. "Behind there." Troi knew now that it was a woman whose terror she had shared. The woman was sleeping now, but whatever had started her terror and then her grief was still there. They could drug the woman, but when she woke, the emotions would still be there, raw and waiting to suck her down. Would they swallow Troi up again, as well? The counselor didn't know. She could not remember when a stranger's pain had so affected her.

The door at the far end of the room opened. An Orianian stepped through. She was bare-faced, with the typical high-boned cheeks and huge luminous eyes. She was dressed in orange surgical dress. A doctor perhaps?

The woman did not see them at first. Her eyes were downcast, staring at something she carried. The orange wrapped bundle was the color of the surgical gown and so small that it would not have filled Troi's two hands. The Orianian woman looked up at them, almost in slow motion. Her eyes were pale brown, large in her face, but filled with unutterable sorrow.

Troi looked away from that haggard face, but the emotion did not leave. It was not a matter of eye contact, but of the woman's need. Her despair reached out for Troi like a blanket, wet and gray and suffocating. Troi pushed the emotion away. She could not accept this woman's pain. In any case, it wasn't this one who had woken her.

"Guards, who are these people, and how dare you bring them here?" There should have been anger in her voice, but there was none left. It was as if the despair had eaten everything else.

The first guard went to one knee before the woman.

"Dr. Zhir, this is the Federation ambassador and his party. This one," he pointed at Troi, "is a healer of some kind. They said they could help."

"You know no one is to enter this place on the night of a birth. You know that."

The second guard, Breck, went down on one knee beside the first. "Dr. Zhir, Colonel Talanne gave orders that the ambassador is to be denied nothing. He is to have full access."

"I am sure she did not mean for you to bring strangers into our holy places."

Picard stepped forward. "Dr. Zhir, we meant no harm. My counselor was awakened by the pain of one of your patients. We want only to help."

Doctor Zhir laughed, an abrupt, bitter sound. "Help? You cannot help us. No one can help us, Federation Ambassador. Our sins are too great." She hugged the tiny orange bundle to her chest. It made a small protesting sound, almost a cry.

"We are here to stop the war, Doctor. Surely that will help."

"Stop the war if you can, but it is too late for our race."

"I do not understand, Doctor," Picard said.

"What sort of healer are you?"

"I would be called a mind-healer," Troi said.

Zhir nodded, slowly. "Then you know what is in this room. You know what our greed and hatred have done to the children."

Troi shook her head. "The guards say the babies in the tanks are dead." She glanced at Picard. "We don't understand."

"I think it is too late, Ambassador. I think that even

40

if peace happens tomorrow that race is doomed, but you don't believe that, do you?"

"No, Doctor, I don't. You will find most humans believe a great deal in hope," Picard said.

Zhir stood a little straighter. Her thin face became smooth and calm. She had made some sort of decision, and with it came a moment of peace. "Come, Ambassador, let me show you why I have given up on hope. Look upon the sins of Oriana."

"Doctor, it is forbidden," the first guard said.

"I am a doctor, I am allowed, and they are strangers. Our laws do not hold them."

"Are you sure, Doctor?"

"Colonel Talanne said to show them everything. Well, by the withered leaf, I shall."

The two guards still kneeling on the floor laid their foreheads on their bent knees. They covered their faces with their gloved hands.

Zhir stepped around the kneeling guards to stand next to Picard. Worf started to move between them, but Picard waved him back. "It's all right, Lieutenant, I trust her."

Doctor Zhir stared at him for a moment, a puzzled expression on her face. "You are either a fool or a wise man to be able to decide who to trust."

"We come to make peace for your people, Doctor. Trust must begin somewhere."

She nodded. "Yes." She stared at Troi. "The guard said you were a healer. Is that true?"

"I am a healer of the mind, yes."

The doctor laughed, that same abrupt and almost ugly sound. "Oh, we need such healers as yourself. There is so much I cannot heal. Perhaps you could alter their minds so they do not care if they are healed or not."

"I would be glad to help in any way I can."

"Do not promise until you see the task I set you, Healer," Zhir said. "Come closer, you and the Federation ambassador, come and see what I hold in my arms."

Troi moved forward to stand shoulder to shoulder with the captain. She felt Zhir's fear, disgust, anticipation.

Doctor Zhir balanced the orange bundle in the crook of her right arm. With the left hand she began pushing back the cloth. A tiny fist thrust into the air. Tiny feet kicked free of the bundling. Troi leaned forward to touch the smooth reddish skin. Soft, almost furlike in its texture, like that of all newborns.

The cloth fell away from the face. A tiny mouth opened wide with a high-pitched and keening scream. The rest of the face was smooth skin, blank as if all the parts hadn't been put together yet. No eyes, no nose, only a thin red slit of a mouth.

Picard took a sharp breath. He steadied himself, Troi felt the effort it cost him. "Is this typical?"

"Typical?" the doctor repeated, "yes and no. We have many deformities. The pollution has contaminated our water, air, the ground. All our food, our world, is poisonous to us. And it does this." She began to rewrap the crying baby.

Troi stroked a tiny fist. It reacted, grabbing her finger, squeezing. "What will happen to him?"

"He will go in one of the vats," the doctor said, "and we will reconstruct eyes and a face. We will build him into a whole person."

"Do you have to do this with many of your children?" Picard asked.

"Reconstruct them, you mean?"

"Yes."

"Most of our children in the last ten years have been beyond saving. The deformities were too serious. Few women even carry a baby to term. Their bodies are too full of poisons to support life."

"But we saw Colonel Talanne's son, Jeric," Troi said.

"Yes, Jeric." The doctor shook her head. "I do not explain miracles. I am merely thankful for them. This," she held the tiny baby closer, "is what we usually find if we are lucky."

"The guards called this the place of lifeless children," Troi said, "but they aren't dead."

"We can keep them alive, but we cannot bring them to life," Doctor Zhir said.

Troi frowned. "I don't understand."

"We have the technology to keep them from dying, but we cannot cure what is wrong. We cannot help them become real children. Children that can walk and run, laugh and think. They are alive but they are not. Do you understand?"

Troi stared round the room, at the hundreds of boxes. "You can't cure them?" she made it a question.

"No, we cannot cure them, but we can repair some of what is wrong," the doctor said.

Picard stared at the boxes and at the kneeling guards. The enormity of the room, the slurping of liquid going through tubes, the faint hum of electricity, all washed over him in a cool horror. Troi could feel his instant sympathy with this beleaguered doc-

43

tor, his instant repulsion at the contents of the room. "As soon as possible I would ask your permission to have my ship's doctor beam down and look at your . . . children. There may be medical techniques that could aid you."

"If you could truly aid us here, then it would be a powerful thing to bring to the peace table."

Picard nodded. "I understand."

"I am a doctor in a world of perpetual war and disease and deformity. There are not many doctors left, most of us became other things." She rocked the crying baby until it stopped. "The pain, you understand."

"It was your pain I felt, part of it, anyway," Troi said.

"You felt my pain?" Zhir said. "And it woke you, brought you here?"

"Yours, and the woman who gave birth tonight," Troi said.

Zhir smiled, ever so slightly. "You have given me hope, and I curse you for it. I thought I had given up such useless thoughts, but there it is, hope, the last refuge of madmen and dreamers."

"Would you like me to see the mother tonight?" Troi asked.

"She is sleeping. Better that she sleeps as long as she can. It will be a long time before her son comes out of this room. Breck there," she indicated one of the kneeling guards, "was one of mine, not so different from this one. Though he did heal better than most. Almost all of the people below twenty spent some time in this room." She shook her head. "Go, go, I must put this little one to bed."

"I have your permission to send my ship's doctor as soon as she becomes available?" Picard asked.

Doctor Zhir nodded. "There is always room for another doctor on Oriana, Federation Ambassador. Now please go." She spoke directly to the two kneeling guards. "Rise, the sin is covered."

The guards uncovered their faces then looked up, blinking into the light.

"Escort the ambassador and his people out of here."

"Yes, Dr. Zhir. We meant no intrusion," the first guard said.

"Hope is never an intrusion but often a lie." She smiled again to herself and spoke softly to the carefully wrapped baby. Troi could not hear what she said.

The guards stood and began herding Picard and the others toward the far door. "You heard the doctor, we must go now." There was fear in his voice, as well as respect.

Doctor Zhir pressed a panel on the wall and a silver drawer popped open. Zhir was speaking softly to the baby.

The guards almost physically pushed them toward the door. Only Worf's warning glare kept them from it.

Dr. Zhir began to sing clear and soft, but it carried. A song Troi did not know. The whispering echoes of the babies, hundreds of babies, thoughts, ragged bits of dream responded to the singing. Troi felt a brush of pleasure, like a whisper of happiness from the babies.

Doctor Zhir was singing to the lifeless children, and they heard her. Her voice, her . . . love for them.

The corridor outside seemed somehow wider,

fresher. Everyone was relieved to be out of that room. Everyone. Troi was no exception, but she could still feel Dr. Zhir singing. Not the words but the feelings —grief, horror, pain, but under it all like something new . . . hope. The last refuge for madmen and dreamers.

Chapter Four

PICARD, TROI AND WORF were just outside their room when a guard hurried toward them. The Orianians pointed rifles at a nearly running figure. He or she, displayed empty hands. "Please," the voice was male, "I am Breck and Colonel Talanne has sent me to find the Federation healer. A mind-healer."

"What has happened?" Picard asked.

"The general's son, Jeric, he is . . . not well," the guard said.

"What is wrong with him?" Troi asked.

"I know not. Colonel Talanne ordered me to fetch the mind-healer from the starship. She said only that her son is ill and in need of help."

"Counselor?" Picard said.

"He is telling the truth, Captain. He is worried about the boy." Troi stepped out from between the still cautious guards. "I am the . . . mind-healer. I will come with you."

47

"No," Worf said. "It could be a trap."

"He believes what he's saying," Troi said.

"He could have been lied to as well."

"No," Troi said.

"Captain, this could be a ploy to separate us. The counselor could be used as a hostage."

"If I understand the word properly," Breck said, "we do not take hostages. To hide behind a nonwarrior is an act of cowardice."

"You use assassins and poison," Worf said.

"Yes, but not hostages," Breck said. He seemed to find nothing wrong with his code of honor. Poison, but not hostages. Interesting.

"Lieutenant, we must trust our hosts," Picard said.

The look on Worf's face said plainly how far he trusted their hosts. Picard chose to ignore it. "Counselor, do you feel safe going to the aid of this child?"

"Yes, Captain."

He nodded. "If you could help the general's child, it might help negotiations."

"Understood, Captain."

"But that is not worth sending you alone. Lieutenant Worf, you may accompany Counselor Troi."

"I agree someone should accompany her, Captain, but what of your own safety while I am away?"

"I managed to stay alive long before I met you or Commander Riker. I think I can manage a short time alone. Besides, the Orianian guards should be able to stave off the attackers until your return."

Worf frowned. "Your safety is not a laughing matter, Captain."

"I am not laughing, Lieutenant Worf."

The guard who had come to fetch Troi was shifting

from foot to foot. "Please, Colonel Talanne was most insistent. Will you come now?"

"Yes," Troi said, "I'm coming." She followed the guard down the hallway, the opposite way from the nurseries. Worf trailed behind her like a frowning shadow.

The boy's room was nearly identical to the one where Troi had awakened—was it only an hour ago—only the wall hangings were different. Scenes of nearly life-sized children playing games. Beautiful Orianian children. Children like Jeric, not like the babies in the nurseries. There were no wounds or deformities here. The running, laughing children were as perfect as the flowers they picked.

Had Oriana been like this once? The vibrant green trees, the flowers like melted rainbows covering soft, rolling hills. The golden-skinned children with their liquid, bright eyes. Laughter, play, life.

Troi stared at the two bodyguards in their ever-present face masks and goggles, their rifles. What had happened to this planet, these people, to make them destroy everything? Surely, nothing was worth such total destruction.

Talanne sat on the edge of a sleeping mat holding her child. Jeric cried softly, his small hands clutching her loose blouse. She was stroking his silky hair, whispering, "It's going to be all right, Jeric. The healer is here now. She'll help you." Talanne met Troi's eyes as she said the last. She wanted her words to be true, but she feared they were lies.

In that moment Troi wanted to help the boy, not just for his own sake, or for the peace talks, but to

49

take that haunted look from Talanne's eyes. The look that had seen too much that was bright and wondrous wither and die. Troi knelt beside the mother and child. She spoke softly, "Jeric, can you look at me?"

The little boy peered at her through his mother's arms. His large, brown-gold eyes shimmered with tears.

Troi smiled at him. "Did you have a bad dream?"

He nodded solemnly.

"Can you tell me about it?"

He just blinked at her.

"It's all right, Jeric," Talanne murmured. "Tell the healer what you dreamed."

The boy's fear was fading, replaced by puzzlement. He didn't understand the question.

"Jeric," Troi said, "did you see scary pictures in your head?"

He nodded.

"Can you tell me what the pictures looked like?"

He nodded. Talanne held him tight, as if her arms could keep him safe.

"I saw Bori."

Troi looked a question at Talanne. "It is . . . was his sentinel," Talanne said.

Troi nodded. "What was Bori doing?"

"He was talkin' to a man."

"Could you hear what they said?" Troi asked.

Jeric shook his head.

"They just stood and talked?"

He nodded.

"Nothing else?"

Jeric shook his head solemnly, eyes too large for his tear-stained face. He was telling the truth as far as he knew it. But it wasn't the whole truth, just the truth as his conscious mind understood it. Underneath, in the subconscious, was another truth. Down where his nightmare had come from, Jeric knew why seeing two men talk was terrifying. But he was not ready to face what he had seen. Troi thought it likely that Jeric had seen his sentinel die in defense of his life. It was a terrible burden for one so young.

Troi patted the boy's hair. He just stared at her with large blue eyes. His skin was still fear pale, but he didn't remember why two men talking should fill him with such dread. "May I speak with you in private, Colonel Talanne?" Troi asked.

"Of course." Talanne's concern for her boy was like a sharp push in Troi's gut. Talanne might be the perfect warrior as most of the Orianians were, but she felt real fear, normal mother's fear for her child. Troi thought that was a good sign all on its own. If the Orianians loved their children, then peace was possible.

Talanne settled Jeric on his sleeping mat. She smoothed his fair hair onto the silkiness of the pillow. She handed him a stuffed animal that looked vaguely like a horse, except it was bright red with delicate embroidery covering most of its body. The embroidery was images of leaves, flowers, trees. The stuffed animal, like the wall hangings, spoke of artistry, grace, softer things than war.

Jeric clutched the toy in his small arms. "Rest, my little love. I have to speak with the healer. I'll be right back," Talanne said.

The boy didn't cling to her. Rather, he lay, tightly clutching his toy, and said, "Right back, Merme?"

Talanne smiled. "Right back, I promise." She kissed him gently on the forehead and stood.

Troi walked to the other side of the room with the woman trailing behind her. Worf stood near the door with the other guards. He looked at Troi, his eyes flickering back to the boy. She could not read his mind exactly but would have bet that Worf was thinking about his own son. Alexander, more than anything else, had softened the Klingon, made him able to sympathize with a parent whose child cried out in the night.

When Troi was sure the boy would not overhear, she asked, "Was Jeric close to his sentinel?"

"Yes. Bori had been his personal guard since he was born," Talanne said.

Troi was surprised. The changing of the guard had seemed so random. "Is it usual to have a personal guard?"

"Every leader and each member of that leader's family has at least one personal guard. Someone who is loyal to that one person above any other loyalty."

Troi thought of something. "Is that why Breck is almost always with our party? Always with Captain Picard?"

Talanne smiled. "Yes."

She would have to remember to tell the captain that they had their own trained Orianian sentinel, a personal guard loyal to them. "If a guard is loyal to one person, does that mean he, or she, would put that single person's safety above the good of others?"

Talanne nodded. "Exactly."

Troi wondered if that made discipline a problem, but she wanted to know about the boy for now. "So, Bori would be intensely loyal to Jeric?"

"Yes."

"Have you discovered what happened? Why he took Jeric outside?"

Talanne shook her head. "Not yet." She sighed. "And truthfully, Healer, we may never know, unless Jeric himself remembers. The warriors that could tell us what happened are both dead."

"Do you believe that the guard betrayed your son?"

"I can't think what other purpose would be served by going outside. Everything is dangerous outside; the air, the water, the ground itself is so contaminated that what little food does grow is deadly. But we eat it anyway." Her face seemed suddenly older, lines around the mouth deepening with bitterness. "We eat and drink the poison that slaughters our children. I lost three children before Jeric. They never even drew one breath of life. The last baby was the worst, so badly mangled that the doctors could not save him. I prayed for him to die."

She stared at Troi, her dark eyes searching the counselor's face. "Do you have children?"

"I did once," Troi said.

"A death?"

Troi nodded. The pain of her own son's death could still come back to bite at odd moments.

"If you have lost a child, then you understand," Talanne said.

"Yes," Troi agreed. "I understand."

Talanne reached out impulsively and took the counselor's hand. "What is wrong with my son?"

"I believe he witnessed the death of his sentinel. From what you've told me, I have to agree with you. Bori was going to betray Jeric, but I think that at the last minute he couldn't do it. In fact, he may have

53

died defending Jeric's life. I'm certain Jeric witnessed his death. He doesn't remember right now, but subconsciously, he does." She held Talanne's hand in both of hers. "The dreams will get worse, I'm afraid. But he needs to remember. It will help him to heal the wound. But do not rush him, let him remember in his own time."

"We have told him that Bori is dead. Was that wrong?"

"No, but do not speak of it anymore than you must in front of him. This dream is the first step for him to remember on his own."

"Do you think Jeric will be able to tell us why they were outside?" Talanne asked.

"I honestly don't know."

Talanne nodded. She gave Troi's hand a last squeeze and withdrew her own hand. "Is there nothing you can do to help him?"

"Not really. I would like to talk to him during the day. I might be able to help him remember more gently through therapy, but the mind is a delicate thing, Colonel Talanne. It heals best in its own time."

"But he will heal. He won't always wake screaming?" The woman stared at Troi, her need to hear a positive answer tripped over Troi's skin like a vibrating string. And as so often happened in her work, Troi couldn't give a definite answer. "I believe he will heal. He is very young. Children often recover more quickly than adults."

"But you can't promise, can you?"

Troi wanted to say yes, she wanted to fill that frightened core inside Talanne. That little pocket of fear and protection that wrapped around Jeric in his mother's mind. But Troi could not, would not lie. "No, I can't promise."

Talanne nodded. She put her hands over her eyes and took a long shuddering breath. "This blasted war touches everything, everything." When she took her hands down her face was still constricted with grief. Her body was calm but her face still betrayed her inner chaos.

Troi stared at her, waiting for the woman to spend as much effort to control her facial features as she had her body and voice, but it did not happen. Talanne was convinced that no one could tell she was in pain, even though the grief was plain on her face. Troi realized then that the Orianians always wore masks, always. They didn't understand facial expressions. That meant that if they were bare-faced, their emotions could easily be read by a certain Federation ambassador.

Colonel Talanne thought she was showing a mask of indifference. Her vibrating fear was tucked behind a wall of lies. Lies that sounded hollow even to herself.

"Thank you for coming so promptly, Healer. I am most grateful." Her voice was utterly calm, but grief flickered behind her lovely eyes.

"I was glad to come. If you need me again, I will be here."

Her face constricted with an effort not to cry, but her voice did not betray her. "Thank you again. I will see him to sleep. You will be meeting with my husband tomorrow morning. I will be there. Good night, Healer."

"Good night, Colonel Talanne," Troi said. She had

been dismissed abruptly. But Troi understood. Talanne was holding onto her dignity with both hands. It was only a matter of moments before the second highest ranking Torlick officer broke down and cried. Talanne wanted them gone before she did.

A guard opened the door, and Troi started to walk out, but Worf stopped her. "I will go first and check the hallway."

Stepping outside, Worf was relieved to be able to do something tangible. This talk of children and emotional scars had made him uneasy. Ever since they had beamed down to Oriana, he had felt out of his element. Diplomacy was not his strong suit. He half-wanted a confrontation, something real and physical to take the taste of grief from his mind. Colonel Talanne's worry for her son made him think of Alexander.

Worf pushed thoughts of children from his mind. He had work to do. Searching the hallway, he found it empty except for the constant colors. He had grown weary of the bright, screaming paintings.

"It is clear," he said. Troi walked out beside him, and the door closed behind them. They were left alone in the night-silent hallway. Worf could hear the blood rush in his own veins as he strained for any sound of trouble.

"We'd better report back to the captain," Troi said.

"Did you learn something?"

"Every important government leader has a personal sentinel that has loyalty first to the person they guard."

"It would make discipline difficult," Worf said.

"I suppose it would. Breck, the guard that always

seems to be with us, is our personal sentinel or perhaps the captain's."

"Does this mean that this guard is loyal to the captain before his own people?" Worf asked.

"I believe so. I also learned that the Orianians love their children."

"Does that surprise you?"

"They value their children, Worf. I think that what's happening to the children is one of the major reasons this peace negotiation has been called."

"Does the captain know this?"

"Not yet."

Worf nodded. "You have learned much."

"I hope so," Troi said. She looked back at the closed door. A look passed over her face as if she were listening to music that he could not hear. He would have bet she was sensing some emotion. Was she feeling the child's fear? The mother's sorrow? Not for the first time, Worf was glad that he did not share Troi's gift.

They had not gone far when a man stepped around the corner. He was short, thin, almost childlike. He was dressed in full mask and a plain brown cloak.

Worf stepped in front of Troi, using his body to shield her. "Who are you?" he demanded.

The Orianian held his hands palm upward to show them empty. Then he spread the cloak out for Troi and Worf to see that he had no weapon. He was the first adult besides Dr. Zhir that they had met who was not armed. "I am called Audun."

"Are you Torlick or Venturi?" Worf asked.

"Neither." He was still walking toward them.

"Stand where you are," Worf said. Worf drew his phaser and pointed it at the man's chest. He appeared to be unarmed, but Worf knew appearances could deceive.

"I mean you no harm."

"Worf," Troi said, "I don't feel any hostility from him. If anything, he's afraid for his own safety."

"As he should be," Worf said. But he listened to Troi's words. If she said the man wasn't hostile, she was probably right. But Worf did not lower his phaser.

"He isn't afraid of you, Worf, but of . . ." Troi moved out from behind the Klingon and took two steps toward the man. "You're afraid of being discovered. Why?"

Worf tensed, fighting the urge to grab Troi and make her stay back behind him, where it was safe. But you could only protect crew members so far, they had to be free to do their duties. So he kept the phaser trained on the stranger and let Troi risk her life.

Audun smiled. "We heard there was a mind-healer with the ambassador. I did not believe it. It has been a long time since we had such a one among us." He took a step toward Troi, hand outstretched.

Worf gripped Troi's shoulder and drew her back toward him, the other hand still pointing the phaser at the man. "What do you want, Audun, if that is your name?"

The man laughed. "So suspicious. You must love our leaders." He let his hand drop back to his side, slowly. "I am a Green. Has no one mentioned us?"

"No," Worf said.

"They thought they could hide us away like they hide our dying children." The bitterness in his voice was plain, no empathy needed.

"Please, I must speak with you but not here. If I am discovered . . . they will kill me."

"You would lead us to some secluded place," Worf said.

"Some place more private, yes."

"An ambush." If it wasn't a trap, it was at least suspicious. The man was obviously hiding something.

"No, I swear to you, we mean no harm to anyone, not even our enemies. You bring the possibility of peace. Do you know how long we have prayed for such a thing?" Audun held out his hands as if begging. "Please, you must hear what I have to say."

"We hear you," Worf said.

"But . . ."

"He means us no harm," Troi said.

Worf shook his head. "No, Counselor, it is too dangerous. He talks here and now, or not at all."

Troi, as always, was too trusting. They had nothing but this man's words, and his emotions to guide them. Worf did not trust either.

"Please, Audun, speak to us," Troi said.

He lowered his voice, darting a look behind him down the hallway. "You do not understand. I will be killed on sight if they discover what I am."

"And what is that?" Worf asked.

"I am a bioengineer. If a person is even suspected of genetic manipulation, they will be killed. No trial is needed."

"Why?" Troi asked.

He darted another look around the empty halls. "I was a scientist. My specialty was biotechnology. They wanted me to use my knowledge to kill. I refused.

There are many of us, mostly scientists, doctors, others, who believe that our technology should be used to heal this planet not to destroy it."

"Commendable," said Worf, a growl creeping into his voice. He made no effort to hide his suspicion.

"Some members of our group were the first to tell our leaders that the planet was dying. Nearly three decades ago, our people predicted what has happened. Many of the people blame us for what is happening to the planet, because we predicted it. They are frightened and they need someone to hate. So they hate their enemies, and they hate us."

"That is a fine story, but what does it have to do with us," Worf said.

"Worf!" Troi said.

He ignored the counselor and kept his eyes on the man. She was worried he would insult the man. Worf was not.

"We have a way to clean the water of this world. We want to offer that to the two warring sides. The Greens want to be part of the new peace."

"The water on Oriana is lifeless. How can you clean it?" Troi asked.

"We have developed a bacteria that eats the pollutants but leaves the naturally occurring impurities alone."

"I do not trust him," Worf said.

"I do," Troi said. "Can you explain this process in more detail?"

"Yes, but . . ." he looked up and down the corridor, afraid, "Yes, if it means my death, I will tell you all."

"No," Troi said. "We will take you to a place of safety."

"What are you saying, Counselor?"

"He must speak with the captain."

"No! It could still be a trap." The thought of taking a stranger into the captain, the Federation ambassador, when assassins were everywhere, was out of the question.

"I would know if it were a trap," she said, firmly.

He trusted the counselor, if she said it was safe, it likely was, yet . . . "Even if I allowed you to endanger the captain," Worf said, "how would we keep the Orianian guard from taking this man prisoner?"

"The guards are loyal first and foremost to the people they guard. Loyal beyond any other allegiance."

"They will just allow us to consort with their enemies?" Worf said.

"Yes," she said.

He glanced down at Troi, then at the Orianian. He did look helpless, so tiny. Worf was certain he could break the man's spine over his knee like a stick. But you did not have to be muscular to be a good assassin, in fact looking helpless could be an asset. "I do not think this is a good idea."

"We have to hurry before any other Orianians see us," Troi said. She walked up to Audun before Worf could stop her. He watched her stand within easy reach of the man, and block his line of fire in one smooth motion. Worf ground his teeth just a bit. She was probably right, but she was making it difficult to guard her.

"You must explain all this in more detail to the Federation ambassador," Troi said.

"Truly?" Audun asked.

"Yes."

Audun gripped her hand tightly. "I am grateful to you for believing me."

"If you can purify the water of Oriana, it is I who am grateful."

"If we are to do this foolishness, we must get out of sight," Worf said. Leading the way, Worf hoped they would not run into any other Orianians. It would not help the peace process to have a pitched battle between the Federation party and the local bodyguards.

Worf gave a small, bitter smile. No, that would not do at all. He ushered Troi and the Orianian down the corridor. His phaser was still in his hand, on stun. Did Troi know the position she had put them in? He doubted it. She let her heart lead her head at times. Perhaps all empaths were like that.

Worf could not afford to let his feelings color his caution. He watched the empty corridors, tension riding up his spine. Troi and the man spoke quietly, smiling. If this Audun were telling the truth he could be a great help to the negotiations. If he were an assassin Troi would know. Troi had learned much this night that could be helpful. Worf watched the hallways for signs of trouble, and felt just a little useless. In a world at war he had thought to be comfortable, but their system of honor was too strange. War without honor was not a fit occupation for any warrior.

Chapter Five

GENERAL BASHA sat in a high-backed chair, made of black plastic. The back of the chair was far taller than the general and had looping black curls that formed fantastic shapes. It looked like a throne that had been partially melted and allowed to cool.

A desk of the same black plastic spilled away from him. The top was utterly clear as if no work were ever done on it.

The general's gold-ivory skin was mottled by bruises along the right side of his face. The delicate skin, the long, almost birdlike bone structure was covered in deep purple-black bruises. The color was startling against the paleness.

A long gash had been stitched over his forehead. Surely this wasn't the best the Orianian's medical technology could do? If a doctor could rebuild a baby's deformed face, Troi thought, surely they could heal bruises and wounds better than this.

Talanne stood to one side of the chair. Bodyguards stood to attention on either side. The two guards that had escorted the Federation party inside the room moved to stand just in front of the general. A last guard stood near one wall, closer to Talanne than to anyone else.

Breck and another Orianian guard that had been assigned to the Federation party took up posts on either side of Picard. Worf protected his back, but . . .

"Captain," Worf said, he leaned into Picard as if to whisper, but the Klingon's deep voice was not meant for whispering. "They have one more guard than you do. It is a deliberate insult."

Picard nodded. "I am aware of that particular Orianian custom, Lieutenant Worf."

General Basha waved a hand. "Cratin, go." He spoke carefully out of the left side of his mouth, trying very hard not to disturb his bruises.

"General Basha, I assure you," Picard said, "it is not necessary."

The general did not repeat his order. He merely glared at the guard. The look on that once beautiful face was frightening.

Troi could feel the weight of Basha's personality. It was a strange phenomenon that she had felt around some races, humans included. The truly great leaders had an almost psychic force to them.

The guard did not hesitate. He bowed very low and left the room without a word of protest.

"There, Captain, is that . . . satisfactory?" Basha said. He had to swallow between words. His pain was evident, but it was nothing like yesterday.

"Very," Picard said.

Troi realized it wasn't General Basha's physical

pain that had hit her so hard the day before, but the general's rage. Today he was calm. The anger was still there bubbling and hidden, but Basha was in control today. How unusual was it to catch General Basha so totally out of control? Very, if what Troi was sensing was correct. So why would such a steady man show himself to the Federation ambassador bloody and panicked? The panic and rage had been real, but there had been no effort to control them. The man sitting before them now was a man of iron will and nerves of ice. Why had he lost control yesterday? Troi would bring her findings to the captain later in private. For now, she watched and tried to learn more.

Talanne touched Basha's shoulder. There was quiet tenderness in that touch. It was like being allowed a glimpse into something very private. He started to nod but stopped in mid-motion. It hurt. "As you can see, Captain Picard, my husband is in some pain. If it is acceptable, I will do much of the talking for now."

"Of course," Picard said.

"There is a reception planned for this afternoon. The Venturi faction will be represented there."

"What of the Green party?" Picard asked.

General Basha's anger flared through him like a hot wind, but his face never betrayed it. He spoke carefully, each word an effort. "The Greens have no part in our government."

"They are a part of your people, General Basha. Can any peace last if all the people are not represented?" Picard said.

"The Greens will not be a part of this peace," Basha said.

"They wish to bring biotechnology to the bargaining table, General. They have a way to clean this

65

planet's water. Surely *that* is a valuable bargaining chip."

"NO!" The anger in that one word was enough to scald.

"Basha," Talanne said, "if they can truly make the water pure again . . ."

"No."

"General Basha, you came to the Federation for peace. You and the other leaders realized that war was killing not just the warriors, but the planet." Picard stepped forward, Worf moved with him to flank him. Basha's guards moved forward as well.

"I will be all right, Lieutenant. Thank you for your concern."

Worf started to protest, but Picard shot him a hard look. The captain had the ability to say much with a glance Troi noted. Worf stepped back in place.

"General Basha, Colonel Talanne, we have seen the nurseries. We have seen the lifeless children that are not lifeless at all."

Talanne stiffened, clutching her husband's shoulder. He winced at the strength of her grip. His own face remained impassive, guarded.

"That is a forbidden area, Captain. You had no right to be there," Basha said. He stared at the remaining guard that had accompanied them inside. "Tell me."

The guard went down on one knee, much as he had to the doctor. "General Basha, Colonel Talanne gave orders that the Federation ambassador was to have access to all areas."

"Is this true, Talanne?"

"Yes." Her voice was very soft as she said it.

66

"Very well, you have seen our greatest shame. It makes no difference."

"If the Greens' biotechnology can clean your water of the poisons, then perhaps they can clean the air. It is your planet that is killing your children. Even if the war stops today, the planet will not recover overnight. It will take decades. Would you turn down anything that would speed that process?"

"I will not deal with the Greens," Basha said.

"Why not?" Picard asked.

"They deal with demons," Basha said.

Picard just blinked at him, his uncertainty wriggling along Troi's skin. She herself didn't know what to make of this new information.

"They deal with demons?" Picard asked. His voice was careful to make no insult of the question.

"Everyone knows that they do unholy things. They twist the very stuff of life, deforming our babies, while theirs grow healthy!"

His hatred was like some ugly black thing inside Troi's head. It crawled over Troi's skin and filled her with revulsion. It was rare, but sometimes a person's hate was so strong that it was almost physically repulsive.

"I found the Green's representative to be intelligent and thoughtful. A man of science, not superstition."

"Then how do you explain their children being healthy while ours die?" Basha asked.

"I have no answer for that, General, but I have spoken with the Greens, and I believe they can help this planet."

"I have given my answer, Captain Picard." His

voice was low and rage-filled, each word carefully bitten off.

"You would turn to off-world strangers for help, but refuse aid from your own people?" Picard asked.

"The Greens are not my people. I am Torlick. They are my people."

Picard shook his head. "If that is what you truly believe, General, then there will be no peace."

Basha frowned, winced. "What are you talking about?"

"As long as you see yourselves as separate people, you cannot work together. You must put aside old hatreds and work as one people, not fractured groups."

"I do not understand," Basha said.

Again, Troi knew he was lying, but it was a lie of politeness. His rage was like a great hovering warmth in the room, ready to swoop down on the captain.

"We are Torlick, they are Venturi. We are not the same people."

"Except for the colors of your cloaks you are the same people. Your language, most of your customs, your physical appearance is the same. What is it that makes you two separate factions?"

The general struggled to stand, pushing himself upward with his one good arm. "How dare you pass such judgments on us. We are two separate people. We want peace. We do not want to embrace our enemies." Basha's anger had found a focus, and it broke against the captain like heat-lightning. Picard seemed not to notice. Troi felt scorched just standing nearby.

"I do not ask that you embrace your enemies,

General Basha, but you must know that you cannot have peace in the midst of hate."

"Our hatred of each other has been built over centuries of fighting, Captain. Everyone in this room has lost parents, children, brothers, sisters, to the enemy. How can we forgive that, or they forgive us?"

"It is not a matter of forgiveness," Picard said. "It is a matter of practicality. Your world is dying because all your technology has gone into causing death instead of preserving life. If you do not stop now, it will be too late. I ask you, General, is winning the war worth killing all the people on this planet?"

Picard took a step forward. The guards moved in on either side to eye each other suspiciously. "Is winning a war worth the death of not just the children in the nurseries, but all the children? We have met your son, Jeric. He is a bright, strong child. Would you trade his life for your hatred?"

"He is right." Talanne's voice was soft, but clear.

Basha turned to look at her, but the movement was too quick and he nearly groaned aloud with pain. Talanne moved toward him, as if to help him. He stared her into immobility. "So you speak against me."

"No, husband, I speak for our child and for myself. The fighting must end or all will be lost. Everything. Jeric looks at the wall hangings and asks what a tree is, or a flower. He doesn't believe me when I tell him the pictures of dozens of children playing together is true, not a made-up story. Our son doesn't believe that that many healthy children could exist."

Talanne stepped toward her husband, fingers touching his bruised cheek ever so gently. "Husband, we must make peace, and it must last."

69

Basha's face softened. His love for his wife flared like a comforting flame inside of Troi's head. Something inside of him let go, released some old hatred. The anger faded, replaced by an emotion Troi was beginning to closely associate with the Orianians—sorrow. "What would you have me do, wife of mine?"

Talanne smiled and stepped back. "Listen to the Federation ambassador, and invite the Greens to the peace talks."

"NO."

"Basha, remember the stories your grandmother told us about swimming in water outside under the skies. Water so pure you could swim in it, and catch animals out of it, and eat them. Jeric, or his children could go swimming under the sky."

"You do not know that their technology will work," Basha said.

"And you do not know that it won't," she said.

He stared at her for a moment or two, then turned back to Picard. "It seems you have an advocate among my own people. An advocate I happen to trust. Very well, the Greens may send three representatives to the banquet this afternoon."

"Thank you, General Basha," Picard said.

He almost smiled. "Do not thank me." He half-fell into his chair. Talanne rushed forward to help steady him.

"My husband is tired," Talanne said.

"When our ship returns to orbit, we will be happy to give medical assistance," Picard said.

"It won't be necessary, Captain," Talanne said. "It is our custom to save serious healing for the children and life-threatening injuries. Pain is to be endured by a warrior without complaint, but we need our general strong and well for the peace talks. He will be healed in time for the afternoon banquet."

Picard nodded. "I am relieved to hear it, Colonel Talanne."

"Now please go and let us tend him."

"Of course." Picard turned to leave. All the guards pivoted on him, taking up their posts. His flash of irritation was very clear to Troi. "I hope these peace talks go quickly," he whispered to Troi, "I don't know how much longer I can stand to be the center of so much attention."

Troi smiled. "They are only doing their duty, Captain."

"I suppose so," he said, but he frowned at Worf's broad back. Picard was having to take smaller steps than normal to keep from treading on the Klingon's heels. Worf was being very cautious.

Troi hoped Captain Picard was right and that the precautions were excessive. The image of General Basha's battered face flashed across her mind. Troi suppressed a shiver. Perhaps Worf was being too cautious, but then again, perhaps not.

Chapter Six

PICARD LOOKED AROUND the nearly packed room. Lieutenant Worf and Breck were practically glued to his sides. The two other Orianian guards were nearly as attentive. It was . . . embarrassing. Worse, even, than having Riker fuss over him. Only Counselor Troi seemed at ease, but it wasn't often that Picard could detect anything but peace in her delicate features.

The banquet room wasn't much bigger than their sleeping quarters had been. Breck had explained, "Smaller rooms are easier to defend."

All the Orianians wore simple jump-suits in the respective colors of their groups. The Torlick in black with sparkling gold braid. The Venturi in crimson with white blocks of color in sleeves and leg. The Greens wore unadorned blue. There was no insignia to mark rank. This was to minimize the chance of assassination. An assassin simply had to know his victims on sight. Unless of course, he just waited and watched the bodyguards. Their concern and watchfulness was obvious. It made hiding rank insignia worthless. Perhaps it was an old custom that predated the bodyguards?

Audun made up one of the three Green representatives. He had been eloquent last night. Picard had not needed Troi's empathy to see the emotions skate across the man's face. Audun was a man dedicated, not just to the salvation of the Greens, but of all the Orianians. He was the first leader that Picard had met who didn't consider this an "us or them" problem. Audun wanted a united people, because only then could the planet be healed. It was the attitude that Picard was determined to foster in the Torlicks and Venturies. He hoped that the Greens' forgiving attitude would be an example to the rest.

Audun smiled and moved as close to the captain as the guards would allow.

"Oh, for goodness sake," Picard said. "Give me room to breath, Lieutenant."

"Captain, I . . ."

"That is an order."

Worf gave a very curt nod, then stepped back. The other guards did as well, having been convinced earlier that the Klingon was in charge.

Picard smiled at Audun. "I enjoyed our talk last night."

"As did I, Captain. May I introduce my fellow Greens? Marit and Liv." Marit was a short woman with nearly solid brown hair. Liv was tall and slender and almost white-blond. The women smiled and nodded.

"We are very grateful to you, Captain, for allowing us an opportunity to participate in these peace talks," Liv said.

"It is I who am honored. Your work in biotechnology rivals the Federation's."

Liv blushed, bowing her head.

"She is not accustomed to strangers," Audun said. "We have learned to keep to ourselves. It is safer."

"Was there trouble?" Picard asked.

"None, but until today we were members of a dangerous subversive organization. Traitors. In time of war, traitors may be shot on sight." He smiled as he said it, to take the sting out of the words but . . .

"You were hunted like animals?" Troi asked.

"Sometimes, Healer, sometimes," Audun said.

A gong sounded in clear, ringing tones. Everyone in the room turned to see General Basha standing in front of a long table. It was laden with food.

General Alick, head of the Venturi faction, stood just out of reach, behind the table, as well. He was wider through the shoulders and waist than Basha— the closest Picard had seen any of the Orianians come to being fat. But it was hard fat, muscle disguised under bulk. Picard would have guessed that many enemies had judged by outward appearances and been outwitted and out maneuvered by the slow, bulky-looking general.

"Welcome all," General Basha said.

"To this place of peace," General Alick said.

"Eat and drink without fear," Basha said.

"We stand on neutral ground," Alick said.

"And it is against our most sacred laws to defile neutral ground," Basha finished.

It had taken Picard nearly three hours to arrive at

the compromise they had just heard. Both Alick and Basha had been determined to have the "honor" of opening the peace talks.

All the food on the table was bite-sized or slightly bigger. There were no plates. Napkins were to be used strictly for dabbing at hands and mouth. They were not to be used as plates. Plates allowed the sprinkling of poison. If you picked up one item of food at a time and ate it right away, no one could tamper with it.

As the food was laid out indiscriminately and no one had any idea who would be eating what, it was safe, except from random tampering. And the Orianians did not believe in random assassination. That was considered rude.

Lieutenant Worf had said, "I am glad to see the Orianian assassins have some honor."

Picard hadn't been sure if the Klingon was serious or being sarcastic. He couldn't recall ever hearing Worf use sarcasm before.

There was a pile of Styrofoamlike cups. Each guest was to use one cup, then throw it away, again to lessen the chances of poison. Picard stared at the pile of cups and wondered how much energy and failing natural resources had gone into making them. All to be thrown away.

He sighed. One problem at a time. Peace, then the planet's salvation could begin.

"We have a special honor for the Federation ambassador," General Basha said.

"The Torlick and the Venturi have worked together on a surprise for the ambassador," General Alick said.

Picard looked from one to the other, unsure what was about to happen. But that the two warring factions had worked together on anything was a miracle.

Two guards wheeled in a tray with what looked like an old-fashioned urn on it. Basha and Alick took places on either side of the small wheeled cart. The two men spoke in unison like an a capella choir. "Captain Jean-Luc Picard, the Venturi and the Torlick wish you to know we are not entirely uncivilized."

"We have worked together to secure something that your dossier said you preferred," Basha said.

"Working together on this small matter," Alick said, "is perhaps preferable to fighting about it."

Both men smiled. Picard wondered how much fighting had gone into even that short speech. He came forward, motioning his own guards back with an impatient hand.

"If you will be so kind as to get a cup, Ambassador," Basha said.

Picard did, vowing not to throw the cup away after he had used it only once. He held the cup under the spigot. Alick turned a small handle, and steaming liquid poured into the cup.

Picard raised the cup near his face. One whiff and he felt better instantly. The warm, rich smell alone was comforting. He smiled broadly, "Earl Grey tea. I am impressed, gentleman, at your knowledge of my habits and your willingness to cooperate with one another."

Basha and Alick exchanged glances. Alick motioned Basha to speak first. Basha bowed to acknowledge it. "Ambassador Picard, we are learning that perhaps there are worse things than working together."

Alick smiled. "Well said."

Picard breathed in the sweet steam of tea and hid his amazement. They were being civil to each other. This dinner was only the preliminaries. The real peace talks began after dinner, when darkness fell. It was an Orianian custom to negotiate at night when conditions for fighting were not ideal.

"I am most gratified," Picard said. "And please join me in a cup of tea. Let it symbolize the beginnings of working through our difficulties together without violence."

Basha whispered, "You were not there when we had to decide who spoke first. There was almost violence."

Alick grinned almost sheepishly.

"Almost is a beginning," Picard said.

They helped themselves to cups, and when all three had a steaming, brownish-green cup of tea, Picard held his cup aloft. "My people have a custom called a toast. It is to celebrate any great and happy occasion. I propose a toast to the bravery of General Basha and General Alick, the bravery of all the Torlick and Venturi. It often takes more bravery to talk peace than to fight. To peace and prosperity for this planet." Picard bowed to the two leaders and took a drink. After a moment's hesitation, many in the room with cups followed his example.

"You will have to explain to me this thing called a toast more fully later, Ambassador," Alick said. He was standing beside the captain. He was smiling.

Picard smiled back, and for the first time since he had set foot on Oriana, he felt optimistic about his mission. "I would be happy to tell you more of our customs, General Alick . . ."

The smile left Alick's face. He blinked rapidly, shaking his head as if to clear his vision. One hand grabbed for his chest. "Ambassador . . . I don't feel . . . Aahh!" He groped as if blind. The cup with its tea fell to the carpet. Picard reached out to the man. Alick's hand convulsed on Picard's arm.

General Alick fell to his knees, dragging Picard with him. "Get a doctor," Picard yelled. Picard had a sense of people running, frantic movement. He had eyes only for Alick. The man's heart was beating so loudly that Picard could hear it, pounding like it was trying to come out of his chest.

Troi was beside him trying to help hold Alick's convulsing body. Picard stared at her in horror over Alick's twisting body. The man's hands clawed at Picard as if begging him to do something. Picard wanted to ask Troi if she heard his heartbeat. It was so loud, louder than his own heartbeat.

Guards in Venturi red and white pushed Picard and Troi back. They tried to hold Alick's body still, but his muscles and limbs jumped as if they had separate lives of their own.

Even pushed back several feet, Picard could still hear the monstrously furious thumping of Alick's heart. Troi was beside him, one hand on his shoulder. Her black eyes were wide and horror-filled.

Picard wondered wildly, could she feel the man dying? Could she feel it?

A woman dressed in orange surgical garb rushed into the room. The convulsions had already quieted. He lay very still.

"I can't hear his heart any longer," Picard said, he didn't know he'd spoken aloud, until Troi answered,

"He's dead, Captain. He's dead." Her voice held such soft horror.

Picard placed his hand atop hers, giving comfort to the counselor. He was still too numb by the quickness of it all to believe it. Alick had been talking to him, had been fine. What in blazes had happened?

The doctor chased the Torlick guards back and bent over the still form of General Alick. She checked pulse, respiration, then ran a small scanner over the still form. She looked up at the waiting people, and very clearly in the utter silence of the room her voice carried. "His heart has burst."

"What do you mean, his heart has burst?" Basha asked.

"I am scanning for vital functions. His heart has blown apart. There is no repairing it, or reviving him. He is gone."

"He was as healthy as I am," Basha said.

"Yes," another voice said, "but now he's dead and you're alive." It was a Venturi in red and white.

"What treachery is this?" another voice called.

Picard pushed himself to his feet. He was so numb his hands tingled. It had all been so sudden. The peace mission was in shambles before it had begun. War was going to break out while he stood helpless. No, there had to be a way. "General Alick wanted peace, believed in it. He gave his life because someone here was more afraid of peace than of war. Would you dishonor General Alick's memory while he lies barely dead at your feet?"

The Venturi averted his eyes and could not look directly at Picard. "I want no dishonor on our general."

79

"Good. Then we must continue with the talks as your general would have wished." Even as Picard said it, he wasn't sure he believed it was possible. It was only the initial shock and the fact that he seemed to be the only calm person in the room, that was saving everyone from pointing fingers.

"The ambassador is right," Basha said, "but, by the dead world, I cannot understand what has happened."

The doctor said, "I need to speak with the leaders, please, in private."

General Basha looked surprised, then nodded.

A slender woman in crimson and white stepped forward. "I am the next in command. I will speak for the Venturi now."

"Fine. If the ambassador will join us out in the hallway for a moment."

Audun stepped forward in his unadorned blue. "This affects us all. As speaker for the Greens, may I be included?"

"By all means," Picard said.

Basha closed his mouth on the words he was about to utter, frowning at Picard. "Of course," he said finally.

The leaders and their sentinels followed the doctor out into the hall. For the first time Picard didn't think all this guarding nonsense was funny. It was almost comforting.

"Gentle people," the doctor began, "General Alick was poisoned."

"But that's impossible," Basha began.

"I know all precautions were taken, but nevertheless it was poison."

"How long ago was it administered," Picard asked.

80

"Minutes, no more. Death was nearly instantaneous."

"But we were all standing right there," Basha protested. "How?"

"What was the last thing he drank or ate?"

"Tea," Troi said.

"Did any one else drink it?" the doctor asked.

"Yes," Basha said, "I did and the ambassador."

"Then find General Alick's cup. It must be that."

They trooped back inside and found a nearly silent room. All eyes were on them as they knelt by the two spilled cups of tea. One was Picard's, one was the dead general's.

The doctor pulled a bulky object from one pocket. It had a slender handle and a hand-sized square mounted on the top. Multicolored buttons decorated the square. She touched a button and a faint bluish light pulsed over the cups. The doctor waved the scanner over the cups five times before she sighed and stood up.

She gathered the four leaders around her. "It was poison in the cup."

"What sort of poison?" Basha asked.

"It was a plant alkaloid. There are minute bits of plant fiber in the cup. It is not tea leaves." She shook her head. "The plant fragments contain a thousand times more alkaloid than any naturally occurring plant."

"Are you saying," Basha said, "that it was no natural plant?"

"I am saying I cannot explain the toxicity of the plant alkaloid in these plant fragments."

General Basha turned to Audun. "Does your biotechnology include a process to grow such a poison?"

Audun pulled himself up to his full height, still not reaching to the general's shoulder. "There are enough poisons on this planet without growing more."

"Answer the question," Basha said.

The new Venturi leader was standing very close to Audun. "Yes, Green, answer the question."

Audun looked to Picard. He could only nod. "You must answer the question," Picard said.

"I do not know the true nature of the doctor's findings but, yes, we could grow such a plant. But we would not do it. We do not believe in violence."

Basha stepped very close to the smaller man. "You did it. You and your peaceful technology." His words were very quiet, a whispered hiss.

The new Torlick leader said, "They must pay for what they have done."

"Agreed," Basha said.

"Nothing has been proved against them, yet," Picard said.

"It was a bioengineered plant alkaloid," Basha said. "Who else would have access to such a thing? No one else has tampered with genetics for over a century."

"I do not know. But why would the Greens kill General Alick? What would it gain them?"

"People who twist the very babes in their mother's wombs do not have to have a reason," the Venturi leader said.

This is absurd, Picard thought, but aloud he said, "You need proof before you can accuse them of murder."

Basha was staring at Picard, a look on his face that the captain did not understand. It was like an idea was growing behind his eyes.

Troi came up beside Picard and put a hand on his arm. "Captain, I must speak with you."

"It was you who insisted on the Greens attending this party, Captain Picard. And you were the last person to speak with the Torlick leader."

Picard didn't understand for a moment, then the awful implications hit him. He was too outraged to be frightened. "What are you saying?"

"He was standing right beside you when he drank poison. The poison was not in the tea, or you and I would be dead. It had to have been administered."

"I am a Federation ambassador. What possible motive could I have for poisoning General Alick?" He let the anger at the ridiculousness of the accusations flow into his voice.

"I do not know," Basha said, "but we will find out. If it is acceptable with the Venturi leader, we will put Picard and the Greens in one of our cells."

The woman nodded. Her face was very grim. "That would be most acceptable. General Alick was so pleased that our two sides were working together on this. Perhaps the general can bring us together to do one more thing."

Basha bowed. "I would be honored."

"What are they talking about, Captain?" Worf asked.

"I'm not sure," Picard said.

Troi tightened her grip on Picard's arm. "Captain . . ."

"Guards!" Basha yelled.

The new Venturi leader called, "Guards." The room was suddenly flooded with uniforms. "I arrest the Green delegation and Ambassador Picard for the murder of General Alick."

Worf and the three other guards formed up around Picard and Troi. The Orianians that had been assigned to Picard did not hesitate to draw rifles on their fellow Orianians.

"Wait," Picard cried. "Wait!" He stepped out from behind Worf's broad back. "General Basha, Venturi Leader, I had nothing to do with this. I do not believe the Greens did either."

"You would say that," the Venturi leader said.

Picard looked down at the floor, then quickly up, trying desperately to think of some way out of this. The situation would have been ridiculous except for the corpse lying on the floor. It was absurd that they thought a Federation ambassador could have participated in an assassination, but the faces of the Orianians were grim. They believed it. "Don't you need proof before arresting a Federation ambassador?"

"If your guards do not stand down," Basha said, "we will need no proof whatsoever to kill you all where you stand. This is war, Captain, and this," he motioned to Alick's body, "is treason."

"We will not resist," Picard said.

"Captain, I cannot let them take you," Worf said.

"Yes, you can, Lieutenant, and you will."

"I am responsible for your safety."

"I am still your captain, and you will obey a direct order. Holster your arms, Lieutenant, now!"

The Klingon frowned down at him, hands clinching and unclinching on his phaser. "Captain, please . . . " The last was said through gritted teeth.

"No, Worf, we cannot fight our way out of this. We are here on a peace mission. We are trying to show them that violence is not the answer. Fighting now would not help us prove our point. Put up your weapon."

Worf gave a long sigh, but put up his phaser. The other guards followed his lead.

Picard turned back to the waiting leaders. His pulse was a little rapid. Everything was going wrong at a breakneck pace. He could barely keep up with it. "I am ready to go, General. We will not fight this injustice at this time."

"Wise of you, Captain, I would hate to explain the deaths of the entire Federation party. As it stands, only you will be executed."

Picard said, "Worf, don't!"

The Klingon took his hand away from his phaser, but the glare he gave the waiting Orianian guards made them step back, just a bit. "I cannot allow you to be turned over for execution, Captain. Surely, that is a failure of my duty as your bodyguard."

Picard fought an urge to smile, but it wasn't hard to fight. "When will this execution take place?" His voice sounded very calm, normal. Years of practice.

"In three days, unless proof of your innocence can be found."

"I am a mind-healer," Troi said, "and I can read emotions. The Greens and Captain Picard were as surprised as everyone else when the general fell ill."

"I understand loyalty to your leader. There is no shame in that," Basha said.

"I am not lying to save the captain. Don't you want the real murderer found?"

"You have three days to find proof of another murderer. Unless that proof can be found, your captain and the three Greens will be executed on the evening of the third day."

Picard's eyes widened just a bit, but otherwise he took the news stoically. What else could he do? He turned to Troi. "Counselor, do not worry. You and Lieutenant Worf must simply find the culprit. When there is proof, the executions will be stopped."

"Captain . . ."

"No, I will be fine. We will solve this mystery without violence. Intelligence and peaceful investigation will win out." He looked at Worf as he said the last. "You are now in charge of this peace mission, Lieutenant Worf. You are the acting Federation ambassador."

"But Captain . . . " Worf said.

"Remember your duties, Ambassador Worf, and remember you represent the entire Federation."

Worf drew himself to his full height. "Yes, Captain."

Picard looked into Troi's large dark eyes, and said, "Remind him occasionally, Counselor, that this is a peace mission." He managed to smile softly at her.

She smiled back, but her eyes gave her away. "We'll find the truth, Captain."

"I have the utmost confidence in you both." He turned to the waiting guards. "I am ready to go."

The three Greens were already surrounded by people in both Torlick and Venturi uniforms, working together to punish the murderers. Perhaps peace was still possible, if they could find the real murderer. Of course, chances were very good that it was one of the warring factions, which would start the war all over again. Would it be better for the peace mission if Picard and the Greens took the blame?

No. The Greens could save this planet, rebuild it. Even if the fighting stopped, the planet was still dying. There had been too much damage for easy solutions. The Greens had to be included in this peace. That meant they had to be cleared of these charges.

Picard stood beside Audun, behind a wall of guards. He could see Worf's head towering above the others in the room. The Klingon was watching him with fierce, dark eyes. Picard wondered what the lieutenant would do if he and the counselor could not find proof. He doubted the Klingon would allow his captain to be executed without a fight. If the *Enterprise* would hurry back, perhaps there would be other options, but for now they were on their own. Unless the ship returned, it was up to Worf and Troi to find the real murderer and proof enough to convince the two sides.

He had absolute confidence in Worf and Troi, but all the same he hoped the *Enterprise* would be returning very soon.

Chapter Seven

THE ALIEN VESSEL hung in the blackness of space. It was roughly oval, with one end bulbous, the other ending in a soft point. It was twice the size of the *Enterprise,* a huge, silver ball, with opaque silver windows decorating much of the ship.

Commander William Riker sat on the bridge of the *Enterprise,* staring at the Milgian vessel. Their distress message had stopped abruptly about an hour before. Now, they weren't moving. "Data, are there life readings on that ship?"

The android sat at his post, spine rigid. His pale fingers danced over his console. He blinked, then swiveled his chair to glance at Riker. "Yes, Commander."

A tightness in Riker's stomach that he hadn't known was there, eased. To have come all this way to find a dead ship would have been beyond words. A failed rescue was always one of the worst failures. "How many people left alive?"

"Over a hundred, sir," Data said, his voice rising at the end with that small lilt, that was nearly the only inflection the android ever showed.

They had arrived in time. Very good. He glanced back at the ensign who was filling Worf's station on the bridge. "Ensign Chi, hail the alien vessel. Tell them we have arrived to give whatever assistance is needed."

"Aye, sir, hailing the alien vessel now," Chi said. His dark up-tilted eyes scanned his control board.

Almost immediately, Chi said, "They are answering our hail, Commander."

"On main viewscreen," Riker said.

The screen flickered to life. The distress call had been without visual. The alien's skin was pale blue. His head was made up of soft squares, while his mouth was a deep slit in the center. The eyes were scarlet, like fresh blood—startling against the blue of the skin.

His torso seemed to have no neck at all. He looked like a body builder gone mad, huge square shoulders meeting just under the chin.

"I am Commander William Riker of the Starship *Enterprise.* We heard your distress signal. What is the nature of your emergency?"

The voice was almost painfully deep, as if dragged out of the wide throat. The words seemed slow, as if the alien were speaking at half-speed. "I am Captain Diric of the Milgian vessel *Zar.* Our engines have malfunctioned and are a day away from imploding."

"Is there a way to repair?"

"No, we would ask you to take off the families and civilians, so they will be safe."

"Gladly. How many people would that be, Captain Diric?"

"Fifty, though some are injured. There have been explosions in sections of the ship. Internal fires. Three of my people have died."

"Then you will want to evacuate your entire crew?" Riker asked.

"No, we do not believe in abandoning a ship. When our ship dies, it will not die alone. It is our way."

Riker blinked, not sure what to say. There wasn't time to argue philosophies about the sanctity of life. He would try later to convince the captain to beam aboard. Right now, he had people to save.

"With your permission I will send an away team over to you. Do you need medical help, or extra engineering officers?"

"Medical aid would be most appreciated. I have every confidence in my own chief engineer but again, any aid is most appreciated."

"We will contact you as soon as we are ready to receive your people," Riker said.

"Most kind. I will meet your away team." The screen went blank.

"Communication has been cut off, Commander," Ensign Chi said.

Riker wanted badly to lead the away team himself, but he was acting captain, and he had no right to endanger himself. He watched over Picard's safety too tenderly to risk himself now. It would set a bad example for the captain when he returned.

"Data, take an away team and beam over to the *Zar*."

"Aye, Commander, with permission, until we ascertain the stability of the *Zar's* engines, I suggest a minimal away team. I would include Dr. Crusher and Geordi."

"Agreed." Riker smiled, "Make it so."

Data raised one pale eyebrow. "Dr. Crusher and Commander La Forge, this is Commander Data. Please meet me in Transporter Room Three. We will be looking at injuries and malfunctioning engines. Please pack accordingly."

Geordi's voice came out of empty air. "On my way, Data."

"I'll need ten minutes to gather materials," Dr. Beverly Crusher said, her voice spilling out of nowhere.

"That will be acceptable, Doctor. Data out." He turned without another word and left the bridge.

Riker began giving orders to prepare for fifty rescuees. He trusted Crusher to have left the medical preparations for the injured in good hands. A good leader was often only as good as his crew. Riker trusted everyone to do their job.

Watching the viewscreen, he wondered what the alien vessel looked like inside. He hoped there would be time later to view the ship personally, if they could keep it from blowing up. A big if . . .

Data, Geordi, and Dr. Crusher appeared in a large smooth hallway. The walls were the same gray-silver of the outside of the ship and perfectly smooth, rising perhaps five meters to a peaked ceiling. The shape echoed the outline of the ship.

Captain Diric was waiting for them. His squarish bulk nearly filled the broad corridor. The Milgian looked like he was formed from a child's building blocks and moved forward in slow, ponderous movements, reminiscent of his slow, crawling speech.

Geordi wondered what they sounded like to the Milgian. Were their voices incredibly fast and high-pitched? How alien were they to the aliens?

Data stepped forward. "I am Lieutenant Commander Data of the Starship *Enterprise.* We have come to give aid."

"Most welcome," Diric said, each word said as if in slow motion. Geordi fought an urge to shake his head, as if he could speed up the words by giving his ears a good kick.

"Our medical facilities are this way." As he turned, the robes over his squarish body showed burn marks.

Dr. Crusher went forward, nearly touching the alien captain. "Are you injured, Captain?"

"A little," he said. He turned his head toward Crusher. It was unsettling to see his head turn when it looked like he had no neck at all.

"May I help you?"

"No, a small injury is nothing when my ship is dying."

"Please, you are in pain."

"No, if I have allowed my ship to die, then I must suffer with it."

"But I may be able to heal you?" Crusher said.

"No, thank you."

"Surely you would be better able to guide your ship and help your crew if you were completely healed," Crusher said, softly.

Geordi resisted an urge to applaud, good thinking on the doctor's part.

Diric seemed to think about this for a minute, then made a small movement with his spadelike hands. "No, thank you." He moved off down the passageway.

Data followed him.

Crusher didn't move for a moment. The look on her face was one of exasperation. "I never . . ." She seemed at a loss for words.

Geordi patted her shoulder. "You tried."

"I just hope that all Milgians aren't so stubborn. It could make being a doctor obsolete."

He smiled. "You know the old Earth custom. The captain goes down with the ship."

She nodded. "I'm not going to stand by while lives are lost needlessly. I don't care if it is their way." There was a set to her face, a grim determination in her green eyes, that made Geordi very glad she wasn't after him.

They hurried to catch up with the slow moving Captain Diric and Data. The two were walking in absolute silence. Perhaps Milgians didn't feel anymore need for small talk than the android did.

Diric paused beside a piece of corridor that seemed to bulge outward just a bit. He passed a hand in front of it, and the wall opened, peeling back like a curtain. He lumbered inside, and they followed.

The room was uniformly dark. After the silver-brightness of the hallway, it seemed dingy. Milgians of all sizes lay on the floor with sheets over them. Geordi had assumed that all the Milgian would be the same blue shade as the captain, but some were pale yellow, and a few various shades of red. The Milgians looked like a box of crayons spilled onto the floor.

A slightly smaller, yellow version of their captain walked among the wounded. The yellow alien still dwarfed any of the humans. "Which of you is the doctor?" The voice had the same slow measure, but there was lilt to the end of words. Female? Geordi honestly couldn't tell. For that matter, why had he assumed that Captain Diric was male?

"I am the doctor," Beverly Crusher said. She came forward, the emergency medical kit slung over her shoulder.

"Good, I am the only doctor for the whole ship. I am pleased for any assistance." The yellow alien started to kneel beside one of the patients, but instead of bending knees, she seemed to melt. Geordi couldn't see under the long robes, but the movement looked like the lower half of her body had quickly melted, then solidified when she was low enough to touch the patient.

Crusher exchanged a glance with him. Even Data had his head cocked to one side, as if something interesting had happened. Beverly overcame her surprise and knelt by the alien doctor.

Geordi searched the room and found all the Milgians had odd heat patterns. What he could only assume were injury sites were a bright screaming red-orange. The cooler the pattern, the healthier the Milgian. What was their normal body temperature? It had to be lower than a human's.

Crusher ran a scanner back and forth over the first patient. The alien doctor flowed back to her solid looking feet and moved on.

Geordi moved forward to stand by Dr. Crusher. "How is . . . she?"

"Burns over seventy percent of the body, but they

have some sort of cell structure I've never seen before. It's almost as if the structure isn't solid."

"Like when the doctor knelt down. It looked like she melted."

Crusher nodded. "It's as good a word as any, I guess. The temperature readings are all over the place, depending on which part of the body I'm registering, as if different parts of the body are compartmentalized."

"Compartmentalized?" Data said, standing just behind them. "Separate?"

"I think so." She stood and motioned the two men back from the patient. She lowered her voice to a whisper. "If this patient were any humanoid I'd ever met, he would be dead. Parts of the body are nearly burned away, but those sections seem to have been shut down, and the rest of the body seems fine. In fact, there's shock that I can read."

"Can you help the Milgians?" Data asked.

"I think so, but their internal structure is like nothing I've ever seen before. It will be difficult to know what to do."

"But you can help them?"

She nodded. "I'll beam over to the *Enterprise* with the worst of the injured. And prepare my med team for some very unusual patients."

"Very good, Doctor," Data said. "If you have everything under control here, I believe Geordi and I would be of more use in the engineering section."

"I don't know about under control, but yes, we will do everything we can."

"Good. I leave you to see to medical matters. Come, Geordi. We will ask Captain Diric to take us to engineering."

Geordi fought an urge to give a mock salute, but he knew Data wouldn't appreciate the joke. Though it wouldn't be for lack of trying. No one tried harder than Data to have a sense of humor.

"Captain Diric, with your permission, we would like to see your engines. Perhaps there is something we can do to help you."

"My Chief Engineer Veleck is most competent, but a captain's duty is to his ship, and if anything can be done to save it, then of course, you may see the engines." His voice sounded tired or perhaps sad.

Geordi glanced around the room at the more than twenty injured, some of them very small, children perhaps. Against one wall were three large covered forms, no heat, no anything. Geordi knew death when he saw it. He never needed to take a pulse, once the corpse was old enough to cool. Suddenly, he understood the sorrow in Diric's voice.

The engine room was huge, full of flowing silver-gray tubes and open structures. It was like being inside a huge architectural display. Everywhere were flowing lines, arches, metal formed into shapes delicate as lace. Geordi saw them through a colored prism of structural details. But he had a sense of the wide open beauty of it. It was one of those times when he wished he could simply see.

And just as Dr. Crusher had never seen cell structures like those of the Milgians, La Forge had never seen any metal like this. He wasn't even sure it was metal. But it couldn't be anything else.

Geordi searched the vast space for the engines, but there were no heat patterns that he could detect. The room was cold, empty. All right, if there wasn't any infrared radiation, there would be some sort of wave particles. Engines had to run on something.

Geordi turned in a slow circle, concentrating. His VISOR responded to his efforts. Bands of color, cell structure, stress points flared along the metal. He could see the metal flowing in upon itself, forming strong melded joints that were flawless. But there were always stress fractures, blemishes where metal was joined. Even metal that had been forged into a single piece showed signs of imperfection to his VISOR. Geordi lived in a world where he could see all the flaws, and there were no flaws in this metal.

Geordi ran his hand down one curved beam. The surface was like cool, metallic silk. It had almost a furlike quality, a texture that wasn't visible to his VISOR, but his hand picked it up. The metal wasn't metal at all. Exactly what it was, Geordi didn't have a clue.

A small Milgian moved out from behind a particularly thick band of "metal." To Geordi's eyes he was simply a hodge-podge of temperature variants and strange shifting auras. All races had shifting patterns, but the Milgians were scintillating, a constant wave of colors that nearly made La Forge dizzy.

He turned away from the Milgian, to look once more at the metal structures. There were no moving parts, no heat, no fusion, no anything that he could understand. For all Geordi knew, the Milgians were lying, and this whole place was a recreation area. Maybe that was it. Maybe this wasn't engineering at all, and they hadn't been prepared for his VISOR seeing through the ruse.

He shook his head. No, he just had to accept that he was in the presence of technology so different from his own that he didn't even know where the engines were. Suddenly, he was beginning to wonder if he would be any help at all.

The Milgian that walked toward them was much smaller than the captain. He was a dark rich blue, like a sky before night fall. Black streaks decorated the tough outer skin of his body.

"This is Chief Engineer Veleck," Captain Diric said. "These are two Federation officers, Chief Engineer La Forge and Lt. Commander Data. They have come to help our ship."

It was only with the Milgian nearly standing in front of La Forge that he was able to see the scarlet lines on his wounded body. "You're injured. Dr. Crusher would be happy to help you."

Veleck made a small motion with his hands, Geordi assumed it was his version of a shrug. "I am chief engineer. If I cannot heal my engines, then I cannot allow myself to be healed. Is this not your way, as well?" There was the faintest edge of question to the low voice.

"Well, no," Geordi said. "Don't you think you could perform your duties better if you were completely well?"

"My engines are dying, I will die with them." There was no hint of reproach, or doubt, or even fear. Fatalism at its best crept through the Milgian's voice.

"If you could show us your engines, perhaps we could help heal you both," Data said.

"Quite right, Lt. Commander," Captain Diric said. "Veleck, show them what they request. I will refuse no help."

The captain's voice said plainly that he didn't believe the two men could help. Geordi stared up at the supposed engines and wasn't sure either. However, Data moved forward smoothly, with no doubts. He wasn't programmed for them.

Geordi took a deep breath. He knew Data couldn't feel uncertainty, but somehow just following his friend's confident walk made him feel better. If there was a way to help, they would find it.

The closest thing to a solid object in the room was a curved mess of "metal." It swirled in upon itself. Geordi stared at it, but couldn't find a beginning or an end. It was like a Mobius strip, a snake eating its own tail.

Data leaned forward, running a pale hand down the structure. "What method of propulsion do you use?"

Veleck stared at them, blinking tiny eyes. "The ship wishes to move, and it moves."

Geordi and Data exchanged glances. They waited for more explanation, but the alien engineer remained silent. He seemed to think that his explanation was complete.

"Explain further please," Data said.

"I do not understand," Veleck said.

"You have not given us sufficient explanation of your propulsion systems."

"The ship wishes to move, and it does. There is no more explanation."

"Let me try, Data. Um, Veleck," Geordi began. "What makes the ship want to move?"

"We do."

If Geordi could have, he would have rolled his eyes. "Okay, how do you make the ship want to move?"

Veleck glanced over their heads at his captain. "I do not believe I understand the question."

"Nor do I," Captain Diric said.

"Allow me, Geordi. Captain Diric, you say that your engines are in danger of imploding. Could you explain this damage to us?"

"The center of our engines is not functioning properly."

"Could you be more specific?" Geordi asked.

Veleck seemed to think about that for a moment. "If I knew specifically what was wrong, I could fix it. But the damage is too extensive. It is irreversible."

"If you do not know specifically what is wrong, then how do you know it is a problem with the engine core?" Data asked.

"We are not sure," Veleck said, "but unless the damage can be repaired, the engine will consume itself in a matter of hours. The engines are the heart of the ship, and the ship will die."

Geordi ran his hands over the cool metal. It had a texture almost like . . . skin. "Is your engine alive?"

"Please to explain the question?"

"Are their biological components to your engine?"

"There is cell structure similar to living tissue in our engine, yes."

The strange readings he'd been getting suddenly made sense. It was like looking at a giant puzzle and suddenly having all the pieces fall into place. "It isn't a communications problem. Your engine really is eating itself alive."

"This is what we told you," Veleck said.

Geordi stared up at the complex structure and asked the only question he could think of. "How does a living engine make a ship move?"

"We have told you. It wishes to move, and it does."

La Forge was beginning to feel like he was caught in a logic loop. "But . . ."

"What Commander La Forge is asking is for a detailed explanation of how your engine functions. Alive or inanimate, the question remains the same."

"How are they to help us, Diric, if they do not even understand the simplest basics of our science?" Veleck asked.

For once, Geordi could only agree. The ship was in danger of imploding, and everyone on board would die. And he didn't have the faintest idea what made the ship run, let alone what was wrong with it.

He took Data to one side, while the Milgians argued about the wisdom of having aliens in the ship's engine room. "Data, how can we fix something when we don't even understand how it works?"

"That is a problem, but we must do all we can or lives will be lost."

"Do you understand how these engines work?"

"No, but perhaps a doctor would be in order?"

"What do you mean, Data?"

"If the engines are indeed alive, then perhaps Dr. Crusher could heal them as she heals the Milgians."

Geordi patted Data on the shoulder. "That is a brilliant idea."

Data cocked his head to one side, "Really."

Geordi shook his head, and pressed his comm. "La Forge to Dr. Crusher. We may have another patient for you."

Chapter Eight

WORF STOOD IN FRONT OF the far wall of their sleeping quarters. His hands were clasped behind his back so tightly that the muscles in his arms quivered. Rage threatened to choke him. He was Klingon and his heritage threatened to eat through his brain and come pouring out of his fists. Muscles tight, he wanted to strike out in a mindless rage. Everything had been going well one moment, and then the next moment: chaos. The entire situation had slipped through Worf's fingers. The captain was imprisoned for murder, under a death sentence. What kind of security officer allowed such things?

The Orianian guard assigned to the captain had trailed after them, at a distinct distance. Breck seemed in no hurry to approach the new ambassador. Ambassador? Ambassador Worf. It would have been funny under other circumstances. A good warrior knows his own strengths and weakness. Worf knew without doubt that he was not made for diplomacy.

But they could not afford enraged pouting now. There was no time, Worf knew, but what he wanted more than anything right now was to drown his helpless feeling in a good solid fight. Though he heard Troi's light footsteps come up behind him, he did not turn around. He was still not under control. She sighed, softly, and stood to one side.

He could see her out of the corner of his eye, but he pretended not to. Worf did not trust his voice yet. He stared as hard as he could at the wall hanging in front of him. It was a lovely scene, the graceful branches of a tree heavy with some pink fruit. Large fluttering insects danced on a breeze that must have been sweet-scented. It was very lovely and something Worf normally wouldn't even have glanced at. Now he tried to memorize it. He treated it as something he would have to report in detail to the captain.

He closed his eyes and tested his memory. Yes, he could report it in detail, as if it were a room, or the scene of a crime. Worf opened his eyes. His rage was contained. It bubbled under the surface, warm and somehow reassuring, but he controlled it. He was Klingon and that, for Worf, meant the greatest challenge was always within, not without.

With the anger contained, the self-doubt flared stronger. Worf knew his weak points, diplomacy was one. And this was not the situation he would have chosen for his first diplomatic effort.

"Worf," Troi said quietly.

He stiffened and glanced at her out of the side of his eyes. "Yes." The word was almost a growl, yet he had not meant it to be.

"Worf, I know you are angry and worried about the captain. We all are, but we have only three days to find the real murderer."

He whirled on her, nearly yelling. "Do you not think I know that?" He stopped himself, taking a deep breath. Troi's concerns had to be as great as his own, and she was his friend. She did not deserve the brunt of his anger. He stepped back from her. "The captain should not have ordered me to let him go. I should have died trying to keep him safe. Instead, I allowed him to be led off to slaughter. It is unthinkable."

"What would you have done? Fought them all?"

"Yes!"

"You would have been killed and perhaps taken us all with you. Is it honorable to cause the deaths of your friends?"

He turned away from her. "I cannot allow the captain to be executed while I stand by and do nothing."

"What could you have done?"

"I could have fought." He said evenly.

"Fighting would have gotten you killed. It would not have helped Captain Picard. The captain was right, Worf. We have to solve this by peaceful means. We cannot let the Orianians provoke us. A peace conference is no place for violence."

"General Alick would not agree," Worf said, turning back to stare at her. "His death was very violent."

"I was there," Troi said. An emotion Worf rarely saw flitted across Troi's expressive face—anger. She swallowed hard, and Worf watched the ship's counselor fight for control.

Seeing Troi so affected helped steady Worf more than anything else.

"I felt him die, Worf. His terror, the pain . . . " She stopped in mid-sentence. Pain showed in her eyes, her tears gleaming like glass.

"Counselor," Worf said. He stared down at her, wondering how to show he understood, without acknowledging he had seen her lack of control. One thing both of them valued was control. "I did not realize you felt his death. I am being foolish to think my honor is the only thing being compromised. Are you all right?"

She smiled at him, and nodded. "I'm fine. You are the acting ambassador now, Lieutenant Worf. What are your orders?" She stared up at him as she said it.

His anger was still there, and she would feel it, but Troi would also know he was in control of it. He was a Klingon among humans, he was a master of eating his own rage.

"Thank you, Counselor, for reminding me of my duties. We must find the real killer of General Alick. It is the only way to save the captain. And we must find a way to continue the peace negotiations."

"Agreed," Troi said.

"Who gains from this death, that is the proper question," Worf said. He had absolutely no suggestions for how to begin the negotiations again. The first Federation ambassador was under arrest for the murder of an Orianian leader. Why would the Ventures and Torlicks listen to the second ambassador?

"I would say the Torlicks, but this war is killing them, as well. Would they really sabotage the future of their entire race to win a war?"

"Races have done so many times, Counselor. After we have rescued the captain, forged a lasting peace, and returned to the ship, I will loan you some books of military history. I believe you will find them . . . enlightening." His doubts about the peace did not show in his voice. Worf was pleased with that. If Counselor Troi could sense his self-doubt that was one thing, but he wanted no one else to know.

"Um . . . thank you, Worf. I'm sure I will find it unique reading."

"Did you feel deception from any of the Torlick faction?"

"I don't know."

"You don't know?"

"The death was so overwhelming that it blocked out everything else. The murderer could have been standing right over the body while it was happening, and I could not have told you."

"But you told the Orianians that you felt the Greens knew nothing."

"I did sense only confusion from them, but it was faint."

"So you are saying that your empathic powers were not at their best?"

Troi smiled, then nodded. "I suppose so, yes."

"Then the Greens could be guilty, Counselor. They could have done exactly what they were accused of, and Captain Picard's involvement was accidental."

"But why would the Greens kill the leader of the Venturi faction? For the first time in over twenty years the Greens were being given a chance to rejoin their people. To help build a lasting peace. It is what they have striven and sacrificed for. Why would they sabotage it?"

"You heard Audun, Counselor. His people have been hunted like animals, killed on sight as traitors. Hatred is a good motive."

Troi had to agree with the last statement. "If hatred is the motive, Worf, the Venturi hate the Torlicks too."

"Yes, but theirs is a hatred among warriors. I do not understand why they would turn to poison when they could kill each other on a field of battle."

"May I add something, Lieutenant?" Breck asked.

"You may," Worf said.

"It is not the method of your enemy's death that matters but that he is dead. We are a more practical brand of warriors than the Klingons."

"Do you believe it was your own people?" Worf asked, surprised that he would voluntarily point the finger of blame in that direction. The Orianians seemed to have no sense of racial loyalty.

"I do not have an opinion. I am a sentinel, nothing more. I do as I am told."

"Why are you helping us against your own people?" Worf asked.

"I am a sentinel, Lieutenant. If a person under my care is killed then I will die as well."

"I don't understand," Troi said.

"If Ambassador Picard is executed I will be dead soon after. If I do not do the decent thing and kill myself, someone will probably kill me. A sentinel that fails so completely is never trusted again, Healer. I would be an outcast at the very least. Most sentinels who face this option, choose death."

"So it is not out of loyalty to our captain, but fear for your own life, that you help us?" Worf said. Somehow that made Worf trust Breck just a little bit more. Self-preservation he understood. This strange shifting loyalty was a total mystery.

Breck made that familiar palms out gesture that passed for a shrug. "I will agree with all you say."

Worf frowned at the phrasing of it. "If you betray us I will kill you myself."

Breck stared up at the imposing figure, and a slow smile spread across his face. "I would expect nothing less, Ambassador."

Worf gave one curt nod in acknowledgement of the new title. Captain Picard had made him ambassador, Worf was determined to live up to Picard's expectations. "The woman who is now in command of the Venturies, do you know her?"

"By reputation," Breck said.

"Would she have murdered Alick to gain control?"

Breck thought about that for a handful of minutes, then nodded. "She might. But not for ambition's sake alone."

"What do you mean?"

"Some of our people felt that the peace was a betrayal of everyone that had given their lives for the war. There was much argument on our side. I think it would be similar in the Venturi camp."

"You mean she killed him out of honor?"

"Something like that, yes," Breck said.

"But Worf," Troi said, "if honor dictated the peace conference be stopped, anyone in the room could have wanted to poison the leaders."

"The healer is right," Breck said. "Honor is motive for everyone."

"Then if everyone had a motive, we must find out who had the opportunity," Worf said.

"You mean, who could have poisoned the general's drink?" Troi asked.

Worf nodded, once down, once up. "Could anyone here see General Alick constantly?"

"I was watching for dangers to Ambassador Picard," Breck said. "Alick's safety was someone else's duty. I saw nothing."

"Counselor?"

"I don't know, Worf. I was standing right there. But I can't think of anything out of the ordinary."

"This is not possible," he said. "We were all right there, and you tell me none of us saw anything."

Troi and Breck exchanged glances. The sentinel had the grace to look embarrassed.

Troi spoke first. "Perhaps one of the other Orianians did," Troi suggested.

"Yes," Worf said. Here was something he understood. Interrogation was part of security training, and as a Klingon he had special talents in the area. "We will question those who were near at hand."

He turned to Breck. "We will need a list of all the people that were at the banquet."

"But Worf, there must have been over thirty people. We only have three days. The questioning alone could take that long," Troi said.

Worf turned to the counselor and stared down at her. He was on secure ground once more. It was the way Worf preferred things to be. Uncertainty was too close a cousin to fear for any Klingon's honor. He knew how intimidating he could be to most people who did not know him. He would use that on the Orianians. "I will question them personally. It will not take that long."

"Worf, what are you planning to do?"

"To find the real murderer and save the captain."

"You're a Federation ambassador now, Worf. You also have a duty to this peace mission. You can't bully these people."

He stiffened a little. "I am aware of my duties, Counselor. I have not forgotten my role as ambassador, but for the moment I think we should plan how to save the captain." He glared at her. "And I never bully anyone."

Troi gave a small nod from the neck. "Good, then I won't have to keep reminding you."

The glare deepened into a scowl. Troi smiled sweetly at him, and he turned away with a snort. He knew his duties, he just wasn't sure of his priorities. His instinct was to concentrate on freeing Picard, but Worf suspected the captain would want the mission to be first. But as of this moment Worf had no solid idea how to win back the trust of the Orianians, so he would deal with what he did understand.

"Can you get me a list of all banquet attendees?" Worf asked of Breck.

"Easily."

"Then go and do it," Worf said.

Breck started to make a Torlick salute, but stopped himself in mid-motion. He finished awkwardly with a bow and left. When he was gone Worf turned back to Troi. "Do you trust him?"

"I think so."

"You think?" He couldn't quite keep the surprise out of his voice. He had rarely heard Troi be so uncertain.

"The Orianians seem to be able to either block my powers or . . ."

"Or what, Counselor?"

"They are unemotional."

"Like Vulcans."

"No, Vulcans have emotions but have learned to control them. They are often unreadable, but there are flickerings of emotion. I can feel the strain, the strength of their control. With these people it's sometimes as if they have no emotions at all. Breck seems to find nothing wrong in working with us against his own people."

"Do you not find that strange?"

"Yes, but it isn't strange to Breck. He truly believes that his loyalties still lie with the captain."

"But can we trust him, Counselor?"

"With most things, yes, but . . ." She shrugged. "I can't read his deeper thoughts. I don't know why."

"And that makes you suspicious?"

"The Orianians talk of a variety of empathic powers as if they were once common among the people. I believe the Orianians have a great reservoir of untapped empathic and possibly telepathic abilities."

"Why untapped?"

"I don't know. I've never met a race with so much potential that doesn't use it. It's almost as if there is something tangible keeping them from using their abilities."

Worf shook his head. "I do not trust any warrior that works against his own people so easily. You cannot read him. I do not trust him."

"But you sent him to get the list?"

"That is something that is easily checked, Counselor. And if he deliberately leaves a name off, then we have somewhere to start."

"Worf, you really are a detective."

"I may not have Data's or the captain's love of mystery fiction, but we Klingons have our versions of such things."

Troi smiled at him. "When we are all safely back on board the *Enterprise,* you must tell me of the Klingon version of Sherlock Holmes."

Worf nodded. He understood that her statement was a vote of confidence—not if, but *when* they returned safely to the *Enterprise.* Though it changed nothing he felt better knowing Troi had faith in him. "Earth's Sherlock Holmes is too cold for me. Betan-Ka on the other hand, is a detective with spirit and emotion."

"What would Betan-Ka say about our mystery?"

"We have too many suspects and too little time."

Solving the murder was going to be difficult but at least he had a place to begin. With the peace mission . . . Worf would call a meeting with the Orianians and hope for inspiration. Perhaps Troi would have some suggestions. Worf knew he would have to act quickly on both fronts.

"More direct methods may be called for, Counselor, if we are to cut the suspect list down in the time we are allowed."

"We may find clues," she said.

"Klingons do not look for clues first, we secure confessions. It is a much more effective system."

Chapter Nine

THE CONFERENCE ROOM was set up with two long tables on either side, and a shorter table in the middle. The tables formed three sides of a rectangle, with Ventures sitting on one side, Torlicks on the other. Ambassador Worf sat in the center of the small table, while Troi sat to his right, and Dr. Zhir to his left. Breck stood at their backs like a good sentinel. In fact, Worf noted that bodyguards were so thick in the room there was almost no standing room left.

Surveying the meeting he had called, Worf felt a little like he had opened the bottle and let out a genie he wasn't at all sure he could control. It had been Troi's powers of persuasion that had gotten Dr. Zhir to aid them. He had not had the words. Captain Picard should have made Troi the ambassador—she was more suited to it.

No, he could do this. The captain had faith in him. Troi had faith in him. It was cowardice to be so apprehensive. He was a Klingon warrior and could face death with a glad heart. He would face speaking to this hostile crowd with the same bravery.

He leaned over to speak softly to Troi. "What are they feeling, Counselor?"

"Basha is against this conference. I believe only Talanne's intervention got the Torlicks to this meeting. The new Venturi leader, General Hanne, doesn't believe in peace, but she is here out of respect for Alick's memory. She thought a great deal of Alick."

"So both sides wish the war to continue."

"Both leaders do," Troi said, softly.

Worf sat back in his chair, nodding. He had formed this plan to help persuade the Orianians that even with the assassination, peace was possible. No, not possible, imperative. Worf had to make them understand that an honorable peace was their only chance for survival. He took a deep breath and stood.

The bodyguards rustled like a field of corn in a sudden wind. Hands moved for weapons, but none were drawn. Worf knew that Picard would have led by example and left his phaser in the room, but Worf also had to ensure Troi's safety. He was still head of security, no matter what other title he bore. Besides, the Orianians respected strength.

"I have called you to this meeting to discuss peace."

"We saw how the Federation discusses peace," General Hanne said. Her voice held contempt and anger.

Worf turned to the Venturi leader. "Captain Picard's guilt has not been proven. Nor has the Greens'."

"You are grasping at daydreams, Ambassador

114

Worf, if you believe the Greens innocent," Basha said.

Worf looked at the Torlick leader. "I see you do not believe Captain Picard guilty anymore than I do."

"He is guilty. Without his intervention none of the Greens would have gotten near General Alick," Basha said.

"Yes," Hanne said, "Picard arranged it all very neatly."

Worf fought the urge to raise his voice, and spoke very slowly and calmly, and hoped the effort did not show. "Ambassador Picard arranged nothing. He is not guilty. I do not know the Greens well enough to assure you of their innocence, but of Captain Picard's innocence, I have no doubt."

"You would say that," Basha said, "He is your leader."

Worf took a deep breath and let it out slowly. They were arguing in circles. "Regardless of what you believe of Picard, or the Greens, their guilt or innocence does not change why you called in a Federation ambassador."

"We did not call the Federation in to assassinate our leaders," Hanne said. "We can do that on our own."

Worf ignored her with an effort. He clasped his hands in front of him and tried again. "Your planet is still dying. Neither the Venturies or the Torlicks will survive if your world dies. You are facing genocide, or has that changed since the arrest of Captain Picard?" Worf stared around the room, making eye contact with as many of the leaders as he could. Some were masked and he could not read their expressions, but it did not matter. He looked at them anyway.

"Did the arrest of Picard and the Greens purify your water? Did it cleanse your air and make it breathable again? Did it undo all the damage centuries of war have done to Oriana? Did it bring your children back?"

General Hanne would not meet Worf's eyes. Basha stared at him, a flush of anger creeping onto his golden skin. Talanne stared at him, her face eager, as if urging him on.

"How many of you in this room alone have lost children; not to the war, but to disease, deformities. The poison you have spilled into the air, the ground, the water—that is killing more of you every year than fighting. More children die every year than warriors."

"That is not true," someone shouted.

"It is true," Worf shouted back, and his voice filled the chamber, echoing. "And I have proof of it. Dr. Zhir." He sat down so he would not dwarf the slender woman.

She stood, peering out at the group almost nervously. "You all know who I am. Many of you were my patients. I sang you to sleep when you were too badly deformed to live outside the containment wall."

"We all know and respect you, Dr. Zhir," Basha said. "Your work is well known to us. You are the savior of our children, and we are grateful."

"If you are truly grateful then listen to this man," she motioned at Worf. "He offers you a chance for peace. A chance that our race may not die out."

"We do not know Dr. Zhir," Hanne said. "We respect our doctors, but she means nothing to us."

"I am Torlick by birth, but I am also Orianian. If we do not do something now, I will live to see the destruction of our entire race. The poisons in our

116

atmosphere do not care what color cloaks we wear. The poisons do not care who is right or wrong. They kill indiscriminately. And the ones they kill most often are the children." She turned to Hanne, pointing. The bodyguards shifted nervously.

"How many healthy births have the Venturies had this year?"

"I do not know."

"Last year?"

"I do . . ."

"For the last five years, the last ten years, how many?"

Hanne glared at the doctor. "I do not know."

"You do know, maybe not the number, but you know. We all know." Her voice carried throughout the room. "I thought I had given up. I was caring for the children because they were in pain, but I knew it was hopeless. Our race was doomed, killed by our own hands. Then I met the Federation ambassador, and his mind-healer. They returned to me something I had lost. No, something I had given up. Hope. They gave me back my hope. Hope that this world, our people, are not lost."

"It is a moving speech," Hanne said, "but it changes nothing."

"That's right," Dr. Zhir said, "it changes absolutely nothing. If the two of you do not begin to talk peace here and now, nothing will change, and in ten years there will be no Torlicks, no Venturies. We will all be dead."

"You exaggerate, doctor," Basha said.

"No, General Basha, I do not. The deformities of our children grow worse. Most women cannot even become pregnant. Those that do, miscarry, or give birth to hideous things that I pray will die, because I cannot save them. There have been things born into my arms that haunt my dreams. We are killing our children. Without our children we will die as a race, both sides. It will not matter who is right, or wrong, or who won, or who lost. There will be no one to care, because we will have poisoned Oriana. This planet will die and the few struggling remnants of our race will die with it."

Dr. Zhir hesitated for a moment, then said, "I did not think I could still care so very much." She set down to a room that had grown utterly still.

Worf waited a moment, then stood. "Your planet will die, your children are dead and dying, let peace save them both."

Hanne cleared her throat sharply. "The Venturies are willing to talk peace, but not yet. If Picard was acting alone with the Greens, then his death will cleanse the honor of the Federation. If he is innocent, then again, we can talk peace with the Federation. But if Picard names the rest of you as accomplices, or that this was a Federation plot, then there will be no talks, no peace."

"I agree with General Hanne," Basha said. "Prove Picard innocent and we will talk peace, or let him die as the single Federation traitor, and we still talk. We understand that you are not responsible for every member of your party. We have all had ambitious traitors in our midst."

Worf wanted badly to defend the captain, but he held his tongue. The captain was innocent—they would prove that, shouting would not help. "So," Worf said, "if we prove Captain Picard's innocence, you will talk peace."

"Yes, or let him die guilty without naming you as accessaries, and we will talk peace," Basha said.

Worf did not say it would be a hot day on Rura Penthe before he let Picard die to save this world. Perhaps, as a Federation ambassador, he should have been willing to sacrifice his captain, his friend, to save an entire race. But Worf did not lie to himself about his motives or his priorities—humans tended to do that, but not Klingons. He knew where his loyalty lay, and it was not with the Orianians. It was with Captain Jean-Luc Picard.

Chapter Ten

WORF STOOD TO ONE SIDE of Troi's delicate figure, watching the face of Dr. Stasha, the doctor who had first examined the murder scene. Worf normally didn't feel so imposing, but there was something about the doctor that made him think of a dog that had been kicked once too often.

She had small features: eyes, mouth, nose, all in the middle of her face. There was nothing wrong with her face, everything was perfectly symmetrical, but still the effect was crowded. Her face looked like a piece of dough that someone had pinched in the middle. Everything had been scooped to the center. Her large, shining eyes, so typical of the Orianians, were almost bulging as if the eye sockets did not quite hold them.

Now that he had seen two of the "lifeless children" brought back to life, Worf recognized the signs. Dr. Stasha had floated in a metal coffin for how long? Worf could not conceive of spending childhood floating, hooked to machines, then coming out close to normal. How could you recover from something like that? Or did you? Could that be why the Orianians had so little respect for life and honor? Did something happen to them while they floated in the vats? Was something unnamed lost in that horrible waiting?

"We need to know what you have found, Doctor." Worf said. He meant it as a request. It sounded like an order.

Dr. Stasha did not seem to be offended. Perhaps she was accustomed to taking orders. "We have done a genetic scan of General Alick's cup. We have four separate genetic types already matched with their donors."

"But I was standing right there, Doctor," Worf said. "No one passed the general's cup around the room. Four people could not have touched it."

"I did not say that they touched it, Lieutenant Worf. Do you know what dust is, Ambassador?"

Worf frowned down at the slender woman. "That is an odd question. I do not understand its importance."

"I am not explaining myself well, please forgive me." The doctor took a deep breath, clasping her small hands in front of her. Worf did not need Troi's empathic gifts to see the woman's nervousness. Was the doctor merely nervous about what had happened, frightened of him, or was she hiding something? Worf would try to be less threatening and then they would see.

"Dust is formed out of the minute particles of living tissue as it sloughs off: dry skin cells, hair follicles, bits and pieces of living matter. Just by

121

standing close to an object, almost all of us leave little particles behind. If allowed to accumulate, the particles become dust. Thus, there were tiny genetic bits from four different people in, or on, the cup in question."

"Whose?"

"General Alick's, of course; Liv's, one of the Greens; General Basha's; and Ambassador Picard's."

Worf shook his head. "How did you match these samples?"

She blinked, then nodded. "Of course, you would want to know." She turned to a spotless white counter top that held only a bulky object, which was nearly a perfect rectangle. Small knobs protruded along the sides. Stasha removed the top of the rectangle to reveal eyepieces.

"This is our genetic matchmaker. We find it very useful in tracing bombs and assassins. We do try and kill the people that are directly responsible for any terrorist activity. We are not indiscriminate butchers." She said the last without looking at Worf, but there was the tiniest bit of protest in her voice.

Stasha pressed her face to the eyepieces and adjusted the knobs to either side. "The sample on the left was taken from the murder scene. The right is a sample extracted from the people after the event, so we could try and match it."

She looked up from the matchmaker. "Please, see for yourself. The matches are perfect."

Worf crossed his arms across his chest. He fought an urge to glare down at her. Perfect matches, indeed. "How are we to know which samples came from the poisoned cup and which were collected afterwards?"

"Worf!" Troi said.

"What?"

"Please excuse the ambassador and myself for just a moment, Dr. Stasha?"

Stasha bowed her acknowledgment.

Troi grabbed Worf's arm and pulled him to the far side of the room. "Worf, you practically accused that woman of lying."

"She is obviously nervous about something. If she did tamper with the evidence, then hinting that we suspect her may make her admit it. Besides, it is important to assume that everyone is lying."

"For heaven's sake why?"

"Everyone lies. It is the fifth rule of Betan-Ka's principles of investigation."

"Well, you can't let her know you think she is lying."

Worf frowned down at her. "I did it deliberately, Counselor. I want her to know I suspect her."

"Why?"

"It will make her nervous without threatening her. You did warn me not to bully people."

Troi pursed her lips into a thin disapproving line. "Accusing people of crimes without some proof is a form of bullying. Dr. Stasha has been nothing but gracious to us. We do not need to alienate her without good cause."

Worf thought about that for a moment. He had not yelled, or so much as raised a hand, and still Troi said he was too harsh. "Very well. We will do this your way—for now." He walked back towards the waiting doctor. Troi followed him, like an apprehensive shadow. The counselor seemed determined to keep him reined in. He was beginning to feel like Picard when Riker urged him once too often to be careful.

"You may show us how your machine works," he said. He stood very close to the Orianian. She seemed frail beside him and aware of that frailness. Good.

"Perhaps you would care to look first, Healer," Stasha asked. She carefully avoided looking at Worf. Her slightly bulging eyes held a visible anxiety.

"I am the Federation ambassador, I will look first, Doctor." He wanted to add, "or do you have something to hide," but he resisted.

"Of course, of course, I meant no insult." Her anxiety was almost painful to watch. Real fear chased through her eyes. Worf did not understand. He had not even raised his voice to her. He glanced at Troi to see if she was picking up anything more, but the counselor's attention was focused on Dr. Stasha. Troi never even met his eyes.

"These controls help adjust the view through the eye pieces." Stasha pointed to two knobs on either side of the box. "The upper will adjust the fit of your face to the machine. The lower is for focusing."

Worf pressed his eyes just over the viewer. Two indistinct blurs met his eyes. As he brought the vision into focus, lines formed. Gray, black, white stripes solidified before his eyes. There were too many bands to count, all squished together. The pieces looked identical, but still . . .

"Whose sample is this?"

"The Green woman, Liv."

"Is there a way to bring the samples together, to let them touch?"

"Of course, so sorry that I did not think to explain it." Stasha moved forward. She hesitated as if unwilling to brush against Worf, but she reached out a tentative hand, pointing. "There is a small lever here to shift the platform."

Worf bent back over the scanner, and carefully shifted the pieces closer and closer together. They met nearly perfectly. The small defects were an accident of having to cut and paste the genetic material. The samples themselves were as close to a perfect match as Worf had ever seen. There was no mistake. If he could trust Stasha, then Liv had left traces in the poisoned cup.

If they could trust Stasha? Worf frowned. He did not trust her. Her anxiety, even fear of him with so little cause, had to have a reason. How could they trust the Orianians not to tamper with the clues? How could they trust Captain Picard's life to strangers? Especially strangers that were so easily frightened and Worf suspected, easily manipulated.

"It is a match, Counselor."

"If you would like, I can show you Ambassador Picard's samples next?" Stasha's voice was tight with anxiety, almost a squeak.

He glanced at Troi, but she was staring at Stasha as if the woman had done something unique. Troi's concentration was nearly pure. What was the counselor sensing from the doctor?

"Show us Ambassador Picard's samples," Worf said. He tried to keep his doubts off his face. He did not trust Dr. Stasha's clues. No one was this afraid without reason. Picard was innocent, there could be no proof otherwise, unless it had been manufactured.

Stasha placed more slides into the scanner. "It is ready for you, Ambassador." There was a hopeful lilt to her voice, as if she had decided to be nice to him.

125

Be nice, and perhaps the storm that she feared would not come.

"Thank you, Stasha." Worf tried to respond to this new attempt at bravery. Let the woman think he was fooled. If she were trying to frame Picard, nothing would save her.

Troi glanced at him, she was trying to convey something with her eyes. What? She was trying very hard to tell him something, it was almost a warning glance. But Worf was being a perfect gentleman. He could not help it if the doctor had something to hide and was afraid.

Even bent over the scanner, Worf could feel Stasha standing almost next to him, almost vibrating with anxiety. Instead of fear, she was trying to please now. Worf did not understand the change in the doctor. He adjusted one of the levers and accidently bumped the woman. She gasped. Worf looked up from the scanner and as gently as he could, said, "Please, Dr. Stasha, if you could stand over there. I need a little room."

"Oh, of course." Stasha moved past him. The woman stood on the far side of the room, near a door that led out the other side. It wasn't the freedom of the hallway, but she wasn't trapped either. Was she thinking of escape?

Worf bent back to the scanner. He would trust Troi to see that the doctor did not leave the room prematurely. The two samples were a mass of lines. It took only moments for the lines to become clear, symmetrical. "Where was Captain Picard's sample found?"

"On the outside of the cup," Stasha said, her voice sounded strained.

Troi glanced at Worf. He fought an urge to shrug. He had done nothing new. Why the woman's fear level was rising so rapidly, Worf couldn't understand. Unless, of course, she had tampered with the evidence. That would explain it easily.

"Are you sure this was Ambassador Picard?"

"It is the only non-Orianian genetic sample we found on the cup."

Worf had to nod at that, of course. It would make it easy to discriminate. Human tissue would be rare on a planet of nonhumans.

"Would you like to see for yourself, Counselor?" Worf asked it, and moved away from the scanner, closer to Stasha. The woman seemed to shrink in upon herself. Worf was very careful to merely stand, hands clasped loosely in front of him. He tried to look nonthreatening, which was harder than it sounded, but he did try. Stasha did not seem reassured.

Troi glanced up once from the scanner as if expecting to find Worf beating the woman with a rubber hose. What was Troi sensing from Stasha? Worf very much wanted to ask, but knew better. Such revelations had to wait for privacy, or the right occasion.

"It does appear to be a match," Troi said.

"All that this proves is that Captain Picard was standing near General Alick," Worf said. He looked directly at Stasha, it was only polite to make eye contact.

Stasha swallowed hard enough for it to be visible. "That is true. Even our own general left trace evidence on the poison cup."

"So this really proves nothing," Worf said.

Stasha nodded too vigorously, like a puppet whose strings had broken. "Of course, it is just one piece of information."

"All information is welcome," Worf said. He

moved toward the woman, not so much a step, as a
subtle motion. Though he had meant nothing by it,
she backed away from him, before he was even close,
her back striking the wall.

"Worf, please!"

Worf glanced back to see Troi's face wild, a mirror
of fear. He had done nothing to the doctor, nothing.
She had tampered with the evidence and her guilt was
ruining her. That had to be the answer, nothing else
made sense.

Worf decided to show Dr. Stasha what true intimi-
dation could be. He strode towards the frightened
woman and never said a word. He simply walked
toward her, like he would walk down a hallway. He
kept his face utterly blank, except for his eyes. He let
all the frustration and anger over the captain's arrest
spill into his eyes.

Worf stood in front of the woman. His hands were
loose at his sides. He lied to her with his eyes, only his
eyes. The lie was, I will hurt you, I will break you, if
you do not help me.

Dr. Stasha was so small, Worf towered over her. He
stepped even closer using his bulk to threaten. There
were so many things you could do short of striking
someone. Fear crawled over Stasha's face. Her bulging eyes darted back and fourth, looking for some
escape.

"Worf, don't!"

Worf ignored Troi's plea. "What do you know of
General Alick's death?" he asked.

"N-n-nothing. I swear it." Her voice was high-
pitched, nearly squeaky with fear. She sounded like a
little girl.

"She doesn't know anything. She doesn't know

anything!" Troi ran forward and grabbed Worf's arm, whirling him around. "You're frightening her for nothing, do you hear me, for nothing!"

Troi was screaming at him, ranting. He had never seen her like this. "Counselor Troi, are you well?"

Troi stopped, a look of puzzlement crossing her features. She just stood there hesitant, a little pale. She touched her fingertips to her forehead. "I don't know."

He took her arm, gently but firmly. "You do not look well."

Troi glanced up at the Orianian. Worf followed her gaze. Stasha was still cowering against the wall, but some expression moved over her face that wasn't frightened at all. "She's doing it," Troi said, at last.

"What are you saying, Counselor?"

"Dr. Stasha is an empath who can project her emotions. She was filling me with fear for herself. It made me want to protect her from you."

"I have done nothing," Stasha protested. Her face was all innocence and fright, but no one was buying it anymore.

"I did not harm her," Worf said.

"But she thought you would." Troi shook her head gently, clutching at Worf's supporting arm. "I feel dizzy."

He turned to glare at Stasha. "Is she harming you now?"

Troi thought about that for a minute, trying to sort out her own feelings from the lingering traces of the woman's. "No, it's just an aftereffect of such a powerful intrusion into my mind."

"Didn't you know what she was doing?"

"I have done nothing wrong," Stasha said.

129

"Silence!" Worf snarled. She shrank, if possible, even closer to the wall. Her eyes shifted from one to the other, frantic to find an ally between the two of them.

"Stop it, Doctor" Troi said.

"Stop what?"

"Your nervousness grates on my mind. Get out of my thoughts."

"I don't know what you are talking about. I have done nothing to you."

Troi stepped away from Worf. She stared at the doctor's pinched face. "Are you an emotion reader?"

"Emotion readers are only legends," Stasha said. "They aren't real."

Troi walked very carefully toward the woman, as if approaching a nervous wild animal. "You don't have to be afraid of me, Doctor. Just answer our questions. We won't hurt you."

"You lie." She whispered it.

"Ambassador Worf has not harmed you."

"Yet," Worf said. He knew it only made Stasha's fear worse, but he couldn't let the woman off free if she knew something. Terrified or not, empath or not, that did not change things.

Troi glared back at him. "Worf, you aren't helping."

"She would not be this afraid of us unless she knew something about the captain's innocence."

Troi spoke in a quiet voice, the voice reserved for children, and patients. "You are what my people call an empath, an emotion reader and a broadcaster," Troi said.

"No, there are no such things. Legends, old soldier stories."

"Stop it!" Troi nearly yelled it.

"I am doing nothing," Stasha said.

"Troi, is she harming you?" Worf asked.

"Stasha is one of the most powerful projecting empaths I have ever been around, and the woman has no idea of her power. Earlier she was doing it on purpose, trying to gain me as an ally, but now it is accidental. She leaks her fear into my mind without meaning to."

Troi took a deep breath and stepped away from the woman. "I don't understand why I can't shield my mind from her."

"Are you all right, Counselor?"

"No, but it is not her fault. She doesn't mean to hurt me."

"I am not harming you," Stasha was almost in tears. "I have harmed no one."

"We are not going to hurt you," Troi said. She glanced at Worf as she said it. Worf nodded his assent. Troi rewarded him with one of her warm smiles.

Worf would not harm the doctor. There had to be another way to find out the truth. Yet, he did not have the stomach to abuse someone who was such a victim.

Breck came in from the hallway. "Colonel Talanne and her guards are here." His eyes widened, and a look of surprise crossed his face. Something in the room had caught him off guard, but what?

"Yes," Worf said. He glanced at Troi for some confirmation. If he had seen it on Breck's face, then Troi must have felt something. The look on her face said she had.

Breck saluted, then walked back to the door. "They are free to enter."

131

"What is wrong with Breck?" Worf spoke low for Troi's ears only.

"I'm not sure. Something he found in this room just now surprised him greatly."

"What?"

"I don't know."

"Not a satisfactory answer, Counselor," Worf said.

"I don't have a better one, Worf."

Talanne swept into the room with four guards at her back. Breck followed behind them. The long, narrow laboratory was suddenly crowded.

"What is going on here?" Talanne asked. Her voice echoed in the room, demanding more than asking.

Worf stepped forward. "We are looking at the evidence collected from General Alick's cup."

"Dr. Stasha, are you all right?" Talanne didn't even look at Worf. Her attention was all for the delicate woman behind him.

Stasha glanced at Worf and Troi, then scooted around them, practically running to Talanne. She hid behind the wall of body guards, her relief plain on her face, almost smug. Had her cringing been an act?

Talanne cupped the doctor's face in her hands, raising the small face upward. She stared into her eyes, seeking something. "Have you been harmed?"

Worf wondered for just a moment if Stasha would lie. He did not trust the woman, but what fell from her lips was the truth. "Not yet."

Talanne nodded. "Good, I was hoping I would arrive in time. My guards told me you were questioning the good doctor."

"In time for what?" Troi asked. She walked forward toward Talanne's bodyguards. Breck moved in her way.

"Not too close, mind-healer. Everyone is nervous. Caution is best."

Troi stared at the sentinel. "We have had a murder. If we are to find the truth, we must stop these elaborate precautions. We must trust each other."

One of Talanne's bodyguards laughed rudely behind his, or her, mask. Talanne silenced it with a glance. "As you say, mind-healer, we have had a murder. It makes trust very difficult for us."

"You said you came in time. In time for what?" Troi repeated.

"Breck, did you inform them of our laws on gathering evidence?"

"No, Colonel, I did not."

She nodded. "It is allowed that you act in your own best interest. But, Breck, Dr. Stasha did not deserve such treatment."

"She has not been harmed," Breck said.

"No," Talanne said softly, "I see that."

Worf stepped into the middle of the room. "I am tired of being talked around, as if I were not here. What did Breck fail to tell us?"

"You are allowed to see all the evidence against your captain. You are allowed to use any means available to ascertain that the evidence gathered is legitimate."

"We were doing that," Worf said.

"But even in cases involving important leaders, no one is allowed to seriously harm, or kill, nonsuspects."

"You mean, Dr. Stasha thought we were going to kill her?" Troi asked.

"Hurt her, at the very least," Talanne said.

Troi turned to Breck. "That's what you were so

surprised about when you came in. You were shocked that we hadn't harmed her, yet?"

"That is why I waited out in the hall with your other guards. We were to keep anyone from interfering," Breck said.

Worf just stared at Breck for a moment. He could hear the blood pounding in his head, a loud sound that echoed the anger he could feel rising up from his gut. "You thought I would harm a civilian, a noncombatant?"

"Forgive me, Ambassador, but yes, that is what I thought."

Worf turned to Talanne. "And you came to stop us from killing the doctor?"

"Yes."

Worf drew a great breath of air through his nose, then let it out very, very slowly. "I am a Klingon warrior and an acting ambassador of the Federation of Planets. I am not an assassin, or a murderer of innocent bystanders!" He let the anger grow in his voice, fanning his rage with words. He wanted to scream at them all. What did they think Klingon honor meant? What did they think of the Federation? They were barbarians and thought he was.

He glanced at Troi and saw horror on her face. She was as sickened by this ludicrous situation as he was, perhaps more. It was not the thought of beating a confession out of Stasha that angered Worf, but the assumption that the big bad Klingon would not be able to resist it.

"Colonel Talanne, are you saying that we are allowed to harm people just because we think they might know something about this crime?" Troi asked.

"How else can you be sure that they are not lying?"

Troi glanced at Worf, his eyes widened. Betan-Ka's fifth rule: Everyone lies. "If everyone is as frightened of us as Dr. Stasha was, how will we ever question them?"

"You make sure they are telling the truth," Talanne said.

"How?" Worf demanded.

"By hurting them until you are sure they are not lying. The law says only that you cannot permanently maim or kill those you question. That is the only law in a case where one of our leaders has been killed."

"You are talking about torture," Worf said. The rage was fading away to be replaced by a sort of wonderment too great for mere surprise.

"That is the word you would use," Talanne said. She was utterly calm about it, as if there was nothing wrong with it. "You seem shocked, Ambassador. I was under the impression that the Klingons were experts at the art of pain and extracting information."

"Klingons do torture when it is necessary," Worf said, quietly, "but torturing civilians is not honorable."

Talanne just stared at him. "You are a strange people. Or perhaps it is living among humans that has changed your attitude."

Worf swallowed hard. These people were not listening to his words. He spoke very carefully, each word clipped and offended. "I assure you, Colonel Talanne, that all Klingons view civilian torture as distasteful. Torture is only acceptable when the person is strongly suspected of some crime, then only if they are a warrior. We do not torture nonwarriors, or innocent people."

"You will not torture the civilians whom you question then?" she asked.

"No." Anger tightened the muscles in his shoulders. But he would do nothing to prove that Klingons were the monsters the Orianians thought. It was they who were monsters.

"Then I do not see how you will ever help Picard. Our people know no other way, Ambassador Worf. They will not help you prove the murderer of one of our leaders innocent. Think upon this, Ambassador: if you prove Picard innocent, then one of us must be guilty. None of my people will willingly help you do that."

"Breck is aiding us."

"His life is as much at stake as Picard's." She stepped through her bodyguards until she was nearly touching body to body with the tall Klingon. "Remember this the next time you become squeamish. None of them will help you without the incentive of pain. None of them."

Worf glared down at her, breathing too quickly, his hands balled into fists. "I am not squeamish."

Talanne smiled. "You are, but because you are new to our planet, and Picard came to help us, I will help you, this once." She stared into Worf's face as she said, "Hold her."

Two of Talanne's bodyguards grabbed the doctor. Stasha made a small cry of protest. "I have not lied. I have not lied!"

Her small, pinched face crumbled into terror. Worf wanted to look away. Such fear should not be seen by a crowd. It was personal and not meant to be shared.

Troi staggered. If Breck hadn't caught her, she would have fallen.

"The healer is not well, Ambassador Worf. May I take her to your room?"

"Troi, are you all right?" Worf cursed himself for not realizing that Stasha's fear would be projected onto Troi again. If it had been strong before, it had to be worse now.

"You can't let them hurt her. You can't let them . . . Can't breathe."

The sharp crack of a slap behind him brought Worf's attention from the nearly fainting Troi to Stasha. She was crying, a heartbroken sobbing. Tears trailed down Troi's cheeks. Worf had to stop this, now.

"We do not want her harmed," Worf said. He started forward, intending to wade through the Orianians if necessary to free the doctor.

The bodyguards drew weapons. Breck drew one as well, and suddenly the room was full of potential death. The faint line from pain to disaster was about to be crossed, unless someone did something.

Troi raised her voice to be heard, and it cracked like a child's. "Is there anything we can do to convince you not to hurt her?"

"She will only lie to you, if I stop," Talanne said.

"Then stop," Troi said.

"We cannot stand by while you torture her," Worf said.

"Then you will do it yourself?" Talanne asked.

"Damn you, woman, don't you understand. She will not be tortured while we can stop it!" Worf growled.

Talanne glanced at the drawn guns. "You would risk your lives to save a stranger pain? A stranger that might clear your Picard?"

137

Worf glanced down, then up. He wanted to wade into the guards and start throwing people. But he just stared at Talanne, letting the anger and frustration show in his eyes. If she feared him, she hid it well. "There has to be an honorable way to clear Captain Picard," he said.

Talanne gave the smallest of smiles. "You Federation people are a strange lot. Let her go."

The bodyguards released the weeping doctor. She stood uncertainly in the midst of so many potential enemies. She was like a rabbit in the midst of a dog pack. There was no truly safe haven. She finally turned tear-stained eyes to Troi. "I swear to you by the fruit of the last tree that the evidence I showed you was exactly what I found. I have not lied to you, and if you come back to question me, I will not lie to you then either."

"Thank you, Dr. Stasha," Worf said. "I believe we have all we came for, Colonel. I think we had all better leave the doctor to her work."

Talanne laughed out loud. "You offer honor and truth, Ambassador. And you expect the same in return." She shook her head. "I wish you luck with your honor and truth, because your Picard will need all the luck he can get."

"I am not honorable because of what it will gain me, Colonel Talanne. I am not honorable because it will impress my enemies. Honor is an end in itself. It exists even if everyone around me is dishonorable. The only honor I must worry over is my own."

"A pretty speech, Ambassador Worf. Let us hope that Captain Picard does not pay the ultimate price for your . . . high ideals."

Chapter Eleven

DR. CRUSHER STOOD IN the engine room of the *Zar*, staring up at the swirling framework that Geordi assured her was the ship's engine. The smooth metal seemed inert, no moving parts, nothing that Crusher recognized as mechanical. She turned back to Geordi and the alien engineer. "And you say that this . . . engine is alive?" Her voice held all the scepticism that she managed to keep off her face.

Geordi smiled almost apologetically. "I know it sounds strange, but if what my VISOR is showing is real, then the engine has more similarities to living tissue than metal."

Crusher shook her head. "I believe you, but I . . ." she glanced at Veleck. "Could we have a few moments in private?"

The engineer glanced at Geordi but turned and lumbered away without a word.

139

When he was far enough away, Crusher turned back to Geordi. "I am having enough trouble understanding the cell structure of the Milgians themselves without moonlighting as an engineer."

"Are you able to heal the Milgians?"

"Yes, now that I've figured out how to modify some of our equipment, but all I can do is surface healing. Any surgery or internal rearranging . . . I'm afraid to operate on them. Their bodies seem to compartmentalize all injuries. If they suffer blood loss, the body shuts off that part of the body, sacrifices it for the survival of the whole. If I start operating on them, I don't know what their natural defenses will do."

"You think that the engines will have the same problems?"

"I just don't know," she said.

"Well, if I'm right, I think that working together, we might be able to fix the engine."

"What makes you think that if they can't do it, we can?"

"I'm sure we can try."

Crusher nodded. "Agreed. How long do we have?"

Geordi turned around to find Veleck just standing across the room. He seemed to be doing nothing. If it had been the *Enterprise* in danger, Geordi knew he would work until the engine blew up underneath him. Every member of the alien crew seemed to have given up already. That was taking fatalism one step too far.

"Veleck," he called.

The alien turned his head without turning his body. It was an odd sensation watching the head turn around independently of the body, like an owl. Again there was that bright band of heat just under the head, as if the turning of the head gave off some sort of energy.

"Veleck, how much time until the engines go critical?"

"Perhaps six hours."

"Six hours," Geordi said. He turned back to the doctor. "If it gets close, you can beam out any time you want. Fixing engines isn't in your job description."

"I've been trying to convince the main crew of the *Zar* to evacuate. They won't leave. They're going to go down with their ship." She shook her head. "Data is still trying to convince Captain Diric of the waste of it all. I was getting too angry to talk to him anymore."

Geordi smiled. "I've been having the same trouble with Veleck here. They all seem convinced it's useless."

"Fatalism is one thing, Geordi, but this is just giving up," she said.

"Well, we'll show them that one thing the Federation doesn't do is give up."

Crusher nodded. "All right, let's do it." She lifted a scanner from a small kit at her side. Crusher raised the scanner over the metallike structure.

Veleck came up behind them. "What are you doing?" His slow as molasses voice was just a bit rushed. It was the quickest speech Geordi had heard him make.

"The doctor is scanning the engine structure."

"But why? Why use a doctor for an engineer's job?"

"Your engine is alive. Our engines on the *Enterprise*

141

are just metal and power. I don't understand how to heal living tissue, the doctor does."

"If your engines are not one with you, then what makes them want to run for you?" Veleck asked.

"Well, they don't want to run. We make them run."

"You enslave your ship?"

Geordi stared at him for a moment, not sure what to say. "Our ship is just a ship, Veleck. It has no feelings, no emotions. It's a machine."

"But isn't your Lt. Commander Data a machine? Do you enslave him, too?"

That was a good question, and Geordi still didn't know how to explain it. "Lt. Commander Data is alive. He thinks and acts independently. Our ship is just metal and power. It doesn't have a life of its own."

Veleck's face wrinkled and was covered in a wash of red heat. Geordi wished he could have seen what was happening to the face, but he thought that the engineer was frowning at him.

Crusher came over to them and Geordi was grateful for the interruption. "You are right, Geordi. The engine is alive. The entire ship is alive. The cell structure is very close to the Milgian's own." She turned to Veleck. "Do you mix biological cells in with your construction materials?"

He frowned again. "I do not understand the question."

"The engines are not merely metal. They have living structures inside them, correct?"

"Correct," his voice sounded uncertain as if he weren't quite sure that it was correct.

"I don't understand how they do it or exactly what it means, but the entire ship is alive."

"Can you find the . . . injury?" Geordi asked.

"Not yet. All the scanner can tell me is that the metal contains living tissue. I haven't even figured out how it works, yet. How can I tell you how it's broken?"

"But will it be an injury?"

"I believe that it will need a combination of medical and engineering skills to heal it, yes."

"Veleck," Geordi said, "do you have healing as well as engineering knowledge?"

"I talk to the engines, and they respond to me." He said it as if that answered the question.

"Then what is the injury? What's wrong with the engines?"

"They are going to explode in a matter of hours," Veleck said.

"We know that, but why are they going to explode?"

"I do not understand the question."

This was not a good time for Veleck to suddenly become coy. "Why did you decide the engines could not be fixed?"

"The injury was too severe to be fixed."

Geordi shook his head. It was like talking to a wall. "Can you show us the injury to the engines?"

Veleck seemed to think upon that for a moment. "I can."

They waited for a moment staring at each other. Finally Geordi said, "Could you show us now?"

Veleck turned and lumbered down a narrow walkway that was barely wide enough for his squarish bulk. The shining silver filigree that rose on either side of the walkway seemed daintier with Veleck passing between them.

He stopped in front of one smooth silver wall. He passed a hand over a spot about chest level to him. There was a flash of heat that seemed to jump from Veleck's hand to the wall. Geordi watched the wall grow hotter and hotter, until it seemed to melt.

"Beverly," he whispered, "what does the wall look like now?"

She leaned into him. "The wall looks like glass. There are lights and controls underneath."

Geordi nodded. "It was almost like Veleck's body became part of the wall for an instant. The heat patterns were identical."

"I didn't see anything like that. His hand just passed over the wall, and it became transparent."

"Come," Veleck said. "This is our control panel."

Geordi stared at the head-high screen. It was cooling even as he looked at it. Swirls, patterns, lights—but none of it made any sense to him.

"What do you think, Beverly?"

"I don't know. It does look more like a medical readout than an engineering screen." She pointed to a pulsing light. "Is that a heart rate?"

"I do not understand the question."

"Could you, please, explain what this panel says?" she asked.

"It says that the engine will implode in less than three hours."

Geordi sighed and closed his eyes, and counted softly under his breath. "How does the panel tell you that, Veleck?"

Geordi fought the urge to mouth the words with him, "I do not understand the question."

"Well, at least now I know I wasn't the only one talking to myself for the last hour," Beverly said.

"I've never had this much trouble communicating before," Geordi said.

"The captain understands exactly what I mean and what I want him to do. He just refuses to do it. Veleck here on the other hand . . ." Beverly let the thought trail off, then said, "Veleck, are there any other engineers to speak with?"

"Most of them were injured. When we all agreed it was hopeless, I sent them up to help with the injured crew members. I stayed behind to see how long I could delay the inevitable."

"I can't believe that it is inevitable. There's got to be something that we can do," Geordi said.

"I do not understand this strange persistence you have with fighting against the truth. The engine will die in less than three hours. Why can you not accept that?"

The wall panel pulsed a very bright red. Veleck didn't see, his back was to it. Geordi stared at the control panel. There was a pattern to the lights and swirls. There had to be. It was only a matter of finding it.

"I don't believe in no-win scenarios, Veleck. It's sort of a human trait."

"It is puzzling, this trait."

"Could we look at more panels?"

"This is the main panel. It will show you what you need to see."

"We need more input before we can understand your engines," Geordi said.

"Very well." He moved along the wall that held the first panel, and a host of panels appeared behind his hand. Every time there was a burst of heat, an exchange of body cells, perhaps. To Geordi it seemed that for a moment the . . . hand had become part of the wall. Dr. Crusher said that to her eyes, it didn't happen that way. But the heat sharing was so intense that it blinded Geordi's VISOR, and the illusion of mixing hand and wall was a good one.

Geordi approached the second wall panel. It was just barely at eye level for him. Veleck stood beside him, staring down at the much smaller man. Geordi couldn't read the Milgian's face, but he seemed to be looming over him. Geordi had an urge to tell him to back up, give him a little room, but it was his ship, his engines. If things had been reversed Geordi probably wouldn't have let some stranger run around his engine room unsupervised.

Geordi touched the clear panel. It still felt more like metal than anything else, but there was a warmth to it, as if blood flowed behind it. Was that the fuel of the Milgian ship—blood, life? Did the ship truly move because it wanted to? Veleck explained it that way, but Geordi wasn't sure if he was asking the right questions. But try as he would Geordi couldn't think of better questions.

There was no rush of heat when he touched the panels. He pressed his fingers to the flashing lights as he had seen the Milgian do, but the cool, smooth surface just sat there. No heat, no spark, not even a change in the swirling, indecipherable patterns. The control panels were ignoring him.

"How do I get them to work?" La Forge asked.

"You pass your hands over them, and they recognize you."

"You mean they recognize fingerprints, cell structure, what?"

"Cell structure," Veleck said.

"So, you're saying that I can't get the engines to do anything because they don't know me?"

"Your hand is strange to them. There are no pieces of you in the engine. But I will do all that you require. You have only to ask."

Geordi sighed and glanced at the doctor. Doctor Crusher shrugged. She didn't have any brilliant suggestions.

"All right, Veleck, show me the fuel monitoring system."

"Fuel?"

"How you know how much energy the engines have?"

"Ah, here." He led them to the fourth panel. It was a mix of mostly red with some orange. It was indeed a very hot screen.

"Is the amount of red an indication of a full reserve of energy?"

"Yes."

"What color would be low energy?"

"Blue."

Three questions, three straightforward answers. They were on a roll. "What panel tells you the health of the engines?"

"Overall health is here." The last panel on the wall was a lurid smear of violet-purple. Geordi could feel his body react to the shade and the intensity of it.

"What color should this panel be? What color is good?"

"Green."

Either he was finally connecting with the alien, or Veleck had suddenly decided to be helpful. Geordi didn't care which. He had an entirely unknown engine system to figure out, diagnose, and fix. All in a little over two hours. Geordi smiled slightly. It was like asking for a miracle and expecting to get it. But Chief Engineer La Forge had made his own share of miracles in the past. What was one more?

Chapter Twelve

ACTING AMBASSADOR WORF stood staring down at the sentinel of the now very dead General Alick. It had been Breck's suggestion to question the sentinel. He was the walking dead according to Orianian law. If they were going to ask him questions it had to be soon, before he chose a way to end his life.

After the scene with Dr. Stasha, Worf was determined that this questioning would go more smoothly. He did not need Troi's urgings to behave in a civilized manner. He was Klingon and deeply offended at Talanne's assumption that he would not mind a little torture. He would show them what Klingon honor meant, even if it meant holding his temper.

Troi sat quietly in a corner, watching the guard. The Orianian was slender even for an Orianian. His gaunt face was dominated by shining nearly doelike eyes that seemed out of place in his starved looking face. A white lightning bolt of a scar marred his face from forehead to chin.

But it wasn't merely the scar that stole the beauty from the Orianian's face. There was something wrong with the way the nose lined up under the eyes. A twist to the thin lips that didn't match the face. Kel looked pinched and somehow uncared for, as if life had been hard, and it wasn't getting any easier.

Worf stared at the deformed face and wondered if there were worse things hiding behind their breathing masks and goggles. Perhaps there was a reason, beyond necessity, for faces to remain hidden. Perhaps many of them looked like Kel underneath. Healed by medical technology but somehow twisted.

Worf stared down at the sentinel, arms crossed over his chest. This man was a warrior, not a civilian, and that made things easier. Worf did not feel the same constraints he had felt when questioning Dr. Stasha. Kel was a warrior, he would not be instantly afraid. Worf hoped that here, at least, was a worthy opponent.

Kel kept glancing up at Worf with brief flicks of his eyes. Kel's thin hands twisted in his lap. The darting glances that he gave Worf betrayed an obvious nervousness. He was very uncomfortable. Worf was puzzled. Were all the Orianians victims at heart?

Breck sat in the far corner of the room nearest the door. There was a Venturi officer in the other corner. She was there to see that no illegal harm was done to the sentinel. True he had failed his duty in the worst possible way, but still he was Venturi and there was still the law.

Breck and the Venturi ignored each other. Their

face masks and goggles lay in their laps. The new Venturi was as beautiful as Alick had been, with white-blond hair and eyes that were the molten gold of a snake's. It was a rule of the interrogation room on this planet that all must bare their faces.

After one brief glance, neither Breck nor the Venturi officer had looked directly at Kel. They looked at anything to avoid Kel's face: walls, Worf's tall form, Troi, anything but their unmasked fellow.

Kel's eyes, too, avoided them. He did not glance into their perfect features. He did not look at Troi, but he had to look at Worf. The Klingon had made that unavoidable.

Kel sat in his small chair, and Worf towered over him. He had found that his height made the Orianian guards nervous, and he used that now to intimidate one guard. Worf stood almost close enough for their legs to touch. He stared into Kel's face without even blinking, as if he were trying to memorize each flaw.

Sweat beaded along Kel's forehead, and still Worf only stood and stared. If just standing and staring would make Kel sweat, then that was what Worf would do. There was no need to do more, when staring seemed to be enough. The sentinel licked his thin lips, darted a glance upward, then down. His hands twisted the mask in his lap as if clutching it would keep him safe.

"Do you expect me to believe that you know nothing about General Alick's death?" Worf's deep voice seemed loud in the stillness.

Kel jumped. "I . . . I know nothing. I have told you everything I know."

Worf leaned over, placing a hand on either side of

151

the chair back. He glared into Kel's face from a few centimeters. "You're lying to us," he growled. "Lying to me."

Kel pushed to his feet, sending his chair to clatter along the floor. He stood to his full height, but still only came to Worf's lower chest. He stood trembling, hands clenched into fists at his sides. His breath came in gasps. "How dare you stare at me like that!" He shouted. "I am hideous, but it is no fault of my own. I would rather you beat me than humiliate me like this!"

Worf just stood there for a moment, staring down at the smaller man. He fought to keep the surprise off his face. Staring was worse than a beating, so be it. He stepped into Kel, forcing the man to step back.

"I will stare at you if I please. You have allowed your leader to be murdered. You have no rights to anything."

Kel's anger collapsed, and his face twisted in the first signs of tears. Was he going to cry? Would a warrior break down in such a manner so quickly? Worf found it hard to believe, but the man's torment was real. He fought an urge to glance at Troi, to see if she felt Kel's pain. But Worf did not need empathy to see the pain tear at the man's twisted features.

Breck stood and spoke softly. "Kel is one of our lifeless children that was saved. Sometimes, it is not possible to heal everything. It is our custom not to look upon them when they are barefaced."

"Why?" Worf asked. "They are only scars, healed injuries. There is no shame in that if the injuries are incurred honorably."

Breck gave a faint smile. "The Klingons have a

different opinion of such things, Ambassador Worf. We . . . we see them as a mark of our shame."

Kel was indeed crying, softly. His tormented face was made worse by the effort not to cry, not to break down.

"Is it against your laws for me to stare at him?" Worf asked.

Breck could not keep the surprise from his face. He glanced at the Venturi officer. Her face was just as puzzled. "No, it is not against our laws to stare at him. But it is . . ." Breck paused as if searching for the right word. "It is rude."

"But not illegal?" Worf asked.

"No," Breck said, "not illegal."

"Then face me, Kel, and tell me what you saw. If you did not poison Alick, you know who did. An innocent man does not break so easily."

"This is too much," the Venturi officer stood. "You are tormenting him."

"I have not touched him," Worf said.

"You are allowed to touch him," she said. "We are warriors accustomed to physical hardship, but you are not allowed to humiliate him."

"I can beat him, but I cannot stare at his face?" Worf responded.

"Of course," the officer said. "It is expected to torture prisoners to wrest confessions, but not this cruelty."

Worf just stared at her for a moment, an idea too horrible for words forming. It was Troi who voiced it. "Do you mean that while we've been questioning witnesses, someone else has been questioning our captain?"

153

The officer spread her hands. She did not know. "It is possible. I am not privy to the ambassador's questioning."

"You mean they are torturing Captain Picard?" Worf asked. He glared at Breck. "Why did you not say something?"

"I thought you knew, Lieutenant."

"Take us to the captain, now!" His voice rolled like thunder in the room.

Breck gave a bowing salute. "I will see if it will be allowed."

"It will be allowed," Worf said, "If we have to go through the entire Orianian army, we will see the captain—now!"

Rage spilled up inside Worf in a warm tide, but underneath the rage was fear. Fear of what they might find. Fear of having allowed harm to come to the captain. A cold, empty, space had opened up inside him. The anger kept him warm, and felt good, but the fear was there. What had been happening to Picard while they questioned witnesses? And why hadn't they asked what treatment prisoners could expect on Oriana? That question haunted Worf.

Worf strode out into the hallway, physically shoving Breck out the door ahead of him. Troi followed without protest. The Venturi officer and the weeping sentinel stayed behind.

This delay would allow Kel to recover himself, to regain control. But it wasn't knowledge of Alick's death that had made Kel nervous, even frantic. It had been showing his deformity, and being stared at. Worf was almost a hundred percent certain that Kel was simply self-conscious. He didn't really know anything helpful. But if Worf were wrong, this might have been Kel's only moment of weakness.

Would they be able to wrest the truth from him later, if there was truth to find? No answers for that, but as Worf strode down the corridor, he didn't care. Suddenly, the murder investigation, the peace treaty, none of it mattered half so much as finding Captain Picard safe and unharmed. And if he was hurt, Worf was not at all sure he wanted to remember that he was Ambassador Worf.

Chapter Thirteen

THE TWO ORIANIANS outside the cell block doors were fully masked and armed. They saluted Breck as he walked up. He returned the salute. "Ambassador Worf to see Ambassador Picard."

"Murderers do not receive visitors. You know that," one guard said.

"This is not a request," Worf said. He moved forward to loom threateningly over Breck and the guards. They gripped their rifles just a little tighter but otherwise didn't flinch.

Breck actually placed a hand on Worf's chest, pushing him back, gently but firmly. "The acting ambassador wishes to discover the health of Picard. It is not an unreasonable request."

The guards exchanged glances. "Murderers are not allowed visitors. That is the law."

"I will see Ambassador Picard," Worf growled. He

pushed past Breck, looming over the two guards like a storm about to break. "I will see him now!" Each word was a low growl, chopped and very certain. It was an order. The guards understood that. They shifted nervously.

Troi felt their uncertainty. They evidently had no orders to cover a rampage by the acting ambassador. . Did they dare shoot him? Defend themselves? Or not?

Worf had tried to get word to Talanne or Basha, to get permission to see the captain. Neither leader had been available. As Federation representatives they should have gone through channels, but Troi agreed with Worf. They had to see Picard, now. The captain was the first human the Orianians had ever seen up close. Torture might not work the same on the captain. They might kill him without meaning to.

Troi hoped the guards' uncertainty would work for Worf, and not against him.

"We were not told that the ambassador was an exception to the law," the guard said.

"Do you wish to tell General Basha that you never received his orders," Breck lied as smoothly as he breathed. Troi knew there were no orders, but the anxiety level of both guards jumped. They weren't sure if they had missed orders or not. This was, after all, an unusual situation.

"We have had no orders," the second guard said. There was a stubborn set to his voice. "If your General Basha wishes the new ambassador to have access to the cells, then let him tell us himself."

"Do you really think that with the Venturi leader assassinated, the general has nothing better to do than come down to the cells and see that his orders are being carried out?"

"We have no orders to cover this . . ."

"Enough of this!" Worf said. His fist lashed out to connect very solidly with the first guard's face. He slid down the wall and collapsed in a silent heap. The second guard started to bring his rifle up, but Breck smashed him in the gut, then followed with a knee to the face. The second guard slumped to the ground, as well.

Worf had disarmed the fallen guard and had no doubts at all about his actions. "Breck, open the door."

"I obey orders," Breck said. He punched a series of buttons near the door. They flashed once, and the door opened. "It only opens one way. It is a safety precaution against people breaking in."

"Once inside we are trapped?" Troi asked.

"Yes."

"It does not matter. We are not here to rescue the captain, only to make sure he is safe. Once that is done, we will wait to be released," Worf said.

Breck made a sound very like a laugh. "I only hope it is that simple, Ambassador."

Worf wasn't listening. He led the way through the door, rifle half raised. Would he shoot guards that got in his way? Troi tried to feel what his intentions were, but the rage, the near panic to find the captain, was masking everything else. Would Worf commit murder to save the captain? Perhaps. But even knowing that, Troi followed them inside. The door shut behind them with a sigh, and they were alone in a maze of small doors and dim lights.

The walls were a crisp, pure white. It was nearly soothing after the conflicting colors of the rest of the Orianian complex. Troi would almost have asked to be jailed if she could rest her eyes on the soothing blankness. It didn't look much like a prison. If it had not been for the many small doors, it wouldn't have looked like a cell block at all.

But the corridors were very narrow, forming a white maze that spread out in every direction. It was dizzying. The white walls seemed to squeeze around them like a fist.

"Which way?" Worf asked.

"I have not been to see Picard, either," Breck said.

"I was not asking you. Counselor?" Worf turned dark eyes to her. His certainty that she would lead them through the puzzle-box of this place was clear and unwavering.

Troi only wished she felt as confident as he did. As soon as she knew they were coming to a place of torture, she began building the mind-shielding she would need to survive. The Orianians' emotions were so overwhelming at times that she didn't know if she could go into the bowels of real despair and still be able to function.

"If I drop my mental protection to search for the captain then I may not be able to filter out the feelings of all the other prisoners."

"We don't have much time," Breck said. He cradled his rifle more securely in the crook of his arm, waiting. Waiting for her to decide whether all this effort had been for nothing.

A shrill scream cut the silence. It was impossible to know if it were male or female. A level of pain had been reached where it made no difference in the voice. The scream came from up ahead in the heart of this white maze, and it decided Troi.

They had to find the captain.

The mind-shield was like a layer of buzzing, made up of her own emotions, like bricks in a wall. She had entombed her mind behind pieces of her own thoughts. She could have shattered the shield with one gentle touch, but Troi knew better. In this place the influx of emotions could drive her mad. It had happened to Betazoids before. There were reasons why empaths avoided torture chambers. Other than the obvious ones.

The buzzing quieted it. Each sound, each emotion faded back into her mind, until there was nothing but that last great shield. A solid blankness, a blessed quietness that all empaths needed as a last retreat. On the other side of that quietness Troi could feel the press of emotions. It was almost physical, like hands shoving against her mind.

She cast that quietness away, like discarding a piece of clothing. Now, her mind was naked to everything. Troi remembered nothing for a moment. Then, there was a voice calling to her, but the sound was very far away. The only thing she could 'hear' was the roar of terror. A screaming, crimson sound that clawed across her mind. Pain had color and shape and texture. Other people's terror rode her, and she could not remember who she was, or why she had come.

Hands were digging into her arms, tight, hurting. It hurt. Her body. Her pain.

"Troi, can you hear me? Deanna!"

That was right. She was Deanna Troi, and all this pain belonged to strangers. Someone was shaking her, hard and harder She looked up into Worf's grim face. Somehow she had fallen to the floor. It was Worf's hands that had brought her back, his small violence that had chased away the pain. He was still shaking her.

"Worf, I'm all right."

"Deanna," the relief in his voice washed over her, soothingly. "What happened to you?"

"There is no time to explain. Please, help me up."

Worf stood and lifted her as he moved, one motion that made her feel like a child in his hands. She clutched his arm as she tested whether she could stand alone.

The pain, terror, despair were still there, but as a distant buzzing. She could concentrate again, feel her own thoughts again. Could she sort the captain's thoughts from all the noise? If the people in the cells had been any other race, she would have been confident, but the Orianians for better or worse were an overwhelming empathic mess.

But Troi knew the feel of Picard's mind, the ordered strength of his thoughts, the cool control of his emotions. Troi knew Picard was a very private man, and as much as he valued Troi, she made him just a little nervous.

It was that nervousness that Troi reached for, that reserve, the solid, familiar core that was Jean-Luc Picard. She knew some Betazoids said people were like tastes in their mind, or smells, but to Troi it was always more abstract than that, perhaps because she was half-human. Whatever the reason, the thing she searched for was nothing so concrete. In fact, in many languages, there were no words for what she sought. It was like walking through the buzzing noise, pushing it aside with your body, like swimming, but that wasn't it either. Words were not enough for the rush of other people's thoughts rippling inside your head.

There—there. Troi stopped and stood very still, though to Worf and Breck she had not moved and so could not be still. Troi forced herself very still inside. There, like a familiar thread, or a piece of music heard from a great distance. Picard; she knew that slightly disapproving calm anywhere.

Troi didn't so much open her eyes as begin to see where her body stood again. "I've found him." Her voice was very quiet and seemed to echo from deep inside her body. It was not easy to make contact with someone who could not reciprocate the mental touch, and to maintain that contact and follow it back to its source while moving through a place drenched in terror.

Troi moved very carefully down the hallway. It was like carrying a glass of water up a flight of stairs. Each movement had to be thought about, not just by her mind, but her body. Concentration had to be total.

"Are there other guards?" Troi asked. Her words seemed slow.

"Two more in the torture area, plus the questioner," Breck said.

"The torturer?" Troi made it a question.

"Yes."

"If the guards come, I can't help you. I can't let go of the captain."

"Understood," Worf said. "Take us to the captain. Breck and I will do the rest."

Troi moved down the corridor, past all the doors. Someone was behind almost every door. The buzzing flowed and faded, parts growing louder as she passed in front of the physical cause of the fear, or sorrow. She saw Picard's thread as a faint white line like the things you see out of the corners of your eyes. She did not look directly at it but around it, and it pulled her forward.

A hand grabbed her shoulder. She stumbled and nearly lost that shining thread. She didn't dare look around to find out why someone had stopped her. If she panicked now, there might not be time to reestablish contact with the captain. Troi closed her eyes. Her job was to maintain concentration. She had to let Worf and Breck do their jobs. If they failed . . . Troi didn't even let herself finish the thought. Nothing mattered but that faint line. Nothing.

Breck's voice came softly, a whisper. "The main torture area lies just ahead. If we must pass through it, then we may be forced to kill."

"Counselor, are we close to the captain?"

She spoke with her eyes still closed, concentrating on that faint line. "Yes." Her voice was thick and slow with the effort not to lose that line.

Worf leaned into her, his breath whispering along her face, "We have only three more doors to either side before we will be forced to confront guards. Is Captain Picard on this side?"

"I don't know. Close, he's very close." Worf's irritation was the faintest of thoughts. She had no time or energy left over for Worf.

"Lead us, Counselor," he said.

Troi moved forward, eyes still closed. She didn't need to see. It was only a handful of steps, and the line merged into a door. She reached a tentative hand in front of her. Fingertips brushed something hard and cool. She blinked rapidly, trying to see what she touched. It was a cell door.

"Behind here, he's behind here." Her voice still held that lazy quality. She felt like she was waking from a dream, sluggish and heavy-headed. The effects would pass in minutes, but while they lasted, Troi felt a step away from reality. Distant and cool as a dream.

"Can you unlock this door?" Worf asked.

Breck didn't answer but gently pushed Troi to one side. He pressed his palm flat to a slightly raised panel of the door. There was a faint pulse of amber light, then the door cracked open with a sigh.

Breck pushed the door inward, rifle at the ready. Worf hissed, "Captain?" The door opened wide.

Picard sat on a narrow bench against the far wall. A look of complete surprise crossed his face. "Lieutenant Worf, what are you doing here? This had better not be what it looks like." His face crumbled to a frown. Anger would not be far behind.

Troi stepped into the room, eyes still not quite focused on any one thing. "We were worried about you."

"We discovered that the Orianians torture their prisoners. They refused to let us see you."

"So you assumed I was being tortured."

"Yes."

"I am glad to hear you didn't come to rescue me." Picard smiled. "When I saw the three of you slink in here, I was sure you had done something foolish. Forgive my doubts."

Worf glanced at Troi. She was more herself, and could appreciate Worf's sudden pang of conscience.

"Well, Captain, there was some trouble in getting into the cell block."

"What kind of trouble?"

The door slammed open, ringing against the wall. Armed guards poured into the room, rifle barrels searching out individual targets. "No one moves," a familiar voice called out.

"That kind of trouble," Worf said.

"What is going on here?" Picard asked of everyone and no one.

Colonel Talanne stepped into the room, a rifle pointing very steadily at the middle of Worf's chest. "That is what I would like very much to understand, Ambassadors."

Chapter Fourteen

PICARD HAD NEVER SEEN a real torture chamber. Staring around the room now, he still felt like he had not seen one. The walls were smooth and white, and everything was spotlessly clean. There were tables with bright silver straps and chairlike devices whose function was unclear. But the room was open, airy. You could almost picture a gentle breeze wafting through the room. Wasn't there a rule somewhere that to terrify you had to look terrifying? It seemed somehow obscene that this sparkling room should be a place of pain.

"Please, Ambassadors, Healer, be seated. Be comfortable." Talanne herself slid behind a neat desk that took up most of the west wall. "I am sorry that there are no other chairs, but lean against anything. I promise it will not harm you." Picard couldn't even figure out what the various instruments did, let alone how they could hurt.

Picard glanced around the room. Breck had taken up his station at the captain's side. For once Picard did not protest. His recent incarceration had made him appreciate the paranoia of the planet. Or perhaps it was watching General Alick die?

Talanne propped her feet upon the desk in an attitude of carelessness that was at odds to anything Picard had seen of her. He glanced at Troi. She widened her eyes a bit. Picard wanted badly to confer with Troi, not just for Talanne's oddly relaxed behavior, but about Alick's death. Picard wanted to know what they had found out and what Troi had sensed. "May I confer with my people in private?" Picard asked.

"I think not," Talanne said. "After Ambassador Worf's display of bravado, I believe we should keep our eyes upon you."

Picard turned to Worf. He tried to think how to phrase his question in front of strangers without embarrassing Worf. He didn't like to question his people in front of others. "What was so important, Lieutenant, that you would risk our hosts' displeasure?"

"We had reason to believe you were being tortured, Captain."

"Tortured," Picard said. He felt his face collapse into surprise before he could stop it. "Lieutenant, are you telling me that you thought the Orianians would torture a Federation ambassador?"

Picard stared at Worf, waiting for an answer. Worf did not look uncomfortable in the least when he said, "Yes, I did."

"Troi, did you believe this, as well?"

Troi was staring at Talanne very steadily, the

concentration almost touchable. She was sensing something. "The Orianians' customs do allow torture of suspects and witnesses, Captain."

"What are the two of you talking about?" Picard asked. He had missed something, sitting in his cell.

"Captain." Worf stood to attention. "We have learned that the Orianians consider torture as part of their," he looked down as if seeking the answer on the floor, eyes widened, "culture."

"In what respect?"

"When we went to question people to discover the real murderer, Talanne herself offered us the opportunity to torture civilians. Innocent doctors who had done nothing but gather evidence from the crime scene."

Picard stared at Talanne. The look on her face was one of arrogance, unreadable, almost amused, but there was a tightness around the eyes that made it all a lie. It was still a masterful effort at keeping a blank face. The Orianians had no talent for it. That Talanne could do it at all meant she was a very quick study. "Is this true, Colonel Talanne?"

"That we consider torture as a normal part of a criminal investigation, yes." The false amusement slipped away, leaving her face bleak. "In fact, if Ambassador Worf had waited but an hour, he would have been right." She stared at Picard, her face calm.

"Excuse me, Colonel Talanne," Picard said, "Are you saying that you do intend to torture me?" It was too absurd to say out loud. There had to be a misunderstanding somewhere.

"You will be interrogated like any other murder suspect, Ambassador Picard. It is our custom."

"But surely, Colonel Talanne, there are exceptions for diplomatic missions," Picard said.

Talanne frowned. "Why should there be?"

Picard made an exasperated sound. He looked at Worf, who said, "I told you, Captain. They are barbarians."

Picard didn't even correct Worf, he was too taken off guard. "Colonel Talanne, I agreed to be arrested but I did not understand your customs. I did not realize that torture was part of . . . your routine."

"Are you saying that you would have fought rather than submitted, if you had known?"

"I honestly don't know."

"You are all very surprised by this," Talanne said. "Why?"

"The Federation does not condone torture under any circumstances."

"Why not?"

"I ask again, may I be allowed to speak with my people in private?"

"I don't think so." Talanne stood in one sweeping motion, her cloak swirling like a solid wind around her. "We have no secrets from each other, surely. Speak the truth in front of us without fear."

Picard gave a small nod. "As you like. Counselor, what do you sense from Colonel Talanne?" He did not look at Troi but watched Talanne. He depended on Troi, but his own observations were always valuable to him.

"She is truly puzzled, Captain. She doesn't understand why we are shocked that they use torture. She feels no remorse or guilt. It all seems very ordinary, every-day, to Colonel Talanne. They have every in-

169

tention of torturing you, Captain." Troi's voice was soft on the last word.

Talanne was wearing her face bare as a compliment to the ambassador. Picard now saw that it was a mistake. The limited control she had of her expression crumbled. Every emotion crawled across her delicate features, plain even to Picard. Surprise, embarrassment. The Orianians had worn masks too long and had lost the knack of keeping blank-faced. But Picard asked aloud anyway, a perverse form of politeness, perhaps. "Is that accurate, Colonel Talanne?"

"Yes," the word was unsure, hesitant.

"You intend to torture me in an hour?" Picard was still having trouble believing it. His diplomatic training didn't cover this.

"Your interrogation is scheduled in an hour, yes."

"We cannot allow this, Captain," Worf said.

Picard's first instinct was to agree, but what would that mean for the mission? What would it mean for them getting out of here alive? The torture chamber was full of Talanne's guards. They were outnumbered two to one, and the *Enterprise* was gone. Even if they fought their way out, where would they go?

"What does the torture consist of," he asked.

"Captain!" Worf nearly shouted it.

"Lieutenant, I need more information before I can make a decision."

"What are you saying, Captain," Troi's voice was breathy with fear.

"Colonel Talanne, what does the torture consist of?"

Talanne watched them all, openly curious. "You mean what will be done to you?"

"Yes."

"I cannot allow you to be harmed, Captain," Worf said.

"Nothing has been done to me, yet, Lieutenant. We are gathering information, that is all."

"Our laws state that a prisoner cannot be maimed or permanently damaged. Our devices are designed for maximum pain but minimum harm."

Worf made a sound very much like a growl. It curved through the room like the beginnings of a storm, and the bodyguards shifted uneasily.

"Lieutenant Worf, at ease."

Worf scowled at the guards but gave a curt nod. "Aye, Captain."

"I give you my word that you will not be damaged. It is only pain, Ambassador. We are not complete barbarians." She made the last word bitter.

"Captain, may I speak?" Troi asked.

"By all means, Counselor."

"Is Captain Picard the first human you will have tortured?"

"Yes."

"Then there could be more extensive damage done than you realize. Human physiological responses may be very different from Orianian."

Talanne nodded. "Yes, that is a very good point. We will be extremely careful. I will supervise the interrogation personally, if that will ease your fears."

"I think I would feel better if you explained the mechanics of your torture devices. Perhaps that way we could understand the process better."

"Well, I don't know, one of the principles of torture is surprise. If a prisoner knows exactly what to expect you have lost some of your power."

"Unless the torture is so frightening, that the anticipation is frightening," Picard said.

"There is that. Very well, I will explain our concepts of pain to you. If it will help."

"It might," Picard said. Frankly if Talanne's explanation was not satisfactory, he wondered if he could in good conscience fight his way out. It would be the death of the peace mission, and perhaps their own deaths as well. Picard did not wish to sacrifice his people for his own self-preservation.

"All our interrogation techniques rely on stimulating the nerves of a particular section of the body." She stepped to a small white object that was about chest high to her. There was a small cage like arrangement on top. "The prisoner kneels and the head is strapped into place. The nerves of the face and skull are stimulated. The worst aftereffect is dizziness, and some temporary memory loss."

She moved to a white frame from which cords dangled at regular intervals. The cords were obviously to bind ankles and wrists. "This reacts on the nerve endings in the skin. The pain is excruciating but once the machine is turned off, the pain stops instantly. There is no lasting damage."

"We cannot trust her, Captain," Worf said.

Picard tended to agree but he had to know. "Counselor?"

"Colonel Talanne believes what she's saying, Captain."

"I would not lie about it, Healer." Talanne sounded offended. "We will do your captain no permanent damage until the execution."

The phrasing was strange, so Picard asked, "What do you mean?"

172

"Assassins are tortured to death."

"You said these devices only cause pain, not permanent injury."

"There are levels of pain that the body cannot tolerate, Ambassador. It is not the injury that kills but the shock. The body's own reaction is the method of death."

"Captain," Worf said, "we must get you out of this place."

"No, Worf, I believe the colonel. I will submit to the . . . interrogation."

"No!" Worf's voice filled the room. The guards drew weapons.

"Worf, no!" Picard motioned his officer to be still. Worf froze with his hand on his phaser.

"Captain, please . . ."

"No, Worf, I will not endanger all of us because I am afraid of a little pain." Picard was glad his voice sounded steadier than he felt. "You are not to try and rescue me, Lieutenant."

"Captain."

"That is a direct order, Worf."

Worf wouldn't meet his eyes. He stared at the bodyguards then back to Picard. "Aye, sir." The words were a growl of anger.

"One more question, sir," Worf said.

"Yes, Lieutenant."

"Counselor, is anyone in this room planning to harm Captain Picard. Do they see him as an enemy?"

Troi's face grew blank, her concentration touchable. She shook her head. "They are doing their jobs. There is some worry over whether torturing him is wise, but no one is angry. It is all very practical."

"Must we discuss all this in front of your guards?" Picard asked.

Doubt flashed across Talanne's face. Did she realize how transparent her face was? She couldn't possibly know, or she would never have shown herself maskless.

"Colonel Talanne?" Picard made it a question.

Her eyes flickered to his face then down. "I don't know. It has been a very long time since this planet has seen a mind-healer of such power. I had heard stories of powers that could look into the very soul, but," she looked away from them, her voice growing soft, "I did not believe."

Picard was tempted to tell her that her face alone gave most of it away. But Orianians were so uncomfortable without their masks that he would not compound their discomfort.

Talanne turned to them, her face guarded, eyes uncertain. "I will allow you to speak in private to your people. The guards outside the cell block should have allowed Ambassador Worf to see you. You are still a Federation ambassador, and you will be accorded the accompanying privileges."

"We would also need to speak with the Greens," Worf said.

Talanne opened her mouth as if to protest, then smiled. "I suppose if we are to execute a Federation ambassador, you must be given full access to everyone involved." She looked suddenly tired. "I will leave orders that everyone is to cooperate with you fully. There will be no other incidents." She stared at Worf as she said the last. "If you have any urgent demands, Lieutenant Worf, simply come to me. I will

174

expedite them without your having to go through all these heroics."

She smiled but it was not pleasant. "You have learned much about our ways this day, and I have learned that not all I hear of Klingons is true." A look of genuine puzzlement crossed her face. "Who would have thought that a Klingon would have any qualms about torture?"

"Honor does not allow harming innocent people."

"Yes, yes, I understand that now. Perhaps if we ever get this mess sorted out, you can tell our warriors something of the Klingon code of honor. It seems all we have heard about is the pain and barbaric behavior. Perhaps," she said softly, "there is more to it than that."

"I would be honored to share the Klingon way with your people, Colonel Talanne." Worf stood very straight, and the pleasure and pride at the prospect of sharing his honor code with an entire race was obvious even to Picard. The captain had never before realized that Klingon honor was almost akin to a religious system. Would he convert the Orianians? The thought of a dual culture based on Orianian and Klingon customs was not comforting.

"You may go back to the ambassador's cell and talk among yourselves," Talanne said. "And then you may question the Greens. Though I will supervise that questioning."

"You are most gracious, Colonel Talanne," Picard said.

"It is not graciousness, Picard, as well you know." She glanced at Troi. "It seems I cannot lie to you, so I will not try. If we do execute you in two days, the

Federation will not be pleased. We are dying from our own war. We cannot possibly win a war against the Federation. My husband does not see it that way, more is the pity."

Picard found Talanne's reaction to Troi's powers refreshingly direct, as was her honesty. Honesty deserved honesty. "The Federation is not in the habit of making war upon," he groped for a phrase, "less advanced societies."

"We are not even great enough to be worthy enemies, is that it?" There was anger in her voice.

Picard sighed. "No insult was intended."

"We may be uncivilized, Ambassador Picard, but unless your people can prove your innocence, two days from now you will die. This puny, backwards planet will have at least one Federation death to its credit." She took the mask from her belt and slipped it over her face. Then she turned a blank, unreadable face to them. "Do not underestimate us, Ambassador Picard. You do so at your very real peril.

"The guards will escort you back to your cell. When you are finished talking in private, then you have only to tell the guards. They will fetch me, and I will go with you to talk to the Greens."

"Thank you, Colonel Talanne," Picard said.

"Do not thank me, Picard, please, do not thank me." With those cryptic words she swept past them, two guards falling into step behind her. Her sharp footsteps echoed into the distance.

It was Breck who broke the silence. "You heard Colonel Talanne. Take us back to the ambassador's cell." His voice held the certainty of an order.

The faceless guards did not argue. They turned almost as one and formed a phalanx around the

Federation group. Breck was very clearly grouped with the outsiders. If he minded, he made no show of it.

Picard found himself almost relieved to be back in the cell. He had not thought that was possible. He had spent all day waiting for news, or anything else. The guards fed him but would not talk to him.

It was like some awful anxious dream. Not only was the peace mission in ruins but he, a Federation ambassador, was thought a murderer. His own possible death was secondary. The total failure of their mission would doom thousands.

The white cell seemed even smaller with Worf's bulk. His head brushed the ceiling. The Orianians hadn't planned for a prisoner of such height. Of course, Worf wasn't the prisoner, Picard was.

"How is the peace mission progressing, Ambassador Worf?"

"I am no ambassador, Captain," Worf growled. "The Venturies and Torlicks are still willing to talk peace but only after the stain upon the Federation's honor is removed."

"What exactly does that mean?"

"Proof of your innocence, or your death," Worf said.

"I see," Picard said quietly. "Then we must find the real murderer."

"We have been trying, Captain."

"What have you discovered, Lieutenant, Counselor?" Picard sat on the pallet that he had slept on. There were no chairs to offer so he waved them to the floor.

Breck slid easily to sit against the far wall, nearest the door. Counselor Troi sat near the captain on a corner of the pallet. Worf remained standing at attention.

Worf gave the report, what little there was of it. "We believe that Dr. Stasha was telling the truth about finding your genetic print on the cup."

"Counselor?" Picard made the one word a question.

"I wish I had more to add, Captain. I don't think anyone has deliberately lied to us, except perhaps General Alick's sentinel. He was extremely nervous and fearful when we questioned him. But it makes no sense for him to have anything to do with Alick's death."

"Why not?"

"If a sentinel's charge is killed while he, or she, is on duty, then the sentinel is expected to commit ritual suicide," Troi said.

Picard glanced at Breck still sitting easily across the room. "If I die, will they expect it of you?"

"Yes, Picard. Our laws are very strict on sentinels who fail their task."

"Though it seems harsh in this case, there is nothing you could have done to prevent this," Picard said.

"It does not matter, Ambassador Picard. Sentinels are one of the cornerstones of our government. There can be no excuses or exceptions. If one failure is allowed, then more will follow."

"You aren't angry about that system?" Picard asked.

"Why should I be?"

To that Picard had no answer. "Have you sensed anything at all, Counselor?"

Troi glanced at Breck. "Yes, Captain, but . . ."

"If you think I am a security risk, I will wait outside the door," Breck said. His voice was even, no offense taken.

"Counselor?" Picard asked.

Troi shook her head. "His life is forfeit along with yours, Captain. It seems . . . unfair to exclude him. Besides, he might be able to answer some of the questions I have about the Orianians."

"Lieutenant Worf, do you concur?"

Worf nodded, one small movement. "Yes, Captain."

"Very well," Picard said. "Proceed, Counselor."

"The Orianians have very strong empathic abilities. I have never been around any race that could so easily breach my empathic barriers."

"Is that what happened the first night, when we saw the room of lifeless children?"

"Yes and no. When I'm asleep, sometimes my barriers are not as strong, and intense emotions do seep through, but never to that degree. It was like the fear, the pain, was my own. One of the greatest fears for a Betazoid is losing self-identity. To be swallowed up by someone else's thoughts and feelings until you forget that they are not your own."

Her lovely face was . . . haunted. Picard had no better word for it. It was not often that the counselor allowed her own worries to show so clearly. "Are you all right?"

"It passes, Captain. I have experienced a few individuals in the past who could intrude upon me in this fashion, but never so many people in one place. And the strangest part is that they don't know they have the ability."

"Explain," Picard said.

"I don't know if I can. It is like they all have these wondrous empathic talents, but somehow it is stunted or hidden, even from themselves." Troi looked at Breck. He sat motionless against the wall, but he was watching her. She had a vague sense of his intense concentration but could not read him.

"Breck, what are the legends of mind powers? What were they suppose to be able to do?"

He shifted, settling more comfortably against the wall. His body language was much more casual than the intensity Troi could feel.

"There have been no true mind powers among our people for over a hundred years. Until I met you, Healer, I thought they were wishful stories for children. Now I am not so sure. I feel strange when I am near you and you use your powers. It prickles along my mind. Why?"

Picard watched doubts pass over Troi's face. Was she debating whether to tell the truth? If so, Picard knew which she would choose. Troi was more comfortable with the truth.

"Many of the Orianians are blank to me, Breck. That means I can't read their emotions, which is highly unusual. It implies an ability to block empathic senses. You are a blank to me most of the time."

"So, you are saying I am an empath or a mind-healer?"

"In some sense, yes."

He smiled at that. "A mind-healer, but why are so many of us blanks, as you call us?"

"Did you feel General Alick die?"

"I don't understand the question," Breck said.

"I felt him die, Breck. I felt his death inside my head. It was horrible, bitter." Troi stopped then spread her hands wide. "I don't have words for how it feels, but it is hideous. It is one reason Betazoids don't go into security work."

"You feel all deaths?"

"Not all, but many."

"You think that the Orianians were originally empaths, but killing forced the talent underground?" Picard asked.

"Yes, Captain."

"Wait," Breck said. He was leaning forward now, making no pretense of disinterest. "You mean this war has killed not only our people but our mind-powers?"

"What were the powers suppose to be able to do?" Troi asked again.

"They could heal the body as well as the mind, though that was rare, only the greatest could do that. No leader ruled without a healer by his, or her, side. They were supposed to be able to talk to the ground, the plants, even the water and trees."

"Talk, how?" Picard asked.

"The legends say they could conjure fruit from bare rock, but I don't know what is myth and what is reality. The stories grew as the healers died."

"But their empathic sense was often tied to the ground, to the planet?" Troi asked.

"Yes. If the stories are even partly true, the most common power was to be a friend of the trees and growing things."

"Does that help you, Counselor?" Picard asked.

"There is something called a sense of place, Captain. Land can have a sense of itself. There are theories it is the imprint of people, but it is often strongest in areas where there are no people."

"Are you saying that the planet itself could be empathic?"

"It is alive, Captain," Troi said. "Every living thing gives off something that death steals from it."

"But a planet, an entire planet?"

"A dying planet," Troi said softly. "Dying like the people and their empathic abilities."

"I do not understand this," Worf said. His voice was a questioning growl.

"I do," Breck said softly. He laughed and it was the first truly free sound Troi had ever heard from him. "We are tied to our planet. As we poison it, we poison ourselves, not by being forced to eat corrupt food, or drink foul water, but directly. We are tied to our world, and as it dies, so do we. And the first thing to die was our tie to the planet we were killing. Our mind-healing."

Troi nodded. "I think so."

"Could you teach me how to use my powers?"

"I believe so," Troi said.

He laughed then, delighted as a child. "We must save you, Picard. Your Federation has too much to teach us for it to end here. If we can prove to my people that killing and destroying this planet has robbed us of our healing . . . all of them, even the ones who want to continue this war, might listen."

"Then we must talk to the Greens," Worf said.

"Agreed, Lieutenant." Picard smiled, slightly. "But I doubt that they will allow me to accompany you."

"Captain, I cannot leave you to be tortured. I cannot . . ."

"You can and you will. Believe me, Worf, if I saw another solution I would take it. But we don't have the firepower to fight our way out. Even if I was willing to allow the peace mission to die in my place."

"Captain . . ."

"Find the real murderer, Lieutenant, clear my name. Perhaps this afternoon's unpleasantness will be the only interrogation needed."

Worf stood in one smooth motion, using only his legs. "We will not fail you, Captain."

"I have no doubt of that, Worf." He carefully did not look in Troi's direction. He did not want to see her compassionate glance. She would know, if no one else did, that he was worried. Two days, and he would die. The worst of it was, the peace mission seemed likely to die with him. And now he had less than an hour before he was going to be led away to voluntary torture. It was ridiculous, but he saw no way out of it.

Picard had always known that death was a likelihood as a career Federation officer, but ending his days executed for murder . . . It was too absurd.

The others went out the door. They would do the questioning. The sorting out of all the horrible implications. Picard would have felt better if he could have gone with them. It was not that he thought he would see something or hear something Worf and Troi did not. It was that once that door closed behind them, all Picard had to do was wait. To wait for the guards to come and take him back to the clean white room, and its devices. But after the pain he would be returned here to wait some more. To wait and wonder. It rankled that he should spend his last hours helpless, and dependent on others, even trusted friends.

"Enough of this," he said to the empty room. "I am Jean-Luc Picard, Captain of the Federation Starship

Enterprise. I am not so easily defeated." Out there was the best security chief he had ever worked with, and the only counselor he had ever trusted with his own thoughts. They were good people. They were part of the *Enterprise* crew, and that meant the best. He was in good hands, the best hands. Picard knew that, and yet . . . he worried.

Chapter Fifteen

THE GREENS' CELL DOOR was near the center of the maze of white corridors. The stark white walls stretched as far as they could see, a tide of prisoners behind identical clean, white doors.

Worf leaned close to Troi and whispered, a rumbling growl that vibrated in her ear, "Are there prisoners behind all these doors?"

She whispered back, "I'm trying very hard not to sense anything, Worf."

He nodded and straighted back to attention. They were all waiting until Talanne could be brought. She had left very clear orders that they were not to question the Greens without her presence. So, they waited.

Troi stood very still in the center of the corridor. She had rebuilt her barriers after the captain was found. She had no choice. The emotions behind the doors were like vibrating static playing along her nerves. Troi felt exposed, or worse yet, diffused. She felt stretched thin, tugged at by every emotion they passed. A planet of unbelievably strong empaths with absolutely no training. It was too frightening.

If the captain hadn't been jailed, awaiting execution, Troi knew that she would have been the one in the greatest danger. So she stood in the midst of the buffeting wind of the Orianian minds and tried to feel nothing.

Worf and Breck stood to either side of her. If someone had simply glanced at them, they might have assumed that it was Troi who was the new ambassador. Breck had tried guarding Worf, but the Klingon had made it clear what he thought of the Orianian's help. So they both guarded Troi.

The problem was that the real danger to Troi was something that neither warrior could protect her from. Only one person could help her walk safely through the pain and despair that was the jails of Oriana, and that was Troi herself.

Sounds came from down the corridor. The guards all turned at full attention to face the noise. A group of three masked and cloaked Orianians came into view. Their black and gold cloaks almost glowed against the whiteness. Troi found her eyes drawn to the color. This unrelieved whiteness was exhausting to the eye. Perhaps that was the point. Even the walls themselves reminded you that this was a prison, as bleak in its own way as the outer planet.

"Greetings, Ambassador Worf, I am sorry to keep you waiting. The guard that came to tell me you were here had some trouble locating me." It was Talanne's voice, but she made no offer to remove her mask and

186

show her face. "Open the door for us." Her voice was quiet, but it was definitely an order.

A guard moved to obey. He, or she, pushed the door wide, holding it with an arm. He stood aside to let the ambassador's party enter.

"Please, enter," Talanne said. "All guards will remain outside the door."

"But Colonel Talanne . . ." a guard protested.

"I have spoken," she said.

"Ambassador Worf," Breck said, "shall I remain outside, as well?"

"Yes." Whether Worf wished it or not, custom dictated that if Talanne had no bodyguards, then he would have none. In fact . . . "We are honored that Colonel Talanne shows such trust in us."

"I am trying to behave like a civilized leader." The bitterness in her voice could have cut glass.

Troi was relieved that even standing next to Talanne, she felt nothing. She was blocking out Talanne's empathic broadcast. There was only a faint buzz like the humming of insects, ignorable if she worked at it. Troi was relieved more than she would admit. But how could she help Worf and the captain if she refused to use her powers?

Worf ducked through the low doorway into the cell. Troi followed him because that was her job, but fear was growing in her, her own fear. Fear of failing her duty out of cowardice.

The harsh, bright light bounced off the glaring whiteness of the walls. The room swam in brightness like burning water in a glass globe. Audun sat against the far wall, his large brown eyes staring dully at the door, as if he did not really see it at all. Liv was huddled on one side, her back to the door. Her shining white-blond hair spilled onto the floor, a line of darkness staining it. Marit lay on her back, one arm slung carelessly outward as if in sleep. But her face was too pale for sleep.

Worf moved swiftly to kneel by Audun. Troi just stood for a moment staring at Marit. The buzzing in her head was growing louder like someone had turned up the volume. *No,* she thought, *no, I can't feel this. Not again. Please.*

Talanne stepped in behind them. Perhaps she couldn't see around them, perhaps it took a moment to realize what had happened. Or perhaps, the full horror of it slid slowly into her mind, because she simply didn't want to believe it.

"Audun, what has happened here?" Worf asked. He was feeling for a pulse on Liv. He did not bother with Marit. The Klingon knew death when he saw it. "Audun, can you speak?" Worf asked.

Troi stepped toward them, slowly. It was like a nightmare where no matter what you did, it was too late, always too late. If only they had discovered the Orianian attitude toward torture sooner. *If only . . .* two of the most painful words. Words that Troi told her clients not to use. *If only:* words to torture yourself with.

The buzzing in Troi's head exploded into a scream. It shattered her barriers like brittle glass. A shriek was ripped from Troi's throat. She whirled and found Talanne just behind her. Another scream tore through Troi and spilled out her mouth. Talanne wasn't screaming. Troi was doing the screaming for her.

Talanne's emotions washed through Troi and swept her away. Horror at Marit's lifeless face. Terror at

188

what had been done, then anger. Anger that grew and fed on itself until it was rage. It burned through Troi and filled her with a desire to hurt someone. For the first time she understood exactly what Worf felt when just destroying something, anything, would make him feel better.

The burning hatred curled in upon itself—self-hatred. Guilt. Guilt like a gleaming sword to cut and leave Talanne to bleed. The anger turned inward and fed on the guilt, like a beast gnawing its own foot to escape a trap. Troi choked on the tears, the rage, the hatred. She collapsed to the floor, sobbing.

The room was suddenly full of guards with drawn weapons. Talanne had not moved. With her face covered, she seemed utterly calm. Only Troi knew what was happening inside, and only now did Troi realize Talanne's empathic gift. The Orianian leader could project all her strong emotions onto other sensitives. She could rid herself of the worst of them, like throwing out garbage. And all of that emotional trash was filling Troi until she wasn't sure where Talanne left off and this person called Troi began.

"Troi!" Someone was holding her, cradling her in their arms. "Troi, can you hear me?"

Talanne's voice came low and calm. "Who was in charge of the Greens' questioning?"

Troi's lips moved soundlessly, mocking the words, repeating them.

"Counselor!" Worf shook her, forcing her to look up at him instead of at Talanne. "Deanna, can you hear me?"

"Who did this?" Talanne's words hissed this time,

189

rage burning through them. Troi repeated the words like an echo. She did not seem to see Worf's face.

One of the guards dropped to one knee in front of her. "Colonel Talanne, we did not know that the Green was so delicate."

"Do you give me excuses!" She slapped him, and he pressed his face to the floor.

"Mercy!"

"You will get mercy," she said softly, Troi repeated it with her. "The mercy you gave that woman." Talanne turned her back on the crouching guard. "Take him to the place of pain."

Worf slapped Troi as gently as he could. She did not react, but her eyes tried to follow Talanne. Worf cradled the counselor in his arms and stood. "I must get the counselor away from here. Stay with the Greens, Breck. See that no harm comes to them."

"As you ask, so shall it be done," Breck said. He backed toward the prisoners, his rifle now pointing out at his fellow guards.

Worf pushed through the guards with Troi's limp body in his arms. He stopped in front of Talanne. "I must take her out of here. She is ill. I charge you with the safety of these people. I left Breck to see that no more harm is done them. You will treat him as a member of the Federation. He is not to be tortured."

"I will see that no more harm is done. You have my word of honor." Troi repeated the words, it was ghostly, as if Troi were not there anymore. Worf held her tighter as if that would help.

"Your word of honor means nothing to me, Talanne," Worf growled the words next to her masked face. Troi winced, spine bowing as if in pain. Worf pushed through the guards into the hallway. Troi whispered, "Go with them, show them the quickest way out of these cells." A second later a guard came out to stand beside them.

"Colonel Talanne bids me lead you out of the prison."

Worf swallowed hard enough for it to hurt. How had Troi known that? How? "Then lead us," Worf growled.

The guard made a half salute, then strode down the corridor, black and gold cloak swinging out behind him. Worf followed, glancing down into Troi's face. Her eyes were wide open, but they looked blind. She didn't even blink. He whispered, "Troi."

He had ordered her to find the captain. He had taken her farther into this place, knowing how it might effect her. Worf had given the orders, but it might be Troi who paid the price.

Every commander knows that when he orders his people into battle there is a chance not all will come back, but Troi was different. Worf could not think of her as a warrior. That should have been an insult coming from a Klingon, but it was not. Worf could not explain it, but Troi was the only friend he had that was not a form of warrior and still he respected her. He had never seen her so much as carry a phaser. She went into battles unarmed, and though she would not kill, she never flinched or considered personal safety first.

She was a warrior at heart, but she had the soul of something gentler. Worf did not understand her completely, but he valued her. To Klingons it was an honor to die performing their duty. Why did it bother him so much that Deanna Troi might die here and now?

Chapter Sixteen

WORF KNELT BY TROI'S SIDE, back at their sleeping quarters. She lay on her sleeping mat, pale and very, very still. With her eyes closed, Worf would have thought she was asleep, but when he lifted her hand, it was totally limp and her skin was cool to the touch.

Worf had piled blankets on top of her, forming them into a cocoon around her cold body. "Troi, Deanna, can you hear me?"

He felt again for the pulse in her neck. The beat of her heart was steady, comforting. Should he take her to one of the Orianian doctors? Would they be able to help her? Or would they only make it worse? No. He couldn't give her over to those butchers.

Worf squeezed his hands into fists and ground his teeth. A low growl of frustration trickled from his mouth. He did not know what to do. This was not a problem for phasers or anger. He stared down at her pale face and felt some of the helplessness that he often felt with his son, Alexander. Why couldn't the world be as simple as battle?

If only the *Enterprise* would return. Turning Troi over to Dr. Crusher would have been comforting. Turning her over to these honorless warriors—Worf didn't like it. How could anyone trust such people?

The image of Marit's dead face was still vivid. They had tortured her to death by accident. Accident! Worf tried to swallow the anger, but he couldn't. Troi was hurt. Picard was in jail. A possibly innocent woman was dead. The planet was dying. The peace mission was in shambles.

Worf stood, walking toward the nearest wall. He stared at the bright, pretty pictures, and all he could see was the woman's dead face. He smashed his fists into the wall, first one then the other, as if he were using a punching bag. Over and over, smashing, hurting. The rage bubbled up from his gut and flowed out his shoulders, down his arms, into his fists, in a red wave. The rage poured out of him, and it felt good.

"No need to destroy the room, Worf."

He whirled. Troi was propped up on one elbow, smiling at him. Worf rushed to her, grabbing her in a huge bearhug. "Deanna, thank Hakkierk!"

Her voice came muffled against his chest. "Worf?"

He pulled away from her, pulling at his chest sash. His control slid into place like a well-worn glove. "I am very glad to see you are better," he said.

Troi smiled up at him. He knew she was sensing his happiness at her recovery but he also knew he did not have to make embarrassing displays for the counselor to know how he felt. It was . . . calming. She was the only "human" he had ever been around whom he was sure would not misunderstand his Klingon ways.

"Are you unharmed?"

"A little weak but it will pass," she said. She scooted around on the mat to put her back to the wall and cozy the blankets around her.

"You know what happened to you, then?"

"Yes," Troi said softly. "Colonel Talanne is one of the most powerful projecting empaths I have been around."

"Projecting empath, what does that mean?"

"All full Betazoids are able to project their thoughts upon others. They are broadcast telepaths, but projecting emotions is much more rare. Instead of being able to sense other people's emotions, they send their own emotions onto other people. In Talanne's case it is only sensitives, other empaths. If a Betazoid with such a talent could not learn to control it, they would be too dangerous for words."

"How so?"

"Say the empath is angry in the midst of a peace negotiation. She could infect all the other delegates with her rage."

"Should Colonel Talanne be barred from the peace talk?"

"I don't know yet. It depends on whether or not she can learn to control her power. She's like all the other Orianians and has no idea she has this awesome ability."

"Are you suggesting the colonel could use her power as an influence for peace?"

"Yes," Troi said.

"Isn't that . . . cheating, Counselor?"

"Worf, all the Orianians are constantly affecting each other. Their talents are almost totally wild. They play off each other now. All I'm suggesting is that we could harness the power and use it, like a tool. Like I use my own talents when the captain is negotiating a treaty. You don't think that's cheating, do you?"

"I had never thought about it," Worf said. "But knowing what the other side is feeling is not the same as making them believe something they do not believe. The peace would only last as long as Talanne could influence them." He shook his head. "No, the peace must be uncompromised."

"You're right. But we have to find some way to control these abilities. I can't keep doing this."

"What happened, Troi?"

"Talanne possessed me. I felt her anger, her outrage at Marit's death. And underneath that was guilt." Troi stared up at him. "Guilt, Worf, like a great darkness eating at her soul."

"She feels responsible as any good commander would," Worf said.

Troi shook her head. "No, it was personal. Whatever she felt guilty over was something specific that she had done."

"What?"

"I don't know, exactly, but she knows something. She knows something about the Greens. We have to question her."

"Do you think Colonel Talanne had something to do with the murder?"

"I don't know. Maybe. But whatever she did, it's something important enough for her to feel an obligation to the Greens. It was as if she had failed personally." Troi hugged her knees to her chest. "I was Talanne for a few minutes, but her feelings were so intrusive that I couldn't catch her thoughts. Guilt, horror, and very specifically directed toward the Greens. Not Marit, but the Greens."

"I will question her, Deanna," Worf said. He stood. "You rest."

"No, I have to be there."

Worf scowled down at her. "You nearly died. I will not risk you again."

"I was not close to death."

"You were badly hurt," Worf said stubbornly. He had no words for injuries of the mind. Troi could be badly and permanently damaged with invisible wounds.

"The greatest fear for a Betazoid is to lose oneself. To be swallowed up until we become the other entity. I became Talanne for a time." She stared down and would not meet his eyes.

"Then you cannot go near her again. It is too dangerous."

Troi looked up at him. Her solid black eyes sparkled with something between determination and anger. She looked so small huddled in a nest of blankets, hugging her knees to her chest, and yet . . . There was nothing small about the look of utter stubbornness in her face. But if she thought she could out-stubborn him, well, Klingons had many talents.

"It is almost nightfall of the second day, Worf. At nightfall tomorrow the captain will be executed for murder. I have to be there when you question Talanne. Now that I know what she is, I can protect myself more actively."

"No, Counselor." Worf said it like it was a reality.

Troi stood, letting the blankets spill to the floor.

"Worf, Talanne knows something important. She's the first person that I've been near that I am sure knows something about this murder. We have less than forty hours to prove Captain Picard's innocence. Without me in the room, Talanne will be the best liar you have ever seen."

"What do you mean by that, Counselor?"

Troi took two steps closer to him, forcing herself to crane her neck upward, but she wanted eye contact for this. "Talanne is a projection empath. She can project her emotions onto others. I and the other Orianians are more in danger, but you are not immune."

"I still do not understand," Worf said.

"I believe that Talanne is a wild talent and doesn't realize what she's doing, but many untamed talents have an unconscious ability to lie in their emotions as well as their words." Troi crossed her arms over her stomach. "In other words, Worf, without me there to tell you if she's doing it, Talanne could lie completely to you, and you'd believe it, because she made you believe it."

"Klingons are not sensitive to empathic messages," he said.

"True," Troi said, "But then Klingons have never come up against a race of empaths with such horribly powerful talents."

"We have dealt with Betazoids before."

"You have dealt with me, Worf. I'm only half Betazoid. There are people on my home planet that could read your mind, your emotions, or plant their thoughts in your mind."

"Truly?" he asked.

"It is all illegal, of course. We have very strict rules

197

governing what empaths and telepaths are allowed to do. But without those laws and the ability to enforce them . . ." Troi shrugged. "It would be a very dangerous world. A world where a few powerful individuals could control most of the population. The Orianians have the potential to do just that, Worf."

"I understand that I need your input, but what is to keep her from possessing you again?"

"I can fight it, now that I know what it is."

"Will there still be danger to you?"

"Yes, but minimal."

He frowned. "I do not like it."

"I am a Federation officer whose captain is imprisoned. You wouldn't deny me the chance to help save him, would you?"

Put that way, what could Worf say? She was speaking of her duty and her honor. "You may accompany me to question Colonel Talanne, but if you begin to feel ill, you must leave."

"I will, Worf, believe me. I have no wish to repeat what just happened. It's horrible for a Betazoid to lose themselves."

"To die with honor in defense of duty is a proud way to die. To lose one's self, as you put it, seems less honorable and more . . . horrible."

Troi flashed him a quick smile. "I agree, Worf. Believe me, I agree."

"I did not mean that your sacrifice would not be as great. I meant that by not dying, your sacrifice would be greater."

"I understand you perfectly."

He honored her with one of his rare smiles. With so many of the crew, even his friends, Worf often felt out of step. But here with this gentle woman, he was understood, perfectly. No explanations were needed. In the midst of chaos Troi was like a center of peace. In many ways Worf valued Troi for the same reasons Picard did. Though neither captain nor lieutenant would ever have guessed it.

Chapter Seventeen

COLONEL TALANNE sat in a small square interrogation room. She was almost completely lost in her cloak and mask. Nothing showed of her, even her small hands were gloved. Was it some subconscious hint that she meant to hide things?

Troi sat in the far corner of the room, as far away from Talanne as she could physically get and still be in the room. Talanne had asked after Troi's health, hoped the mind-healer was better today. Yes, Troi was better today. But fear trickled low in her stomach. She had to force herself not to clench her hands into fists. But she had the training for it. It was part of her job that no matter what was said or done in a session that she, the counselor, could remain outwardly calm. Troi hoped fervently that she would be able to maintain that calm.

Troi had barricaded her mind. When Betazoids first got their powers at adolescence, many were untamed talents. If you worked with them, to help them train, you had to be able to block your mind beyond anything required for daily interaction. But she had never worked with children. Since she was half human, her mind-shielding was not up to the challenge. Of course, Troi had not mentioned that fact to Worf, fearing he'd refuse her access to Talanne.

The woman knew something. Troi was sure of it and they would find out, now, tonight. Captain Picard was running out of time.

Worf stood near the door, arms crossed over his chest. He stared, unblinking, at Talanne. He watched her as if she were some new form of life that he had dedicated himself to studying. The mask was useless before his concentration. She could hide nothing. That was the arrogant confidence that Worf projected into the room.

Troi had seen him do it before. It was wonderfully intimidating. The thing that truly made it work was that Worf believed it. His utter confidence was not a mask. Failure was not a possibility until it was brought abruptly to his attention. He had prepared for this questioning as he would a battle. There was no room for doubt when doing armed combat. Doubt could kill you much quicker than your opponent's blade. Troi, in her own way, had prepared for battle, too.

"Do you know why you are here?" Worf said, his voice was a low rumble. Even when his voice was flat and unemotional, there was a hint of growling anger.

"I know you requested to interrogate me," she said. "I gave you the great courtesy of not bringing any bodyguards to this meeting. I am placing tremendous trust in you." Her voice sounded certain.

But underneath the confidence was a thread of fear. She had left the bodyguards out because there was something she did not want anyone else to know. Troi had the flavor of Talanne's mind, and it was easier to read, almost too easy.

Troi was walking a dangerous line between blocking Talanne's errant emotions and sensing what she was truly feeling. Troi had formed a solid smooth shield inside her head, but in the center was a tunnel. There was a door at the end of the tunnel that Troi planned to slam in place, to seal herself behind, if it became necessary. But the shield was a compromise, flawed because it had to be. So far, so good.

"We understand the honor you do us by coming alone, Colonel Talanne," Worf said. The word honor had a bitter twist on it.

Talanne shifted in her chair as if it were suddenly not as comfortable. Shame flared down Troi's mind. Shame and anger.

"She did not mean to honor us, Worf," Troi said. They both turned to look at her. "The colonel didn't want anyone else to hear her secret. That's why she came alone." Troi let her voice hold all the certainty that she felt.

"Why would you not want your bodyguards to hear?" Worf said. "Why is it safe for us to hear? Do you plan to kill us the way you killed Marit?"

Talanne sat up suddenly, very straight. "I did not kill the Green woman." Her voice shook a little, and sorrow dripped into Troi's mind.

"You ordered her torture. The torture killed her. You killed her," Worf said.

"No!"

"You know it is true," he said.

202

Talanne hung her head, gloved hands coming up to touch her masked face. "Yes, yes, it is true." She looked up suddenly. "But don't you see, everyone connected with the crime had to be tortured." She looked from Troi to Worf, her hidden face still managing to convey anxiety. "Don't you see? I had to do it."

"Who are you trying to convince, Talanne? Us, or yourself?" Troi made the words soft, without reproach, but she dropped the woman's title. Troi could feel Talanne's agony over what had happened. The woman was genuinely grief-stricken about it. Why? She had not known Marit. Or had she?

Troi took a chance. "When did you first meet Marit?"

Worf glanced at Troi, fighting to keep the surprise off his own face. Talanne stared at Troi as if she had sprouted wings. "I do not know what you mean."

Fear boiled through Talanne and poured down the tunnel in Troi's mind. Troi's heart began to beat faster with someone else's panic. No, not again. Troi closed her shielding, solid and smooth and unbreakable. It was like cutting off a hand, so abrupt. The tie with Talanne gone, Troi felt like she'd lost something. A piece of herself. She had almost been part of Talanne again, that easily.

A calm, cold horror swept over Troi. Would her mind barriers hold?

Her voice was still calm, as cold as the fear in her chest. "When did you first meet Marit?"

"At the reception dinner, of course," Talanne said. Her voice had the smallest of quavers to it.

"You're lying," Troi said softly. It was a gamble because with barriers in place, she could not sense a lie. But she had sensed it before. The truth didn't change that quickly.

"Tell us the truth, Colonel Talanne," Worf said. He took two steps away from the wall, arms uncrossing, hands flexing at his sides. His breathing had quickened.

Talanne glanced up at him, then back to Troi. "I am sorry, sorrier than you can know, about the Green's death. I have given orders that no more torture is to be done. It was not really I who gave permission for the torture to begin." She looked up at Worf. "General Basha forged my name."

Troi noticed she had not called him her husband.

"Why would the general do that?" Worf asked.

"I am in charge of all prisoners. It is part of my duty as second in command. But Basha and I have an understanding. He often metes out questioning in my name. Though he never gives death orders. Only I can do that."

"How convenient," Troi said.

"I do not enjoy ordering my own people to death. Unlike Basha, I see them all as my people." She stood and paced closer to Troi. "Even the Greens."

Did she mean it? Troi had no way to tell. "You met with the Greens without Basha knowing about it." Troi made it a statement, though she was far from sure it was true. There was no time to be cautious.

Worf had managed to keep his face neutral. Why shouldn't he be calm? He thought Troi was sensing all this, not guessing.

"I did not betray my husband," she said.

"I did not say you betrayed him, Talanne. I said you had met with the Greens without his knowledge. I am a mind-healer Talanne. You know what that means.

204

Your legends tell of people like me. You cannot lie to a mind-healer." This wasn't strictly true, but most Orianians seemed to believe it.

"No! I did not betray my husband. I would not betray my own people. I obey the laws." She turned to Worf, hands out as if pleading. "I helped make those laws. Why would I break them?"

"Because you believe that the Greens are your people, too," Worf said.

She stepped back from him as if he had struck her. "You use my own words against me."

"You have broken your own laws, betrayed your own people. You are without honor," Worf said.

"And now you have helped kill one of the people you met with secretly," Troi said. "You have betrayed everyone, Talanne. Your own people and now the Greens."

She ripped off the mask and threw it against the wall. It hit with a smack and slid to the floor. Tears were trickling from her lovely eyes.

"What was worth all that betrayal, Talanne, what?" Troi asked.

"Jeric, Jeric!" She screamed the name of her son and burst into tears.

Troi and Worf looked at each other. Worf's puzzled expression matched Troi's feelings. "What do you mean, Talanne? What about your son?" Troi asked.

"I thought you knew everything." Her voice was bitter. "I had lost three children, so deformed at birth that they could not survive. Three dead babies." She stared at Troi. Her large, nearly golden eyes shimmered with unshed tears. "Do you understand what that felt like, mind-healer? Three babies that I carried in my body. Three times I felt life moving inside of

205

me. And three times I gave birth to monsters that could not survive outside of my body."

A visible shudder ran through Talanne's body. Troi was glad she couldn't feel it.

"It was as if I were their lifeline." She stared at Troi, tears sliding slowly down her face. "I was their mother as long as they were inside me." Her arms folded across her abdomen. "But once they were born I couldn't be their mother anymore. I couldn't save them. I had to watch them die." She bent forward, cradling her stomach.

Her voice when it came was low, almost a whisper. Troi was forced to step close to hear it at all. "I could not go through it again. I could not."

"You went to the Greens for help," Troi said.

"Yes," she whispered.

"Tell us," Worf said. His deep, growling voice held none of the threat it had before. In fact Worf's hand was halfway out toward the woman, as if to comfort her. He stared at that offered hand and clenched it to his side. The pain that blazed behind his eyes for a moment was enough to show Troi he felt the woman's pain. Worf understood loss. Even if death was something to celebrate, some losses still hurt.

"Tell us," Worf repeated gently.

Talanne blinked up at Worf, as if realizing that he was feeling some of her pain. Troi wondered for the first time, if that were literally true. Was Talanne projecting her emotions onto Worf?

Troi stared up at Worf. She would have to drop her barriers, and she did not dare. Talanne was in the middle of an emotional storm.

"Most of us cannot even become pregnant," Talanne said, her voice shaky with tears. "You know what happens with the babies that survive." She would not look at either of them as she said, "The dead children. Most can be saved eventually, but they are never the same. Nothing could save my children."

She turned in one smooth motion, drawing the cloak tight around her body. "The Greens become with child much more easily. And their children are healthy, strong." She shook her head. "Much of the hatred of the Greens comes from seeing their smiling children. It is too painful a reminder."

"Why not share technology with them?" Troi asked. "Surely it's clear that they are using some form of biotechnology to help their children."

"To admit that would be to admit that, perhaps, the Greens had been right all along. That we have been killing our own children. No one wanted to believe that. They wanted to go on hating each other and then they began to hate the Greens as well. We were accustomed to hating. It was easier than changing."

"You went to them to help you have a healthy baby," Troi said.

"I did," she said. "And now I have Jeric. I don't regret it, not in the least."

"Marit helped you?"

Talanne nodded. "And now I have let her die."

What could Troi say to that? It was true, in a way. "Does Basha know?"

"No, he is a true Green-hater."

"Audun was our only contact with the Greens. Can you take us to them?" Troi asked.

Suspicion was plain on her face. "Why?"

"We have only one more day before Captain Picard is killed," Worf said.

Talanne nodded. "Of course, you hope the Greens

can tell you something of the biologically altered plant."

"Yes," Worf said.

She stared from Worf to Troi as if trying to memorize their faces. "I have betrayed the woman who gave me my son. I would not betray the Greens again. If you play me false or play them false, I will kill you both, Federation ambassadors or not." Her voice and face were very steady, utterly serious.

Worf gave a small nod. "Understood."

"Good," she said. "It is good that you understand me. I wish I did." She gave a soft smile. She got her mask from the floor and slid it into place, then lifted the cloak hood. She was hidden again, bland and safe. "I will take you to a Green encampment. Perhaps there you will find your answers, as I found mine."

"Thank you, Colonel Talanne," Troi said.

"Do not thank me yet, mind-healer. Your captain is still going to be executed unless you can prove his innocence. You saw how much power I had to save Marit. I will be no help to you unless you find proof."

"We will find proof," Worf said.

"How can you be so sure?"

"Because Captain Picard is innocent," he said.

"I knew that Klingons were violent and obsessed with a strange honor code, but I did not know that they were politically naive." There was the faintest trace of a smile in her voice.

Chapter Eighteen

GEORDI STARED AT the smooth blinking panels. They were pretty. The soaring silver wall flowed upward to curve into the ceiling. It looked more like a graceful sculpture than a control panel. Geordi admired the beauty of it, but the more he studied it, the less he understood it. He felt like he was growing stupider the longer he stared at the thing.

He wanted to open a panel and look inside. Veleck had been horrified. You would have thought that Geordi had suggested cutting the chief engineer's own body open. Barbaric had been the most polite term Veleck had used.

Geordi had never realized how much of his engineering skill relied on either a good diagnostic computer program, or a hands-on approach—take it apart and put it back together again. The computers here were tied into the engines, they wouldn't talk to him either. He felt useless.

Dr. Crusher stood a few meters to his left. She was running medical tests on the control panel, as if it were indeed an injured patient. She had had more luck than Geordi. Because her regular patients frowned on having their skin cut open just for a casual look around, she had tools to peer inside without damaging the outer shell. She turned off the medical tricorder and stared at Geordi. There were tired lines around her green eyes. "I think I may have found the injury."

"What?" Geordi walked towards her eagerly. Maybe this was the break they needed.

"If it were a patient, I would say there is some sort of problem with the immune system. I don't know exactly what it is, but it would be like something entering our bodies and eating all the white blood cells. As the immune system is destroyed, internal organs would shut down. The body would begin closing ranks, trying to stay alive. The one thing I don't understand is why the shutdown of the immune system would destroy the engines. A patient I could keep alive, in stasis if I had to."

"I think I know," Geordi said. "You can't shut this engine off, or even take much of it off-line. The major systems are interconnected—damage one beyond repair and it would be like a house of cards. It's the main reason Veleck won't let me cut into any one system. Damage one part and the entire engine is hurt."

"So if a vital system is destroyed, then it all goes," Crusher asked.

"Yeah."

"I think I can slow down this immune damage, but

210

the real problem is repairing the systems already injured."

Geordi ran a hand along the blinking panel. It ignored him as it had for hours. "Before the engines are stressed to the point of no return."

"And they explode," Crusher finished for him.

"Can you get started on the immune problem?" he asked.

"I've diagnosed the problem, Geordi, but I don't know how to get at it."

"What do you mean?"

"If this was a patient, I would have to operate, invasive surgery. Some of the engine's vital organs are shutting down. Repair or replacement is needed. Can you open the engines to me? Peel back the proverbial skin and let me get at it?"

He shook his head. "The engines ignore me. It's like I'm not here. Veleck touches the panels, and they pulse to life, but they don't know I'm here."

"What can we do, Geordi?"

Veleck must have heard his name for he lumbered out from behind the silver lattice work. "I told you that you could not help us," he said. Even his slow-motion voice sounded tired.

"Couldn't you open the engines up and let the doctor work on them?"

"Our engines would not understand your instruments, or your instructions. You would only confuse them."

Veleck always spoke of the engines as if they were alive, separate beings. Geordi didn't question it anymore. "Then you could talk to the engines for us, explain what the doctor was doing."

"It will not work," Veleck said.

Geordi wondered if there was a Milgian word for pessimist, but he doubted Veleck would get the insult. And besides, Geordi was a Federation officer. He wasn't supposed to insult officers from alien races. Every crew member was in some way a diplomat. He took a deep breath.

"Veleck, we don't have much time left. Can't you just humor us and tell the engines to do what we ask?"

"Humor you? I see nothing funny about this situation."

Frustration burst into anger. Geordi opened his mouth to yell at the stubborn being, then stopped himself. He turned away, swallowing all the words he wanted to say. What he did instead was laugh. A low pleasant laugh.

"I do not understand your humor," Veleck said.

"I think we're all tired," Crusher said.

Geordi nodded. "Yeah, we're all tired." He looked at the large brightly colored alien, the odd unreadable eyes. "Sometimes when humans are upset, they laugh. It relieves tension."

Veleck seemed to think about that for a moment. "Ah, I believe I understand. We do bortak for tension release."

"Bortak?" Geordi asked. Crusher and he exchanged glances.

Veleck's body suddenly glowed to Geordi's eyes. The heat flowed and pulsed from one part of his body to another. His body seemed to ripple like semisolid . . . sand. The heat source faded, and Veleck's body trembled, then if what Geordi was seeing was accurate, solidified again.

"Doc, did you see that?"

She nodded, slowly. "I think so."

"I feel better," Veleck said. "More relaxed."

"I'm glad, Veleck," Geordi said slowly.

A smaller, paler blue version of Veleck lumbered into the engine room. "Chief Engineer, the captain wishes to speak with you."

"Thank you, Engineer Bebit. Stay with our guests until my return."

"Yes, Chief Engineer." The younger Milgian's voice had almost a lilt to it compared to any Geordi had heard before. It sounded almost eager.

Bebit turned to them once Veleck was gone and said, "How may I serve you?"

What did they have to lose? Geordi explained what the doctor had discovered and what they wanted to do with the engine.

"Veleck is correct. The engines would not understand you. Neither he nor I could speak with the engines for you."

Geordi sighed. The tension at base of his neck knotted tighter. Were they going to lose this one? Was the first contact with the Milgians going to be the destruction of one of their ships and the loss of dozens of lives?

"But you might attempt to speak with the engines directly," Bebit said.

Geordi stared at him. "You mean I can talk to the engines, personally?"

"I do not see why not," Bebit said. "It is true that no non-Milgian has ever tried but the principle should cross such boundaries."

"How do I do it?"

"Wait a minute, Geordi," Dr. Crusher said. She

stepped closer to Bebit. "Is there any danger to Lieutenant La Forge?"

"Danger?" Bebit questioned. "I do not think so."

"Geordi, these engines are alive. I don't think it will be like pushing a button."

"Whatever it is, Doctor, I'm willing to do it." Geordi turned back to the smaller alien. Smaller was relative though. He still towered over the two humans. "Show me how to talk to the engines, Bebit."

Bebit walked toward a corner of the smooth wall, if this flowing place had corners. He passed his hand over the wall and a small panel pulsed red and hot. "You must let the engine taste you. Then it will recognize you, and you may talk to it."

"Taste me?" Geordi said. "I don't understand, Bebit."

"Place your . . . hand on this place and the engine will . . . sample you. It will recognize your," he seemed to be trying to think of a better phrase, "your cell structure."

"Doctor?"

"The engines are made up of bits and pieces of the cell structure of the Milgians. I've even found what amounts to DNA that would match Veleck."

"Is your cell structure in the engines, too, Bebit?" Geordi asked.

Bebit's face grew very hot and shifted. It took Geordi a moment to realize he might be smiling. "Yes, all engineers are pieces of the engines. Exactly." He was like a proud parent whose slow child had finally grasped some elementary topic.

Geordi didn't care if the Milgians thought he was slow. He just wanted this to work. "Show me how to let the engines taste me."

"Geordi . . ."

"No, Doc, we're out of time."

She nodded, reluctantly. "All right, but I'll monitor you."

"Glad of it." Geordi smiled to show he was okay, but frankly the thought of something as alien as these engines "tasting" him was frightening and exciting at the same time.

"Just place your hand on this panel, like so," Bebit said. He pressed his own blue hand flat on the panel. It pulsed once almost too bright for Geordi to look at.

"Geordi, my instruments say that Bebit's hand became a part of that panel for an instant. They merged." Crusher looked at him. "Your cell structure won't merge painlessly with that panel."

Geordi flexed his shoulders trying to loosen the tension between them. "I'm going to try, Doctor."

Crusher put her head to one side, her mouth making that lopsided motion that always meant she was not happy. "All right, you have to try, but I'll scan you while you do it. If it starts to damage you, I'm breaking the connection."

"You're the doctor."

"It'd be nice if you remembered that more often," she said.

Geordi smiled, then turned to the panel. "I just put my hand against it?"

"Yes," Bebit said.

Geordi took a deep breath and pressed his hand flat against the glowing panel. It was as smooth as all the others, and at first just as cool. The panel began to grow hotter where his skin touched it, but it wasn't uncomfortable at first. It didn't grow bright like it had

215

with Bebit. The heat seemed almost hesitant, as if it didn't know quite what to do with this new taste.

Geordi waited patiently, hand pressed against the warm panel. The surface grew softly warmer, pulsing brighter and brighter. The heat grew slowly until Geordi felt like his hand was being slow roasted. Now, it was starting to hurt. Gritting his teeth, he kept his skin pressed to the panel. If this was the only way to speak to the engines, he could do it. He had to do it.

"Geordi, your hand is starting to burn."

"I know," he said. His voice went just a little higher from the pain. It felt like the machine was peeling back his skin, pouring molten metal into his veins. A scream was pushing at the back of his throat.

The panel was growing brighter, brighter until the angry red glow was almost blinding. Nausea burned up his throat. He had to scream or pass out. Geordi screamed. Something tingled at his hand almost like a tiny mouth. Something pushed against the burning flesh.

Geordi collapsed to his knees, cradling the hand to his chest. He was covered in a sick sweat, his breath coming in quick pants.

"Geordi." Dr. Crusher was kneeling beside him. She took his hand in hers, gently but firmly. "Let me see."

Huge watery blisters were rising on the palm of his hand and along his fingers. The pain hadn't gone away. It was less, but it was like someone had taken all the blood in his hand and replaced it with molten metal. Now the boiling metal was working up his arm, crawling under his skin toward his shoulder.

216

"You've got second degree burns, and you're lucky it's not worse." Her voice scolded him.

When Geordi trusted himself to talk without gasping, he asked, "Bebit, did it work? Can I talk to the engines?"

"I will ask them," Bebit said. He moved to one of the control panels and waved his hand over it. Colors flowed and chased after his hand, as if the lights could feel his fingers without needing to touch them.

Sharp, cutting pain forced a gasp from Geordi's lips, and his attention was jerked back to his hand. Dr. Crusher was doing something painful to the burned flesh.

"I know this hurts, Geordi, but if I give you painkillers now you'll be drowsy." Her serious green eyes stared at him. "Let me know if the pain is too much."

He bit down on the inside of his mouth to keep from yelling. He swallowed hard, nausea burning at the back of his throat. Geordi had never had a burn this bad before. The pain was incredible for an injury that wasn't close to life threatening.

His voice sounded shaky, but he found himself saying, "I'll be fine."

The expression on Dr. Crusher's face showed plainly that she didn't believe him. Geordi didn't care. Lying about it was the best he could do. He was the engineer. It was going to take both of them to fix this ship, if it could be fixed.

Bebit turned to them, his face still fixed in what passed for a smile. "The engines are eager to speak with you, Geordi."

It was the first time any of the Milgians had used

his first name. It sounded strange from someone he had just met, but they were here to work together, to make friends if possible. It was a start, and Bebit was certainly friendlier than Veleck.

"Thanks, Bebit," Geordi said, getting to his feet with Crusher's help. He didn't feel dizzy, just hurt. "I'm all right, Doc, thanks."

Crusher nodded, and stepped away from him. "I don't think you can take another burn like that."

Privately, Geordi agreed, but they were running out of time. "Bebit, will it hurt me to speak with the engines the way it did to be tasted?"

Bebit's face flared in brilliant red—sad. "I am sorry that you are hurt. It does not hurt me to be tasted. The engines would not purposefully injure you, Geordi."

"I believe you, Bebit, but will it hurt me to speak with the engines?"

"You do not have to touch the panels, only pass your hand above them. Will that harm you?"

"I hope not," Geordi said. "What do I do?"

"Put your hand over this middle panel, here," Bebit said. He splayed his thick fingers wide and the lights flickered, responding. "Do you see?"

Geordi didn't really understand what the lights meant, but he could duplicate the physical movement and hoped that was enough. "Does it have to be the hand that was tasted?"

"That is not necessary."

Good, thought Geordi, lifting his good hand toward the softly glowing panel.

"Do not touch it!" The low scream made Geordi drop his hand to his side and turn around. Veleck stood in the doorway walking forward as quickly as his bulk would allow. "Do not touch it!"

"Chief Engineer," Bebit began.

"Silence! You have almost destroyed this ship."

"But Chief Engineer . . ."

"Get out!"

Bebit didn't argue further. He just turned and lumbered off. His body very cool, no hot spots to glow against Geordi's VISOR. To Geordi, the smaller alien seemed dejected.

"What's wrong, Veleck?" Geordi asked.

"Your cell structure is alien to this ship. If you mingle your cells with ours, it could force the implosion to happen immediately."

Geordi glanced at Crusher, she shrugged. "The ship has already tasted me. It didn't blow up."

"That idiot, Bebit, how could he risk us all like that?" There was real anger and panic in Veleck's voice.

"If the danger was my alien cell structure, that's passed."

"But you were about to speak with the engines." As Veleck walked toward them Geordi saw that the heat patterns on his body were like a kaleidoscope. It was almost dizzying and Geordi had to turn away. He could only assume that this was a pattern of agitation for the Milgians.

"I have to speak with the engines to fix them," Geordi said.

"You do not understand our engines. They are greatly stressed. Trying to speak with something as alien as you are could force them to explode early. Do you understand?" Veleck had moved his considerable bulk between the two humans and the control panels. They were forced to stand back whether or not they wished to.

"In a few hours the ship will destroy itself anyway."

"But not yet," Veleck said.

"All right, let's evacuate everyone to the *Enterprise,* and I'll try to talk to the engines."

"You would risk your own life to save our ship?"

Geordi didn't know quite what to say to that. It sounded terribly heroic and he didn't feel terribly heroic. "I have to do everything I can to save your ship and people, so yes, I'm willing to take the risk."

Veleck stared at Geordi for a moment. The heat patterns had cooled, but Geordi would have given a lot to be able to see the engineer's facial expression. Though, as with most new alien races, the expression might not have meant very much.

"I cannot let you, an alien, risk yourself for my ship. I am chief engineer, I will die with my engines."

"Then stay with me. I'll need all the help I can get," Geordi said.

"We'll need to get the *Enterprise* to a safe distance before you try," Crusher said.

"Yeah. Try to convince as many of the Milgians as you can to evacuate."

Crusher nodded. "I'll try, but this ridiculous determination to go down with their ship . . . I don't know how to get around it."

"It is not ridiculous," Veleck said. "It is our way."

"Any custom that wastes lives unnecessarily is repugnant to me, Chief Engineer Veleck. I'm a doctor; I save lives. And that is more important to me than any custom."

220

"I will not leave my ship when it is in danger," he said.

"I'll go up and try to convince some of the other officers to leave," Crusher said. "I'll be back when I've gotten as many Milgians to safety as I can."

"Wait a minute, Doc. You're going over, too."

"If the engines don't explode and you can speak with them, you'll still need me. These engines are alive, Geordi. You need an engineer and a doctor."

Geordi opened his mouth to argue, but she had that stubborn set to her mouth, a hard glint in her green eyes. In her own way Crusher was just as stubborn as the Milgians.

"All right, Doctor. You handle the evacuation, and I'll try to take a crash course in Milgian engine mechanics."

Two hours later Geordi was back in front of the glowing panels. They had been unable to convince any more of the Milgian crew to abandon ship. Finally, the *Enterprise,* with the few refugees, had warped to a safe distance. Veleck and Dr. Crusher were standing at either side.

Veleck had tried to explain what it would be like to "speak" with the engines, but the idea hadn't translated well. Geordi guessed it was one of those occasions that you just had to experience. Either Geordi would understand once he'd made contact with the engines, or he wouldn't. Either they would blow up, or they wouldn't. Nice to have such simple choices.

"Everybody ready?" Geordi asked.

"A Milgian is always ready to give his life for his ship," Veleck said.

"Sorry I asked. Dr. Crusher?"

"I'm with you, Geordi."

"Here goes everything." He spread his hand over the panel and moved it slowly closer. When his hand was almost touching the panel, but not quite, a tingling shock raced up his arm. Then his whole arm went numb, as if he'd hit the nerve in his elbow, the funny bone.

The engine room receded, as if Geordi were being pulled down a narrow tunnel. Colors flashed and glowed behind his eyes. He tried to shut them, but the colors were inside his head. He couldn't make sense of it and found himself drowning in a whirl of colors—red, blue, yellow, pink, orange. Then suddenly it all made sense. The colors were the engines talking to him.

They had no voice, nothing to hear, and the colors that were visible to the eye were only the outward manifestations, like his own skin. The "talking" went on underneath where you couldn't really see it. But you could feel it.

The engine, for it was one being, was very curious about Geordi. It had never met a non-Milgian. It could read his mind; there was no need for words or even concrete thoughts. It just drank the information directly from his mind.

The engine flowed and pulsed, and Geordi could feel it. His mind ran through circuit boards and conduits. He was one with the engine. It was overwhelming and wonderful, and he knew it would run forever just working with his hands.

"Geordi, can you hear me?" It was Dr. Crusher's voice, floating through the colored language. It was a shock to hear real speech.

"I can hear you, Doctor." His voice sounded very distant to him, almost unattached.

"Are you all right?"

"I'm fine. Why?"

"You've been standing motionless for over twenty minutes. You wouldn't respond to my voice. Veleck wanted to break the connection, but I was afraid it would harm you. If my instruments are correct, the engine is bound to your involuntary nervous system."

"Is that bad?"

"Not as long as it doesn't hurt you." Her voice's concern was a deep violet color washing through the engine's language.

"I'm all right, Doctor. The engine likes me. It's eager to learn from me. I need time to sort out what it's telling me, but I think we're in business. Contact the *Enterprise;* tell them we're okay and we're going to operate on our patient as soon as it tells me what's wrong."

"It's going to tell you what's wrong?"

"Yeah, its name is two long yellow flashes followed by a quick blue dot. Yellow-Dot-Blue." The colors swirled more intensely when Geordi thought of the engine's name. The kaleidoscope of colors whirled around him and dragged him in, and Geordi didn't fight it. He needed to learn how the engine worked, and now it could show him.

Chapter Nineteen

THE CLOAK WAS HOT. And even though the breathing masks were suppose to help you breathe, Troi found herself gasping. Her breathing was loud and labored. Sweat trickled down her forehead. She raised a hand to wipe it away and bumped the mask. Sighing, she forced herself to let her hands drop loosely to her sides. She was supposed to be passing as an Orianian, and they did not rub at their masks or tug at their cloaks.

Worf stood beside her even more uncomfortable, if that were possible. He didn't look like an Orianian. Even cloaked and completely covered, he looked awkward. The hooded cloak was too short and barely hit his knees. They had not been able to find gloves to fit him at all. He hid his betraying hands inside the folds of the cloak. The mask that he had been given on their arrival fit him, but unless he kept the hood tight round his face, well ... He looked like a Klingon done up for Halloween.

Talanne had led them through empty corridors. She was no more eager to be caught than they were, perhaps less. Breck had been allowed on this expedition only because Talanne now considered him a member of the Federation party. It was still unsettling how easily Talanne and Breck accepted his new alliance. A complete change of loyalties, and as far as Troi could sense, neither Orianian thought it odd.

The corridors became rougher, mere blasted tunnels of rock. Worf had been forced to bend almost double. The Klingon made no complaint, but little grunts of effort came now and then.

Troi was a little tall for an Orianian but not much. And though all the borrowed clothing fit, it was still stiflingly hot. The farther into the narrowing tunnels they went, the hotter it became. The air, she noticed, was flat and stale, a touchable blanket that they were forced to wade through.

Talanne's light made huge circular patterns on the narrowing walls. The floor was bare rock, rubbed nearly smooth by the passage of many feet. "What were these tunnels originally for?" Troi asked. Her voice echoed, seeming to come from a different direction entirely. Troi swallowed and stared upward at the dark ceiling. If you became lost down here without a light, not even sound would help you. The echoes would trick you as surely as the darkness itself.

Talanne whispered, but the sound rushed and poured like water in the rock. "No one knows."

Breck made a small sound, almost a laugh.

"You have something to add, Breck," Worf asked.

225

"Only old warrior's tales, Ambassador." His voice was very close to Troi, as if in the pressing dark he, too, felt the need of comfort. "They say these were the tunnels of demons, destroyed before remembered history by our ancestors."

"Tales to frighten children, Breck, not warriors," Talanne said. Her voice held the scorn her face could not show.

Breck did not rise to the taunting. He seemed faintly amused by the whole thing. Amused, and underneath that, nervous. Was he truly afraid of demons? Troi didn't believe that, but for the first time she could feel unease from the man.

"Breck," Troi half-turned to him. "Are you afraid of the dark?" She meant to keep her voice soft, but the echoes betrayed her, sending the whisper rushing through the narrow tunnel.

"I am a Torlick warrior. I fear nothing that walks the ground or flies in the air."

"But do you fear demons?" Talanne called back, her voice soft and taunting.

"I fear nothing." His voice was very firm.

Troi was sorry she had spoken aloud. He was afraid—afraid of the dark and the narrow rock walls. Breck was claustophobic but only in the dark. Troi had come across selective phobias before. People not afraid of heights unless in high manmade structures. It wasn't that uncommon, but somehow the phobia made Breck more understandable. He seemed, for lack of a better word, more human.

"One more short piece of tunnel," Talanne said, then we go outside. Ambassador, Healer, follow me, do not tarry on the surface. The greatest danger is

226

stray pockets of poison air. If we hit one, there is not much that will save us."

"Then why is there no easier way to the Greens?" Worf asked. His voice held just a hint of strain.

"Few of our members would risk coming to a surface area that is not frequently traveled. We tend traveled areas and see they are clear of poison and other hazards. This stretch of deadly ground is the best guardian the Greens could have."

The wall in front of Talanne seemed solid until she saw the light at a certain area. The shadows seemed to peel away and expose a small domed tunnel that was much smaller than the tunnel they were in.

"What do you think, Lieutenant Worf? Will you fit through there?"

Worf had dropped to one knee, so his back could straighten. He stared into the dark hole. "Does it narrow further?"

"No, this is as narrow as it gets."

He moved forward on all fours, tracing the edges of the rough opening with his hands. "I will fit, but it will be . . . tight."

"I will lead the way, then." Talanne bent nearly double and stepped into the tunnel. The light flickered and bounced off the rock like something alive.

"You go next, Counselor," Worf said.

"I think I'll let you go next," Troi said.

"If I become . . . stuck you will be trapped behind me."

"If you become stuck, I can push from behind and Colonel Talanne can pull."

"I hope that will not be necessary," Worf said. His discomfort at the thought of such monumental embarrassment made Troi smile. She was glad he could not see her face. Worf didn't like being laughed at.

Worf crawled into the tunnel on all fours. His shoulders scraped the walls with a rough sound that spoke of scraped skin under the cloth.

Once Worf was inside the tunnel, it was like a cork in a bottle. Talanne's light was gone, swallowed except for a thin glow that haloed Worf's head. Troi and Breck were left in the velvet dark.

Breck's breathing was instantly louder, gaspy. "Why don't you go next?" she said.

"No, I am the sentinel. I will guard your back." His voice was uncertain, full of fear and the beating of his own heart. "Healer, please, let me do my job."

Troi didn't offer again. Breck was afraid, but he would face his fear like a stoic warrior.

Troi crawled into the tunnel, eyes on the thin line of light and Worf's dark bulk. The motionless air was like a hand squeezing at her throat, making it hard to breathe. The rock crushed inward, and sweat broke out on her body. Under enough pressure, Breck, too, was a broadcasting empath. She was on a planet where nearly every person had some wild talent. It was no place for an empath. And the tunnel was no place for a claustophobic.

Worf stopped. Troi tried to peer around him, but the light was just a rim, like an eclipsed moon.

"Why have we stopped?" Breck asked. His voice held an edge of panic that made Troi's throat tighten.

"I don't know."

There was a sound of wind. Troi thought at first she was imagining it, but air was drifting down the tunnel, and a dim glow of gentle yellow light filtered around Worf's body. He began to crawl forward, then disappeared into a blur of light. Troi blinked into the light. All she could see was a glowing nimbus, as if her eyes had gotten so accustomed to the dark they didn't know what to do with light.

"Healer, go forward into the light, please." Breck's voice forced Troi to crawl forward into the near blinding glow.

Hands reached for her, pulling her to her feet. Worf stood beside her, while Talanne was a short distance away, a shrouded figure. Breck came out of the tunnel and leaned against the rock as if to catch his breath. His joy at being out in the open again could not be marred by the desolation around them.

Troi had seen scans of the planet. Raw data, numbers, percentages of this, amounts of that, but the bland information had not really meant anything to Troi. To be told that a planet is dying is awful, but it is an enormity that is hard to believe. You can't hold it in your hand, or feel it. Troi stood staring, and believed.

The sky was a sulphurous yellow, with thick clouds that rolled and boiled as if some giant hand was stirring the sky. Wind streamed around them, tugging at the heavy capes. The heat was breath-stealing but utterly dry. There had been more moisture in the heat of the caves. Here under the poisonous skies there was nothing but air and dirt.

The wind whipped the powdery dirt into miniature whirlwinds. They danced in a ragged circle. Suddenly, Troi felt an unsettling sensation of being watched prickling down her spine.

Worf reached for his phaser, staring at the whirling dustdevils. "Are they real?" He had to yell above the howling of the wind.

"It is just dirt and wind," Talanne yelled back.

"They are watching us," he yelled.

So it wasn't just Troi. Worf felt it, too. It was then that Troi realized the watching was all she could feel. An angry, despair-filled watching. Troi whirled, searching the dry rock walls behind her. There was no one there. She knew that, and yet she knew something was there.

The wind shifted, slinging the whirling dirt against them. Troi threw her arms up to protect herself but it stung even through the protective clothing. Silence made her ears pound. Then the wind was gone abruptly, as if someone had turned a switch.

"Something is wrong," Worf said. His deep voice was loud in the stillness.

"Yes, Klingon, our planet is blowing away before our eyes. The soil that grew the plants, the life, vanishes with each breath of wind."

Troi stepped cautiously away from the hillside to the open stretch of ground. She turned around in a slow circle. There were no other living beings near, save for the two Orianians and Worf. Yet . . .

"There's something here," she said. It sounded vague even to her own ears, but she had no words for the feeling. Troi was often forced to use words that did not clearly convey what she was experiencing.

"Come, Healer, we must not delay our stay upon the surface," Talanne said walking across the dry, rustling ground toward another hill. This one was covered with the skeletons of trees, like the dark bones of some twisted creature.

Worf still had his phaser out, staring around the narrow open space. Breck stepped close to Troi. His hands were playing nervously along his rifle. It wasn't pointed at anything, but it was ready.

"This is an evil place, Healer," Breck said. "It is the eyes of the world you feel."

Troi looked at him. "What are the eyes of the world?"

"Some say it is the world watching us kill it. You can feel that it is angry."

"You feel the anger?" Troi did not try to keep the surprise out of her voice. Breck either didn't hear it, or ignored it.

"Always," he said.

"Do you ever feel the anger of other people?"

"No, why?"

Breck could not feel the emotions of people, but he felt this weight, this thing. Was it the eyes of the world? And if not, then what was it?

"Troi." Worf's voice jerked her attention back to the pale, hot land.

"We must hurry, Healer," Talanne said. "I see a poison storm coming this way. The winds are unpredictable. It could hit any time." She and Worf were waiting beside a door that Troi would have sworn had not been there when last she looked.

Breck gripped her arm and began to lead her toward the others. Troi didn't protest because she had seen the poison storm. A cloud bank was rolling in on the horizon. It was black and a deep emerald green. A shining golden curtain poured from the cloud. Even from a distance of some miles Troi could see white clouds of steam rise from the ground.

"Why is it doing that?" she asked.

"The rain is almost pure acid," Breck said. "The

231

ground boils where it touches." He pushed her into the doorway behind Talanne and Worf.

Talanne's light was a dim beacon down a fairly roomy corridor. But the blackness was just as black as the caves. Troi couldn't feel Breck's fear anymore. All she could feel was the sensation of being watched.

Talanne and Worf waited for them in front of what appeared to be a dead end. Talanne passed her hand over a spot on the solid rock. A piece of it slid out of sight. A breath of air pushed into the dry heat. The air was moist.

Talanne slipped into the dark entrance, taking the light with her. Worf followed, forced to bend painfully low. "Go, Healer, please," Breck said. He nearly pushed Troi through the door. His voice betrayed a breathy fear of the dark, but Troi still felt none of it.

Talanne was waiting to one side of the inner door. She motioned with the light for them to walk farther into the pitch blackness. Worf's form was caught in the light, then vanished. Only the sound of his cloak rustling said that he hadn't simply vanished with the light.

Breck stood at Troi's back. His hand touched her shoulder, and the shock of it screamed along her nerves. His fear was there in his skin.

Troi gasped. His grip tightened. "Are you all right, Healer?" His voice whispered against her hood, thick with fear. The feeling of being watched had vanished when Talanne shut the door, and Troi welcomed the darkness.

"Breck, I'm all right." She moved a little away from him, closer to Worf. The sentinel's fingers moved reluctantly from her shoulder. Breck needed to touch someone, to know he wasn't alone. But Troi needed some emotional space, a breathing room for herself. Too much had happened in the last day, too many emotions, an overload of her empathic talents.

The mind was like the body; it had limits, and Troi was dangerously close to reaching those limits. So much negativity, so much destruction. Death, fear, hatred, anger. Only Talanne's love for her son had been positive, and Dr. Zhir's love for the lifeless children.

Troi shook her head. She needed positive emotions to wash away the negativity, like the body needed to be bathed in cool water to cleanse sweat and dirt away. Troi needed to dress her mind in something that felt good.

"We're at the first outpost," Talanne said. "We must go cautiously from here."

"You said the Greens do not believe in violence," Worf said.

She glanced back at him. The light reflected in the goggles of her mask, glinting like some giant insect. "They do not believe in violence, but they do protect themselves. Just because something is not deadly does not mean it is pleasant."

"You speak in riddles," Worf said.

"I don't mean to," she said. "They don't believe in taking life, but they might hold you prisoner until they had time to move the encampment. Your captain would be days dead."

With that she led the way farther into the tunnels. They had little choice but to follow. The air grew steadily cooler. Even through the protective clothing, Troi could feel the caress of moisture.

Worf's bare fingers traced the nearest tunnel wall. "The stone is damp."

Troi touched it with her gloved hand, and through the tough cloth she could barely sense the cool sensation. "It's not like the other caves at all," she said. "The air feels fresher even through the breathing masks."

"Yes," Worf said.

Breck was pressed almost into Troi's back. But his fear had lessened. His breathing had slowed, almost normal instead of that gasping fear. "Do you smell that?"

"What?"

"I don't know," he said. "It smells like water. But it can't be."

"Why not?" Worf asked.

"Because it smells clean." His voice held a sort of wonder.

Light, the dimmest of illuminations crept into the tunnel. Troi's eyes were starved for light, and even that faint grayness was welcome. She could make out the outline of her companions. She stared up ahead and found a dim, misty glow. A shimmering fall of white light that looked nearly magical against the darkness.

Talanne's caped figure was framed against the glowing light. She turned to look back at them, shining the light onto each of them as if to make sure they were still with her. "Stay there. I won't be long." She walked into the light, becoming more visible as she moved. The colors of her cloak, the stride of her boots, everything was suddenly very distinct. Talanne looked so very real that for a moment, Troi expected her to fade into the light and leave them to darkness.

Breck had moved in front of them, as if he wanted to follow. Or perhaps it was his thought that Talanne would leave them to the dark. Troi wasn't sure anymore. The Orianians could enter her mind and thoughts without a ripple. It was unsettling, but she was becoming accustomed to it. They didn't do it on purpose, most of the time, and meant no harm.

The three of them stood alone in the welcome glow, the darkness pressing at their backs. Troi wanted to walk forward into the light, but again she feared it was Breck's phobia not her own. How could any empath be trained on a planet where the mingling of minds was so seamless?

Talanne appeared in the light again. Two bare-faced Orianians walked at her back. They wore the plain blue overalls of the Greens. Pockets bulged along the arms and outer legs of the suit. They wore what looked like tool belts, which for all Troi knew could have been weapons.

Worf had drawn his phaser, using the voluminous cloak to hide the movement. His fierce readiness beat along Troi's skin. He would not start anything, nor did he actually wish the mission to fail, but his body was keyed for action, violence. The Klingon would be a little disappointed not to put his preparations to use. It was physiologically harder for Klingons to cool their blood.

"They know you are friends," Talanne said. "The rest of the Greens know you are coming. They may become nervous if we keep them waiting."

"Why?" Worf asked.

"If you were Orianians, Ambassador Worf, it would be logical to blame the Greens for your captain's predicament."

"We are not Orianians," he said, softly.

"No," she said, "you are not." There was some-

235

thing in her voice that was almost regret. Regret that even a Klingon could be more reasonable than an Orianian, perhaps?

The two Greens tried to move behind them, to escort them, Troi supposed. "We will follow you," Worf said.

The two Greens looked at each other. "It is our custom to check behind to see that no one follows."

Worf stared down at them. "I mean no offense but I do not want warriors at my back."

The Greens exchanged glances. Puzzled frowns crossed their faces. "We are not warriors."

"Every Orianian is a warrior, so they tell me," Worf said.

One of the Greens smiled broadly. "You will find many things different among us." He patted the Klingon's shoulder, like he was some long lost friend.

Troi didn't have to see Worf's face to know he was scowling. "I look forward to meeting your leaders," he said. His voice growled with a hint of anger, but the Orianian took it as the diplomatic speech it was meant to be.

"Our leaders are most eager to meet the Federation ambassador."

"The leaders that are left," the second Green said. His smooth face was angry. The emotion had thinned the skin along his cheeks and lips, making his face look tight and pinched.

"It is not their fault that Audun and the others were arrested," the first Green said.

"Someone killed Alick, and it wasn't us," his voice held a very final note.

"That is something we have come to find out,"

Worf said "Every second we waste in idle chatter is time lost for our leaders."

The second Green stood a little straighter, a flush painting his face with pink. "Very well then, Ambassador, let us go."

The first Green grinned at Worf and shrugged. "Morei is a little high-tempered."

"There is nothing wrong with feeling loyalty to your leaders," Worf said.

"Well said." The Green slapped him on the shoulder again, smiling.

A low growl slipped past Worf's lips. The Green either didn't hear, or didn't understand. He led the way into the tunnel, still smiling. The suspicious Green slipped into the dark behind them. "I will make sure they are alone." His words held a threat, but Troi couldn't feel any real danger. He didn't mean to harm them. He just didn't trust them. After the way the leading factions had hunted the Greens, Troi couldn't blame him. Besides, Worf didn't trust the Greens, either.

Did Troi trust them? She trusted all the ones she'd met and she'd met five of them—not many. Perhaps most of them felt like the suspicious Green and blamed the Federation for Audun's arrest. Did the Greens know about Marit's death? No. There was no sorrow, not even the initial rage that often precedes grief. The Greens did not know.

Troi suddenly didn't feel nearly as confident about walking into the camp. What would they do when they learned of the death? Death by torture. Would the Greens prove to be as violent as the other natives, if given a reason?

Talanne walked confidently beside the remaining Green. Troi could not sense any fear from her. She, at least, expected no trap. Breck was simply relieved to be in the dim, shining light.

The tunnel then opened into a huge round cavern. A platform of stone wide enough to hold a shuttle-craft acted as the entrance to a broad set of stairs. Everything was carved from the rock, smooth and rounded with the passage of many feet.

Talanne removed her mask, and Troi heard her take a deep breath of air. The counselor didn't need a second invitation to remove the sweating mask. She slipped it over her face, her hair sticking to her face in damp strands. The cool air caressed her skin with cool, moist fingers. It was different from the dry heat of the surface and even the other tunnels.

The smell that Breck had noticed wasn't water but the rich, loamy smell of healthy earth. Green growing things. Life. It was like being caught in a thick cloud of perfume.

"What is that?" Breck asked. He was standing a few steps below the rest of them. His breathing mask had slipped from his hands, and he didn't react. He began to walk down the stone steps, slowly, eyes on something that they could not see.

"It is what our world use to be," Talanne said.

Plants, green growing plants as far as the eye could see. The cavern was thick with vegetation and rich, black soil. Water beaded and dripped from huge leaves. The roof of the cavern was so high as to give the illusion of being a stone sky. Light filtered from banks of shining, white panels set in that distant roof to spread warmth and life on the floor.

Talanne picked up Breck's dropped mask. She spoke softly to no one in particular. "I was the same way the first time I saw it."

The tall trees with the crimson fruit that had played such a prominent part in all the wall hangings grew straight and tall near the edge of the greenery. The trunk was a silvery gray, paler than the paintings had made it.

Troi stood on the stairs, drowning not in Breck's wonderment but in her own. It wasn't the trees, the life, but that this land, this piece of surface was alive. Its being pulsed in her head and played along her skin, as if she had brushed against a person. It was alive. Alive in a way that no tree or flower or piece of ground should ever have been alive.

"The air smells very sweet here," Worf said.

His voice brought her attention back to them. "It's alive." Her voice was a whisper.

"Of course it is," Worf said, "They are trees."

"No, Worf, it's alive, like you're alive, like I'm alive."

"The trees are intelligent?"

"Not intelligent exactly, but aware." She struggled to find the words to help him feel what was pouring through her body. "A sense of well-being, of happiness that plants do not have. It doesn't think like we do, but it is alive. Aware."

Breck had fallen to his knees in the rich green world. He fell forward on all fours, hands buried in a carpet of small, round leaves.

Troi moved down the steps toward him. "Breck?" He was crying. When her feet touched the springy ground, it was like an electric shock. She gasped.

239

"You feel it, too, don't you?" Breck asked. He stared up at her, tears running silently down his face.

Troi could only nod. She didn't trust her voice. The warm heat of life poured through her body until she felt as if she would burst with it. It was so strong that she stared down at her hands, expecting some visible sign to pour from her fingertips.

There was nothing but the sensation prickling over her skin. Nothing visible, nothing to show to Worf. She stared into Breck's face and knew he understood. One flash between them that went beyond words. It was the sharing that she had with other Betazoids. An understanding that none of her human or Klingon friends could share, no matter how hard they tried.

In one moment Troi understood one other thing that she hadn't before. Breck was an empath, but his talent was tied to this rich, living land. Not this particular piece of land, but the surface of this planet. Breck was an earth-healer, a legend. His talent hadn't been apparent because the planet was dead, but Troi felt his mind peeling away. All the protective shields that Breck had been forced to construct, all the things that had allowed an empath to kill others without feeling anything, were fading. His emotions, his mind, were being stripped bare by this pulsing, overwhelming life-force.

"Once it was all like this," the remaining Green said. His voice held a sadness that Troi could not understand. This land, this place, was full of joy, the pure joy of existence. Life for its own sake. How could anyone be sorrowful in the presence of all this?

He came down the steps to stand beside Troi. She was crying and hadn't realized it. Joy was as often tears as laughter. The Green touched her shoulder. "You feel our land?"

His sorrow flooded down her arm, sweeping through her. The loss, the horrible loss. Suddenly, she understood that the entire surface of this world had been like this once. Alive enough to whisper in your mind, to soothe your soul. The Orianians had not simply killed plants and animals, but the land itself. And the land had been their heart.

Breck staggered toward them. "The Greens tend this place. They made it. The land knows them all. It cares for them." Even as he said it out loud, Troi knew that that wasn't exactly the truth. Breck was being forced to put words to things that words could not hold.

"They believe in life, Healer. They could not create this and create the poison that killed Alick." There was a solid certainty to him. The land had told him, and it could not lie.

"I would just as soon question the Green leaders, if you don't mind," Worf said.

Troi turned and stared back up the stairs at Worf. His face was empty of the wonderment, the exhausted joy that showed on their faces. Nor did the sorrow that traced Talanne and the Green haunt the Klingon. He stood alone and apart on the stairs. It would have been the same if Worf had been Picard or Riker. They would not have understood. Troi held out her hand, and Breck took it.

Joy, well-being, happiness—all of it was doubled, amplified. Her skin jumped with the need to feel! She stared into Breck's tear-stained face and was very glad to have someone to share this with. And sorrow

241

for Worf that he could not begin to understand why they stood crying in the middle of a bunch of plants. Some things Troi would not even attempt to explain.

Worf stood on the steps and scowled suspiciously down at the thick vegetation. Troi threw back her head and laughed. Breck's laughter joined with hers, flying higher and higher like birds.

Chapter Twenty

GEORDI PASSED HIS HANDS just above the panel, and the lights pulsed, following his fingers. But it wasn't just the lights that followed his hands. The intelligence that made up the engines followed Geordi's movements. It flowed under his hands like a dog sniffing at him, or a cat rubbing against his ankles. The engine was curious about him. It was studying him as hard as he was studying it.

Geordi had never experienced anything like talking to the Milgian engine. It was as if his hands could touch all the way through the outer metal skin and go inside. His thoughts could travel down the conduits. When he wanted to change direction he had only to wish to move. The engine welcomed him, drew him inside. Geordi could feel its eager energy flowing and pulling at his mind. Was this how Troi felt when she entered the thoughts of another person?

It was wonderful. The engine explained what it

was, but the explanation was too amazing for Geordi to understand completely. The technology of combining living tissue with mechanics was not cybernetics or robotics. The melding of the parts was complete. It was a single organism, not pieces stitched together.

It was a united system, a whole, like his own body. You could no more isolate a single system than he could have taken out his own respiratory system without affecting the rest of his body.

"What have you found out?" Dr. Crusher's words made him jump. His heart was suddenly pounding in his throat.

"Beverly, I forgot you were there. I forgot anything was there but the engine."

She gave a rueful smile. "I noticed."

He smiled back. "Sorry, it's just I'm an engineer and I've never felt anything like this. It's like my mind is the tool and is all I need to do anything. The engine even wants to help. It's incredible."

"I understand the enthusiasm, Geordi, but we don't have much time. Have you found the problem?"

"Not yet. The engine isn't aware of any critical mistakes or breakdowns, but it believes me when I tell it something is wrong. It's helping me search."

"Very cooperative," Crusher said.

"It's not just helpful; it's curious. Don't tell Data, but it reminds me of him. That abstract interest in anything different. The engine isn't scared or worried; it's just curious."

Crusher cocked her head to one side. "It does sound like Data."

"Though it's not anywhere near as intelligent. In fact it seems limited in its reasoning skills. It takes orders mostly, but it thinks about the orders and can question them."

"Does it learn from the answers?" Crusher asked.

"I'm not sure."

"Is there any way for me to talk to it through you? Once you find the problem, it may take both of us to fix it."

Geordi turned to Veleck who had been standing like a bright blue statue for some time. He had made no comment, helpful or otherwise. But there was a great deal of heat fluctuation coming from him. If he had been human, Geordi might have said he was under stress.

"What do you think, Veleck? Could Dr. Crusher talk to the engines too?"

He shifted his square bulk slightly. "She would have to be tasted, and that causes injuries to your outer skin. And there would be the danger, again, of having the engines react badly. We would run the risk of explosion happening now."

Geordi tried to think of a diplomatic way to say what he wanted to say. "The engines don't have a problem with Dr. Crusher joining with them."

"They are not intelligent enough to realize the danger," Veleck responded.

Geordi was beginning to think that Veleck was simply afraid of new ideas. Or maybe he just didn't want to share his engines. Whichever it was, Geordi was running out of time to be polite.

"Is there any way for the doctor to communicate through me then, rather than the engines?"

Veleck was silent for a moment. "There is a link-up that we have used in the past. It has only been used between Milgians, never aliens like yourselves."

"Let's try it," Geordi said.

"Is the doctor willing to take the risk?"

"Risk?" Crusher asked.

"It may harm as the tasting harmed."

Geordi and Crusher exchanged glances. She raised an eyebrow. "I'm game if you are."

"Tell us how to link-up," Geordi said.

Nearly an hour later Geordi and Beverly were standing in front of the lighted panel. Veleck had explained that the link-up was a microprocessor combined with microorganisms. Both were necessary to allow them to speak with the engine in combination. But the link-up itself looked like nothing more than a thin wire. It had been rigged to hang on the side of Geordi's skull. The biggest problem had been that the wire had to be placed inside the skin, like a needle. But it was a needle meant to pierce the much heavier skin of the Milgians. The challenge had been to insert it with a minimum of discomfort and not to pierce Geordi's skull.

The needle lay just below the surface. He could feel it when he moved, the wire tugging and rolling the thin needle. It was an eerie sensation but not really painful. Dr. Crusher had given him a localized anesthetic to remove any real pain.

The wire was very long and trailed from his head to Crusher's face, disappearing under her thick red hair.

"Ready, Beverly?"

Her green eyes were a little wide, but she gave a slight nod.

"Okay." He passed his hands over the control panel. The sensation of falling was doubled. It was as

246

if he were not only falling forward into the panel but backward through the wire into Crusher's head.

She gasped, and the sound vibrated through the wire link. "Geordi, what's happening?"

"The images are the engine's internal functions."

"No, its blood vessels. It's breathing," her voice was an awestruck whisper.

Suddenly, Geordi had the feeling of the entire engine as a giant organism. He saw it not as an intelligent machine but as a living creature with mechanical additions. He realized that he was seeing it as Dr. Crusher was seeing it. It was as if all the systems of the machine were suddenly clearly parts of a life-support system. What he'd thought was a power source was a heart. Everything was the same and different, a melding of machine and life that was truly both.

Geordi didn't need eyes to see this. It was behind his eyes, inside his head where the visuals were coming through. He spoke very softly, unwilling to disturb the link. "What do you think, Doctor?"

"It's amazing." Her voice was as soft as his own. The link felt fragile. Whether it was or not, Geordi couldn't say.

"You are in link-up?" Veleck's voice was jarring. Geordi and Crusher turned as a unit, startled.

"Yes," Geordi said. "We're both inside the engine."

"Good. I will stay with you to make sure there are no ill effects. If you feel any discomfort, you must say so and I will break the link. It was not designed for aliens."

"We know that, Veleck, but thanks for your concern," Geordi said.

The big alien gave a massive shrug, that poured a flush of heat through his body. "I simply do not wish you to risk yourselves in a futile effort."

"If we can save everyone on board this ship, we don't believe it will be futile," Crusher said.

"As you like," Veleck said.

Crusher made a humph sound. Geordi had to agree. The Milgian's pessimism was getting on his nerves. It made him want to prove Veleck wrong— not exactly a diplomatic attitude.

Turning back to the control panel, he was aware of Veleck like a frowning mountain to his left, but Geordi had no trouble blocking him out. The link with Crusher and the computer was overwhelming. The world narrowed down to pulsing energy fields. Liquid coolant shooting through artificial veins. The multicolored lights brightening and dimming as the engine "breathed."

"There, stop." Crusher's voice was soft, inside his head, or so it seemed.

"What?" he asked.

"There." His eyes saw her hand move, but it was like seeing something from the corner of your eyes. All his real attention was inside the engine, only part of him was aware of Crusher's physical form. She was pointing but her hand seemed to move through the pulsing tissue to a darker area. The bright pastel colors were darker here, a livid purple with edges of black. The artery was swollen. As they watched, liquid began to leak in small droplets. They floated through the interior as if there were no gravity, solid beads of black liquid.

"What is that?"

"It's a foreign body. It's been placed inside the

artery. It's the source of the immune system damage."

"Can you remove it?"

"I think so," she said.

Geordi was staring at the blighted area. "Engine, where did this substance come from?"

It did not speak in words like the computer on board the *Enterprise,* but images flashed through his mind. Veleck's face, his desire for an experiment to test stress limits. The engine was like an eager, cooperative child. Veleck assured it that he would fix the damage before it reached critical.

"He tricked it," Geordi whispered. He pulled himself away from the pulsing world of the engines and turned to stare at Veleck. "You sabotaged the engine. You let your own people die."

"Yes." Veleck's deep voice was as soft as it could get, a distant echo of thunder. He slammed his palm flat against the panel nearest him. Pain lanced through the wire in Geordi's skin, tore burning holes through his skull. He heard Crusher scream.

"You are having an unfortunate accident," Veleck said.

The pain was eating through Geordi's face. It felt like his skin was burning away. He fell against the control panels, and the colors went wild. The world was full of burning pain and a kaleidoscope of colors.

The engine was worried about him. Was he well? "No, get help, get the captain!"

Veleck shoved Geordi to the floor. "No, no!" He had released his hold on the panel. The pain vanished instantly, leaving Crusher and Geordi gasping on the floor.

Bebit appeared in the engine room. "The engine

alerted me to an accident?" He stared at the two humans still shaking on the floor. "Are you well, Geordi, Dr. Crusher?"

Geordi stared up at the young Milgian and glanced at Veleck. "I am now."

Veleck whispered, "The engine rejects me." He passed his hand over the control panel and nothing happened. "It will not recognize me." There was soft horror in his voice.

Bebit moved farther into the room. He stared at the fallen humans and the chief engineer. "What has been happening here?"

"He has betrayed us all, that is what has happened," Captain Diric spoke as he entered the room. There were two more Milgians at his back. Geordi could only assume they were security.

"The engine has told me of your treachery, Veleck. Take him into custody."

The two new Milgians moved up on either side of Veleck. He did not protest. "I would not have let the ship die, Captain, you must believe that," Veleck said.

"The engine says you tried to kill it."

"No, I would never do that."

"You deny damaging it?" Diric asked.

"No, but I would have repaired it before time ran out, but they interfered."

He pointed at Geordi and Crusher. They had managed to stand, grabbing onto the silver lattice work to steady themselves. Geordi's head was still ringing. The pain lingered in his body like a bad dream.

"Three of our crew died, Veleck, dozens are injured. Why, why?" Diric asked.

"No, the engine should have trusted me. I wouldn't have let it die. I wouldn't betray my duty as an engineer, not to that degree." He didn't seem to be listening to his captain.

He turned to the younger Milgian engineer. "Bebit, tell the engine I would not have let it die. Please, it must believe me."

"The engine has rejected you," Diric said, "it accuses you of trying to kill it. I do not think it will believe anything you say ever again."

"No," Veleck said, "no, I . . ."

It was slowly dawning on Geordi that Veleck wasn't bothered by the fact that three crew members had died, or that he had betrayed his people. He was only bothered by the fact that the engine had kicked him out, and would no longer respond to him.

"You have betrayed your duty not just to this ship but as an engineer to the engine you helped create. It holds the cells of your body, flesh of your flesh, Veleck, and it rejects you." Diric stepped very close to the chief engineer. "No other engine will ever let you touch it. The mark of what you have done will be passed from one ship to another. It will be encoded on the programming to every engine from now until forever. You will never again commune as an engineer."

The heat patterns were growing dimmer on Veleck, almost as if he'd been injured, and was experiencing shock.

"Redeem yourself as much as you can, Veleck, tell us what was so very important. Why, Veleck, why?"

"I never thought . . . I would never have betrayed the engine. If they had not interfered, I would have repaired."

"Tell me why, Veleck, as your last duty as my chief engineer. Tell us why."

He spoke without looking at any of them, as if he was speaking to the empty air. "If I lured the starship far away from their destination, I was promised alien genetic material." Veleck's heat patterns were turning an icy blue.

"You killed crew members so you could profit?" Diric's voice held outrage.

"Yes, Captain," Veleck said. His slow voice, held a distant quality.

"May I ask him a question?" Geordi asked.

"He nearly killed you both, you are entitled," Diric said.

"Who wanted to lure the *Enterprise* away, and why?"

"A leader on the planet Oriana," Veleck said.

"Which one?"

"I do not know. We each went to great pains to keep our identities a secret, so we could not betray each other."

"Why was it so important that the ship be here, instead of around the planet?" Crusher asked.

"I did not ask. I did not want to know."

Geordi could believe that of Veleck. Had they sailed away and left the away team in danger? He touched his communicator. "La Forge to Commander Riker."

"Riker here, go ahead."

As briefly as possible Geordi explained what little Veleck would tell them.

"Do you think the captain and the others are in danger?" Riker asked.

"I don't know, Commander, but I'm worried."

"Me too, beam up to the ship. We're going to head back to the planet."

"The *Zar*'s engine is still damaged, Commander."

"No," Veleck said, "I can fix it."

"The engine does not trust you anymore," Bebit said. "It will not listen to you ever again."

"I know. I have betrayed everything I held dear for greed's sake. I was even going to give the Orianians one of our weapons to finish their little war." Veleck stared at the control panels on the wall. "But I never thought my engine would reject me. An engineer without an engine is not whole." He stared at Geordi and Crusher. "I can tell Bebit how to make the repair. I will not let it die. Go, help your people. I will do this last honorable thing, then I will await what comes next."

Geordi looked at Captain Diric. "It's up to you, Captain, if you still need us, then we'll stay. If worst comes to worst the *Enterprise* can return to the planet without us."

"We will let Veleck make these small offerings of reparation. He cannot bring back our dead, but he can do this one small thing. Then he will be imprisoned for a very, very long time."

Geordi glanced at Veleck, but the Milgian didn't seem to react to that last bit of news. Veleck had always given up too easily.

"All right, thank you, Captain. It's been a very unique experience."

"You can say that again," Crusher whispered under her breath.

"La Forge to transporter room, two to beam up." The last thing Geordi felt was the warm pulse of the engine in his head, saying good-bye.

Chapter Twenty-one

WORF WAS SURROUNDED by golden-skinned children. Their large, shining eyes stared up at him adoringly. Curious little hands traced the ridges on his forehead. He had tried glaring at the children, but it had not worked. A low growl had only made them giggle, a high, fluid sound.

Worf sat in a small hut that was like no dwelling he had ever seen before. The walls and domed roof were made entirely of plants. Vines, small trees, even what he would term flowers, were all woven together. And all of it was still alive. Worf had seen trees trained to unusual shapes—bonsai miniatures, standards trained against trellises—but the *Enterprise* arboretum had nothing like this.

He wasn't a person who noticed plants much, but these were impressive. Flowers grew and bloomed at the edges of the wall. A vine with huge white flowers like stars climbed up the far wall. The hut had been invisible in the greenery they had first seen in the cave. It was camouflage to make any warrior's heart-beat quicken.

There were twenty huts all hidden in the rich vegetation. But even standing right beside some of the houses, Worf had almost missed them. It was an ideal place for an ambush.

A little girl that couldn't have been more than four had quickly climbed into Worf's lap. Now, he didn't know what to do with her, accustomed to most of the children on the *Enterprise* being wary of him. Perhaps not afraid, but not comfortable either. Certainly not comfortable enough to climb into his lap, lean against his chest, and nearly sleep. Two boys nearly Alexander's age were leaning against his right side. Their eyes were intent, their attention touchable, seemingly interested in the conversation.

The Greens overall leader, Portun, was sitting just in front of him. He, too, was surrounded by children. A very small baby was asleep in his arms. Portun, Worf had learned, was a child-rearer, who tended children while their parents worked.

A small child of perhaps two toddled from Portun to Worf and struggled to crawl into his lap next to the first little girl. Worf was finally forced to help the child settle comfortably. All the children were like this. They expected to be welcomed by any adult, alien or otherwise.

Portun smiled at him. "You have a way with children, Ambassador Worf."

"Thank you, Leader Portun," Worf said. He doubted if his own son, Alexander, would have agreed with the compliment. He knew he did not, but it was not polite to correct the man.

"You wish to discuss the unfortunate accident that befell Alick of the Venturi, do you not?"

"It was no accident, Leader Portun. It was murder." Worf glanced down into the curious eyes of the children. The two oldest boys were old enough to understand this conversation. Most humanoids protected children from such talk. "Do you wish us to discuss this in front of the young?"

"Why not?"

Worf didn't have a good answer for that. As a Klingon he saw nothing wrong with it. "I was being . . . polite."

"And very good you are at it," Portun said.

Worf nodded, acknowledging the compliment. "I do wish to discuss the murder of Colonel Alick."

Portun frowned, holding the baby a little closer to his chest. "I was very disturbed to hear of the incident. We had hoped that the peace talks would be the beginning of true peace. We Greens have no wish to be the last remnants of our race."

"Are you not angry that your people are under arrest . . ." Worf glanced down at the children and finished his sentence in a lower voice, "and are to be executed?"

"Angry, no," Portun said. "Disappointed, yes."

Worf shook his head. "Why disappointed?"

"It was to be the beginning of our forging new ties with the above-ground world. We were to be included in this peace, and we were going to be able to use what we have learned, what we have created, to repopulate our world. To heal it. That this will not happen now is very sad."

"Your people are going to die. They have been

256

accused of assassination. Are you not worried about them?"

Portun's face sobered, the smile fading from his features. "They are my people, Ambassador. I hurt for each of them. They will be gravely missed."

"Are you not planning to defend them?" Worf asked.

"In what way?"

Worf stared around the living walls as if there was some clue as to how to talk to this man. His unshakable contentment was infuriating.

"Leader Portun, do you believe your people are guilty? Is that why you can be so calm?"

"No, Ambassador Worf, my people did not kill anyone. We do not believe in violence. Taking life, any life, is abhorrent to us."

The two children in Worf's lap were almost a comforting weight. The room was full of a warm, easy contentment, that somehow was soothing even to him. "Even if it meant the lives of your children?"

Portun glanced at the children, then smiled wistfully. "If those were my choices, we would be sorely tested. I could let them take my own life without a fight, but . . ." He sighed. "I have thankfully never had to make that choice."

Worf liked the answer. Most people that professed to nonviolence made it a blanket statement, and very often had never even had to choose: life or violence. Portun had thought about it, and was wise enough to know he could not truly know what he would do until he had to choose.

"An admirable answer, Leader," Worf said.

"Just an honest one, Ambassador Worf."

"Did you know that Alick was poisoned?"

"No," Portun said. He leaned a little forward. "We heard only that he was assassinated, and our people and the first Federation ambassador were blamed."

Worf stared intently at Portun's face, wanting to study his reaction to his next words. He wished Troi were with him, but she had gone off with Breck to learn to speak with the planet—whatever that meant. But he was, after all, the acting ambassador. He would do the job alone if he had to.

"The poison was derived from a plant alkaloid. A genetically altered plant alkaloid."

Surprise blossomed to shock on Portun's face. "It cannot be."

"I have seen the test results personally."

"But, you don't understand. Genetic engineering was outlawed over a hundred years ago. It was considered evil, punishable by death. No one but the Greens practice it. Only we would be capable of such a thing."

"I believe you," Worf said.

"You have come here convinced that we made this poison."

"You yourself just said that it could be no one else."

"But . . ." his words trailed off to silence. His eyes were wide, astonishment plain on his face. The baby in his arms whimpered and struggled in its sleep. He patted it absently.

If Portun were pretending to be surprised, he was doing an excellent job of it. Worf believed that he did not know, but that didn't mean no Greens were involved. "Who are your best genetic engineers?"

"No, it could not be one of my people."

"I am not saying that your people killed Alick, but I believe they supplied the poison."

"No."

"May I question your scientists?"

Portun looked directly at Worf for a moment. "I do not know what to say. It seems you must be right and we did make a plant that was intended only for death. But that, too, is against our basic beliefs. Could it not be one of the upsiders?"

"I am trying to find that out, Leader Portun. Help me to clear your people. If it is not one of them, then I can search elsewhere. We are running out of time to save our respective people."

"You are right, Ambassador. If we are involved, the truth must be discovered. You have my permission to question my people. I do not believe in violence to save our friends, but if the truth can save them . . . I believe in the truth."

"Honor cannot exist without truth."

Portun stared around at the children. Most were listening intently now. "I know little of a warrior's honor, Ambassador, but know something of dealing honorably with the land and its bounty. To have made such a plant is to betray that honor."

"I will find the truth, Leader Portun. You can be sure of that."

He smiled suddenly, but his eyes still held sadness. "I have every confidence in you, Ambassador. But suddenly, I do not have such confidence in my own people." He stared straight at Worf. "Isn't that odd?"

Worf didn't know what to say, so he said nothing. There was a saying among Klingons: Silence is one road to honor. And for now it was certainly the kinder road.

259

Chapter Twenty-two

TALANNE LED THEM OUT onto the surface, where the weak sunlight had faded to twilight. The thick, sulphurous clouds were aflame with crimson and violet. The sunset was among the prettiest Troi had ever seen, and yet her stomach dropped into her feet, pulse pounding.

She grabbed Worf's arm. "The executions are scheduled at full dark."

"I know, Counselor, I know."

"We must hurry," Talanne said.

"We have discovered nothing except that the poison must have come from the Greens," Worf said.

"And none of the Greens we've questioned so far were involved," Troi said.

"I will speak with Basha," Talanne said. "I will do my best to persuade him to postpone for a few hours."

Worf nodded. "And we will question the only remaining Greens that we have not questioned."

"Do you think it was one of the ones under arrest?" Breck asked.

"It must be," Worf said.

Talanne strode off across the open stretch of ground, and the others followed. That awful sensation of being watched was still there, creeping down their spines, but now Troi knew what it was.

All planets were alive, but Oriana had been one step beyond just being alive, animate. The planet had been truly alive, intelligent, though in a way that most humanoids would not have recognized. Even the Orianians had not realized how very alive their land had been, until it was too late.

The Greens, through a melding of science and faith, had recreated pockets of what the planet had once been. They had three earth-healers, empaths who were connected with the ground and growing things rather than people. Breck had been nearly overwhelmed when he discovered he, too, was an earth-healer. He had thought himself giftless because there was no surface for him to feel.

The horrible, angry watching was the remnants of the planet's awareness. All that remained was a lingering rage at the violation.

If the Greens, any Green had been responsible for the murder, how would they convince the Torlicks and Venturies that not all the Greens were evil? It would just reinforce all the existing prejudices. And without the Greens, Troi wasn't at all sure the planet and people could be saved. The memory of what the life-force felt like inside her mind, on her skin, was a rush of pleasure—dim but still very real.

261

Breck stumbled as he entered the tunnels, but it wasn't out of fear. He simply wasn't terribly aware of his surroundings. Troi touched Worf's shoulder, and whispered, "Breck is confused about what has happened to him. I don't know if he will be able to fight."

Worf nodded. "I will watch him."

Troi dropped back and let Worf's bulk lead the way through the tunnels. How long until full dark? How long did the captain have? She was worried about Audun and Liv, but truthfully, they were strangers. To think that they would fail the captain . . . No, they would not fail. They could not fail him, not like this.

Once in the main tunnels, with their wall-murals and bright colors, Worf broke into a jog, racing toward the prison. The others trailed behind him, fighting to keep up with his longer stride.

Two different guards stood outside the door to the prison. Talanne stopped their group in front of them.

"Colonel Talanne, what is the matter?" the first guard asked.

"Have the executions started yet?"

"Yes, Colonel, as scheduled."

Worf pushed forward. "We have new information that proves that Ambassador Picard is innocent." It was a lie, outright. They had no new proof. Worf wanted to fight his way to Picard, but guile was better, quicker. If they had to fight from here to the center of the prison maze, they might arrive too late.

Talanne backed him in the lie. "Yes, we have new proof. Would you keep us outside while an innocent man is being killed?"

"No, Colonel, of course not."

"Escort Ambassador Worf and his party to the prisoners. Obey his orders as you would my own. Is that clear?"

The guard saluted. "Yes, Colonel."

Talanne touched Worf's arm. "I will find my husband, since only he has the ability to delay the executions. Keep them all alive until I get back to you. Good luck."

He gave a curt nod. "And to you."

And she was gone, running back down the corridor. Worf turned to the guard. He wanted to scream, but he forced calm into his voice. "Escort us to the prisoners, now."

"Yes, Ambassador. But no one is allowed weapons during an execution. There have been incidents in the past. Please leave your weapon with the guard."

He glanced at Troi. "Worf, we're running out of time."

He handed his phaser to one of the guards. "Now I am unarmed, lead us to the prisoners."

The guard saluted him and opened the door. They followed the guard into the shining, white corridors, leaving the second guard at the door.

"Worf, we must hurry. I feel something, I . . ." Troi swayed and Worf was forced to catch her arm. "It's the captain, Worf!"

"Lead us to the prisoners now, run!" He made it an order, and the guard obeyed, as he'd been told, breaking into a ground-covering trot. Worf was forced to stay at the man's heels, when he could have gone faster. But the maze of the prison was too confusing. There was no time to get lost in it. He cursed softly under his breath, a tightness in the center of his stomach that he could not breathe around.

A scream split the white silence. Masculine, familiar even then. "Captain!" Worf broke into a full run, leaving the others behind. He broke out into the center of the prison alone. Guards whirled, moving in on either side to form a flesh wall to keep him from the captain. Worf was forced to stand there, panting, frozen.

Picard was bound hand and foot to the ivory frame that they had seen earlier. Shining wires ran down to encircle the ropes that held him in place. Waves of electric blue energy poured down the wires. Blue flame licked down the wires, crawled over his skin, oozed out of his eyes, dripped from his mouth. It looked like Picard was enveloped in cold fire. It did not burn, but it obviously hurt.

The others stumbled in behind him. Troi cried out, "Stop it, stop it!"

The blue flames died abruptly, and Picard slumped only partially conscious. He breathed in short panting gasps as if he could not get enough air.

A masked overseer was at the clean desk, observing, but the person pressing the buttons was General Basha. He stood against a small open panel that had split from the white wall. Inside were the buttons, the levers. His attention was steady on the nearly unconscious Audun. He didn't turn as they walked in. Perhaps he hadn't heard; perhaps the horror on the frame was all he could hear.

Liv's wrists were caught in some shiny silver box that was bolted to the floor. A cloth strip had been tied over her mouth. She turned to Worf and Troi, her large eyes even larger than usual, skin pale and sick with sweat.

Audun was kneeling, head caught in the vise like a cage on top. He wasn't gagged. There was no need. Worf knew death when he saw it.

Worf started forward, but guards pressed in on him. He didn't know how long it took for a man to die. Would one more flip of the switch kill the captain? He could not take that chance. And he could not fight his way to the captain, not with Basha hovering over the buttons. His mind seemed to have slowed down, providing the illusion that he had forever to think of a plan. He had to talk his way to the captain, to delay until Talanne arrived. Because now Worf knew. He knew who the murderer was, but he could not prove it.

The observer behind the desk stood to attention and said, "The Federation ambassador graces our executions with his presence."

Basha turned to stare at them. The mask hid his face, but Worf didn't need to see his face to know. "I did not think generals did their own executions," Worf said. His voice sounded terribly calm. Troi moved up beside him, fingers touching his arm.

"Speak freely, Counselor, we are among friends," Worf said. The irony of that statement was not lost upon him.

She looked a question at him, then nodded. She understood, they were buying time. They could not order the guards to lay down their weapons, but Talanne could. If they could delay long enough.

Picard hung nearly motionless, skin wax pale; only his frantic breathing said he was alive.

"I feel panic, fear, hurry, hurry to do something. Something interrupted. Not the torture, not the executions—what? I'm not sure."

"What are you babbling about, Healer," Basha said. "I do not wish you to see your captain die. That would be cruel, and we are not a cruel people."

"What are you hiding, Basha?" Troi asked it softly, taking a step toward him. She had used his name without the title deliberately. "What are you afraid of?"

Worf didn't question what she was doing. He just came, walking at her back, waiting. The guards parted before them. Perhaps it was Troi's words, or their respect for her mind-powers. Or perhaps it was the fact that they had done nothing hostile. Worf trusted Troi to do her job.

"I don't know what you mean, mind-healer. I fear nothing. I am a warrior." But his attention wavered. He glanced at Liv, moving his whole head to do it.

"This is your last opportunity to discover if they are the only traitors. My understanding is that is one of the reasons you torture prisoners, so they can give out names. So why is she gagged?" Troi asked.

"To keep from shouting encouragement to the others, of course."

Liv made a desperate sound through her gag, struggling and pulling to free her hands. A small line of blood trickled down her wrist from her desperate pulling.

"I think she is ready to talk, General," Troi said. "Your strategy has worked. You've frightened her." Troi turned her back on Basha and went to the bound woman. She reached up slowly to undo the gag.

"No!" It was a shout.

"But she wants to tell the truth, Basha."

"No!" He ran forward, toward Troi. Worf smashed his fist into the general's face. The man tumbled backward, hands going to his face.

Basha ripped his mask off. A thin trickle of blood traced the edge of his nose. "Kill them, kill them all!"

The guards moved in like a fleshy tide. They did not question their orders. The anger, the frustration, the helplessness, boiled up from the center of Worf's gut. The rage built, flowed in a hot flash up his chest, across his shoulders, his neck, down his arms. He screamed, an echoing cry that froze the guards for a breathless moment. Then Worf waded into them.

He picked up a guard and tossed him into the crowd clearing a space in front of him. He smashed his fists into two masked faces; one right after the other, the faces fell out of sight. A guard grabbed his arm, and Worf lifted him off the ground. Something hit him hard in the back of the head. He whirled the guard still dangling from his arm. Another guard was standing on a torture device with a broken piece of it in his hands.

Worf tore the club from his, or her, hands and used it on the guard. He used the club like a riot stick to clear the way and it felt good.

A scream echoed over the fighting. Picard was writhing in blue flame again. Basha was at the control panel leaving his people to fight alone.

Worf redoubled his efforts, throwing guards, smashing anything that got in his way. Picard danced and writhed on the framework like a broken puppet.

A shot echoed in the room. Sparks flew from the

control box. Basha jerked his hand back as if it were hurt.

"Stop it!"

Everyone's attention flickered from the fight to Talanne and a handful of guards in the entrance to the torture area. They were all armed. "No more fighting, that is a direct order."

The Orianian guards seemed willing to obey, but Basha yelled, "No, they are here to rescue their captain. You must stop them!"

"Husband, this is a Federation ambassador and his counselor. You can't just attack them. We have the audacity to pronounce a death sentence on one of them. Do not make a worse mistake."

"I will not be questioned, especially not by my own wife."

"If not by me, then who, Basha?" Talanne asked. She walked into the room, the guards fanning out at her back.

"You don't understand."

"I think I do." Her voice sounded tired. "You killed Alick."

"What are you saying, Talanne?"

Troi undid the gag on Liv. The woman took a deep sobbing breath. "I didn't know he would use it to sabotage the peace talks. I didn't know."

"You didn't know the Federation ambassador would use your filthy technology to kill!" Basha said.

"No, you did it. You did it!"

"Liar, filthy lying Green!" He strode toward her, bare face flushed and mottled with rage.

"She is telling the truth," Troi said.

"You would say anything to save your captain," Basha said.

268

"Why were you executing them personally, Husband?"

"They are important prisoners," he said.

"Why, Basha, why?"

"I simply want no mistakes about their questioning. The ambassador said that his lieutenant and the healer, both knew of his plan to kill Alick," he said.

"Did anyone else overhear this," Talanne asked. "Olon, you are my husband's sentinel. You are with him always. Did the ambassador implicate the others?"

A guard stepped away from the rest. He cradled his right arm against his chest. The wrist was hanging at an odd angle and looked broken. The voice that came out was high and light, female. "I will guard your safety in all things but I cannot become a traitor to my people. I heard nothing but the screams."

"You lie!"

"Even your own sentinel will not help you now, Basha. You murdered Alick while you offered him friendship and peace."

"Colonel Talanne," Worf said, "may we go to the captain?"

"By all means."

Worf stepped through the carnage of wounded guards. Troi hurried to Worf's side and they went to the captain together.

He was very, very still. His skin was not white but gray with pain. Sweat soaked his body. Worf touched the captain's cheek with one hand. The flesh was cold. "Captain. Captain, can you hear me? It's Worf."

Troi was crying silently. "Captain, please open your eyes. Jean-Luc, please!"

His eyelids fluttered. His mouth moved but no

sound came out. Worf had to place his ear nearly on top of the captain's mouth to hear the words. "Lieutenant Worf, Counselor, glad you could come."

Troi drew a sobbing breath that had an edge of laughter to it. The relief of hysterics.

"Enough of this," Basha said, "They are the traitors. I don't know how they bribed my sentinel, but they must have."

"Husband, sentinels are honorable. You have betrayed us all. You killed the Venturi leader while he tried to make peace with us."

"It was the only time I could get close to Alick. It was so easy. I had the smallest amount of poison tucked up my sleeve. I turned the handle on the tea urn. I dropped the poison in then, with everyone watching. It was simpler than I ever dreamed." He sounded proud of what he had done.

"We can win the war, Talanne," Basha said. "We can!" He held out his hands to her. "Join me in this."

"No," Talanne said, "no, we can't. Two hundred years of fighting has proved that."

"The Venturi are leaderless, we can win the war."

"No, Basha, no. We cannot," Talanne said.

"Yes, I have bargained with an alien race. They will give us a weapon to finish this war. To destroy the Venturies." He strode to her, hands clenched into fists.

"Who did you bargain with?" Talanne asked.

"Milgians, a race far superior to us and to the Federation," he said. "They lured your precious starship away."

Worf started toward him. "It was a trap!"

"They will not harm the ship. The Orianians do not make war on children, and your ship carries families.

270

We would not deal with anyone that would do such a vile thing. The Milgians do not have any policy of noninterference."

"Apparently not," Worf said. "What could you offer them in return for such a weapon?"

Basha glared at them all. The look on his face was one of fierce determination. Determination not to be wrong. "They wanted the Green technology. They wanted our genetic material."

"How could you promise it to them," Talanne asked. "How could you contact the Greens?"

"This one," he pointed at Liv, "we caught this one. She bargained for her life and gave us enough."

"Enough to kill Alick and blame the Greens," Troi said.

"Yes!" He whirled on Troi. "The Greens could have helped me win this war, but they refused. So I decided that they would help me win this war, one way or another. With everyone believing the Greens murdered the general," he smiled, a most unpleasant smile, "we could have hunted them down and wiped them out. No one would have protested."

"Husband, Husband."

Basha turned to Talanne, slowly. "Don't you understand? Don't you see?"

"Have you never wondered why Jeric is healthy, perfect?"

He frowned. "What are you talking about? We were simply blessed."

"No, husband, it was bioengineering. It was the Greens that gave us our son, healthy and whole."

"You are lying to me."

"No, Basha, I would not lie about our son, you know that."

271

He turned to stare at Audun who was still unconscious, then back to the tear-stained face of Liv. "No, they are evil. She was weak and gave me the means to destroy her own people."

"She is weak, but they are not evil. They gave us Jeric."

He shook his head over and over again. "No, no, I don't believe you. I can't. They are evil." He took a step toward her. "Why are you lying about Jeric? Such wicked lies."

"I swear by all we hold holy that Jeric is a product of Green bioengineering," Talanne said.

Basha shook his head slowly. "No, no." His voice was soft and horror filled. "Our son comes from Green technology?" he whispered it as if it were too evil a thought to be spoken out loud.

"Yes, Husband, our beautiful son."

"Our son is one of them." He stared at Liv. "Our son is a Green. You let this happen. You let this happen!" He drew a small object from behind his back.

Breck yelled, "Don't, do it, General! Don't make us kill you."

That one action, drawing a weapon on the colonel, decided the guards. There was no more hesitation. All weapons in the room swung to point at Basha.

His breathing was coming in harsh pants. Rage and horror showed on his face. Worf watched the man's thoughts flow over his face; it was like reading. Was killing his Green-loving wife worth his own death? The moment seemed to stretch forever, then he threw his weapon on the floor.

The guards rushed forward, pressing him against the wall. Eager hands searched for more hidden weapons. Basha was quickly bound and ringed with guards. His beautiful eyes stared at Talanne, and you didn't need to be an empath to see the hatred.

She had dealt with Greens. She had stolen his son from him, for Basha now felt that he had no son. As simple as that all his love turned to hate. Worf could not understand it. He knew there was nothing that would end his feelings for Alexander. But the look in Basha's eyes was pure and uncompromising. The Greens were evil, anyone who dealt with them was evil—Talanne and Jeric were now evil.

Talanne turned to the guards. "Spread the word there will be no executions tonight. Contact the Venturies. Tell them we know who murdered their leader." She glanced back at her husband. "Tell them we will give over the guilty party as soon as it can be arranged."

The guard saluted her. "As you say, so shall it be, General Talanne."

She nodded, and didn't seem to hear the new title. The Torlicks had a new leader. Worf was betting that this leader would forge a lasting peace. If it could be done, Talanne would do it.

Talanne stared at her husband. He stared back, his hatred nearly touchable. Worf could not see Talanne's face, and he didn't want to. This was a private grief. It deserved not to be intruded upon.

Chapter Twenty-three

PICARD, TROI, AND WORF were standing in the roofed courtyard where they had first beamed down to Oriana. Talanne and Breck, with a handful of guards, were on hand to wish them farewell.

"Are you sure you will not stay with us, Ambassador Worf? I think you have much to teach our warriors about honor."

Worf glanced at Picard, but the captain only seemed amused that the Orianians had insisted on calling them both ambassador. "I am honored that you think I am a worthy teacher, General Talanne, but peace is not a time to train warriors. Your people must learn other paths to honor."

She nodded. "Yes." Her voice sounded almost wistful. "It will be difficult for our people, so many years of fighting. Warriors are not good in peacetime."

"I think you will do well, General Talanne," Picard said. "Saving your planet will be enough of a challenge to keep any warrior occupied."

"And as soon as we can guarantee his safety Portun will be coming to us. He and the other Earth-healers will show us the way to begin healing our planet."

"You have taken the first step by abolishing the law that made bioengineering illegal," Picard said.

"Yes, and the Greens are eager to help the Milgians, as well. The handful of Milgians that had plotted with my husband must have been truly desperate. Their home-world sounds as damaged as our own. The Greens are insisting on a stringent treaty to make sure their science is not misused for war." Talanne smiled at them. "We will be needing another ambassador to negotiate the treaty. Are you sure neither of you would be willing to stay?"

"The Federation is sending out a permanent advisor, General, but I am afraid the *Enterprise* and her crew have other duties."

"Then, fair traveling, Ambassador Picard, Ambassador Worf." She held out her hand to Troi, and Troi took it, though she knew the touch would be intrusive. Happiness, sorrow, but under all was hope.

"We will have mind-healers of our own again. Soon I hope."

Troi smiled. "I know you will. And Betazed will be sending some mind-healers of its own to help you."

Talanne released her hand and stepped back to stand with the guards. Picard touched his communicator, "Three to beam up, energize when ready." He leaned into Worf and said, softly, "Are you sure you don't wish to stay, Lieutenant? We would miss you at tactical, but you could start a new career as a diplomat." There was a very uncaptainlike shine to his eyes.

"No, Captain, I am very happy as head of security."

"As long as you're sure," Troi said.

Worf frowned at both of them. "I do not think I have the disposition to be a good ambassador."

Troi fought the smile that tried to spread across her face. Her eyes were very bright.

Picard cleared his throat sharply, obviously struggling. The tingling rush of the transporter saved both of them from outright laughter.

STAR TREK ®
THE NEXT GENERATION

GROUNDED

by David Bishoff

While answering a distress call from a scientific station in a remote part of the galaxy, the Starship *Enterprise* becomes infected with a mysterious alien life form which feeds on and transforms inorganic materials.

The U.S.S. *Enterprise* begins to gradually disintegrate, and Starfleet is forced to order its evacuation and destruction to prevent the dangerous infection from spreading throughout the galaxy. It's the end of an era for Captain Picard and his crew, who are scheduled for transfers that will split them up among different Starfleet vessels.

But even as the end draws near for the U.S.S. *Enterprise*, Captain Picard begins to formulate a desperate plan to save his ship and preserve his crew - a plan that will force him to defy Starfleet orders and lead him to a confrontation with a malevolent alien force which has the power to destroy the entire Federation.

Coming soon from Titan Books

STAR TREK ®
THE NEXT GENERATION

THE ROMULAN PRIZE

by Simon Hawke

Hermeticus 2 - a planet so shrouded in secrecy that few in the Federation even know of its existence. When a Romulan spy learns of the world, it becomes the centrepiece of a far-reaching Romulan plan to claim Hermeticus 2 as their own.

On routine patrol near the border of the Neutral Zone, the Starship *Enterprise* discovers an advanced Romulan warbird prototype drifting lifeless in space. Investigating the vessel, Captain Picard is drawn into a plot that threatens the very foundation of the Federation. Now, with time running out, Captain Picard and the crew of the U.S.S. *Enterprise* must stop the Romulans before the deadly secret of Hermeticus 2 overwhelms them all.

STAR TREK ®

SHELL GAME

by Melissa Crandall

While on a routine mission to retrieve a research drone for recycling, the U.S.S. *Enterprise* encounters a Romulan space station adrift within Federation borders. Exploring the lifeless station, the crew finds ghostly apparitions flitting at the edges of sight.

Soon the U.S.S. *Enterprise* is also inexplicably without power. Captain Kirk and his crew must now solve the mystery of the strange apparitions before the Starship suffers the station's fate.

The situation becomes desperate when a Romulan warship arrives looking for the station, and the Romulan Commander accuses the Federation of treachery. Before Captain Kirk can save the Starship *Enterprise* from complete destruction, he must avoid becoming drawn into a deadly shell game - a game that will leave no winners and no survivors...

STAR TREK®
THE STARSHIP TRAP
by Mel Gilden

En route to an important diplomatic reception, the U.S.S. *Enterprise* suddenly is set upon by a Klingon warship. This unprovoked assault, Kirk discovers, is in response to what the Klingon ship's captain claims are recent Federation attacks on several Klingon vessels which have disappeared.

Managing to secure a truce, Captain Kirk reaches the reception only to find out it is not just Klingon ships that are disappearing, but Federation vessels, Romulan warbirds and ships from almost every known race are vanishing without a trace.

Now, Captain Kirk and the crew of the Starship *Enterprise* must determine the fate of the missing ships before the entire known galaxy is drawn into a deadly conflict.

STAR TREK®
THE MODALA IMPERATIVE
by Michael Jan Friedman, Peter David and Pablo Marcos

Modala, a peaceful, developing world, is suddenly thrown into turmoil when the government uses alien technology to subjugate the population. Captain Kirk and the U.S.S. *Enterprise* get embroiled in the battle, only to find themselves a part of the revolution.

A hundred years later, the *Enterprise* returns to Modala, bringing with them survivors of that adventure - Spock and McCoy. The centennial celebration is abruptly halted by the arrival of the Ferengi, and Captain Picard must rely on those living legends to help save Modala... again.

The first in a new line of *Star Trek* graphic novels, featuring, for the first time ever, characters from both classic *Star Trek* and *Star Trek: The Next Generation*. With a special introduction by Walter 'Chekov' Koenig.

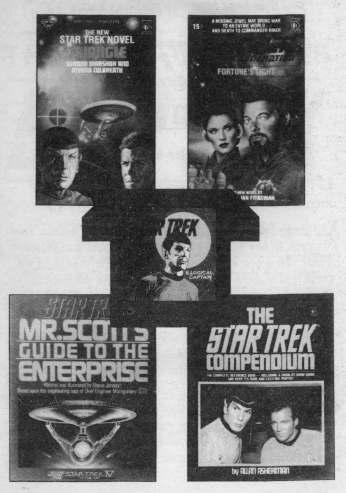

For a complete list of Star Trek publications, T-shirts and badges please send a large stamped SAE to Titan Books Mail Order, 19 Valentine Place, London, SE1 8QH. Please quote reference NG24.